META**WARS**

ORCHARD BOOKS
338 Euston Road, London NW1 3BH
Orchard Books Australia
Level 17/207 Kent Street, Sydney, NSW 2000

First published in 2012 by Orchard Books

ISBN 978 1 40831 460 9

A CIP catalogue record for this book is available
from the British Library.

1 3 5 7 9 8 6 4 2

Printed in Great Britain

Orchard Books is a division of Hachette Children's Books,
an Hachette UK company.
www.hachette.co.uk

METAWARS

THE DEAD ARE RISING

JEFF NORTON

ORCHARD

For Caden

1

Jonah Delacroix loved to fly.

He spread his arms wide and pushed his toes together. He swooped low over the sprawling new digital city of Changhai. The warm wind against his face was virtual, but the thrill in his stomach was real.

In the bustling streets below him, new buildings pixelated into existence and throngs of avatars populated this brave new world. Behind each avatar was a real person whose brain interfaced directly with the internet, generating a digital representation of the user called the avatar.

Jonah lived most of his waking life inside a virtual world called the Metasphere. In this, he wasn't unusual. Most people had gone *meta*.

But now, the Metasphere had a rival.

This fast-growing new world that Jonah soared above was called the Changsphere, and it was drawing avatars from the Metasphere with its higher-resolution graphics, faster servers and infectious sense of optimism. To Jonah, the Metasphere – with its rich, 3D rendering and sharp, lifelike recreation of all five senses – had always seemed more real than the crumbling real world. Inside the Changsphere, however, everything seemed richer and sharper still.

One of the things Jonah loved about the virtual world was the sheer diversity of avatars. They took all shapes and sizes, from the familiar to the ridiculous. As he soared, he saw a cat riding an elephant. On the city streets below him, he spotted a chimpanzee selling apps to a raptor, and a shark strolling on two legs. He noticed two translucent triangles (one isosceles and one equilateral) pulsing as they bickered, and a mallard duck parading three ducklings behind it.

Suddenly, Jonah realised that he had no way of knowing if those avatars below did, in fact, have a real person behind them. They could, for all he knew, be dead.

In the Metasphere of old, some users chose to Upload themselves, digitising all of their memories and storing them in their avatar. They would live on in the virtual world in a state of ignorant bliss, confined to a specific island, the Island of the Uploaded. The uploading process, however, killed the user; every Uploaded avatar had committed suicide to get there. But in return, they were immortal.

Immortal, but not indestructible.

The server farm that stored their memories had almost crashed, and in the nick of time, Jonah had led the millions of Uploaded avatars into the light of the new Changsphere world, where they were now roaming free among the living. For Jonah it was a miracle that the dead could come back to life – or at least a digital life.

Jonah had opened the portal between the worlds two months ago. Looking down, it was hard to believe that back then Changhai had been nothing but a digital grid, zoned for development. In fact, this entire world had only recently come into existence.

Jonah wasn't alone in the sky. He flew past a silver, five-pointed star and nodded his head. 'Good morning.'

'It certainly is in here,' the star replied.

Jonah caught a glimpse of his avatar in the star's reflection. He looked just like his real-world self, gangly with an unruly tuft of dark hair. But what struck Jonah more than anything was how lifelike he looked. The graphics here were so sharp that he could have sworn he was looking into a mirror in the real world, and not at a digital reflection.

Thousands of new settlers were arriving in the Changsphere every day. They were buying up plots of virtual land, building homes and businesses. They were moving their entire online lives here. Jonah shared the optimism of these virtual pioneers as they explored their new surroundings. But to Jonah, the Changsphere represented more than a second chance. It was the one place where his father was still alive.

But not everyone was happy.

Below Jonah, a demonstration was taking place in Changhai Square. He hovered high above to see what the commotion was about. *Why would anyone be unhappy here?* he wondered.

About a hundred avatars had gathered and their angry voices drifted up to him:

'Boycott the Changsphere!'

'Don't support terrorism!'

'Hand back the Southern Corner!'

Jonah felt a surge of anger. *They don't know what they're talking about!* he thought. Part of him wanted to fly down there and argue with them, but he was outnumbered a hundred to one and he knew his voice would be drowned out. Besides, he was on his way to see his Uploaded father.

'Hand back the Southern Corner! Don't support terrorism!'

David Foster grinned to himself. This was going well.

He had started with just a few hardcore Millennials – his own people – but the flash mob he had whipped up had soon gone viral and attracted more supporters through the main portal.

A mangy blue hyena flew into the air and cackled, *'Death to the Guardians! Down with Mr Chang!'*

David waddled through the crowd, urging the protestors to get angrier, to shout louder. In the virtual worlds, David took the form of an emperor penguin. He would rather have been a more imposing avatar like a bird of prey, but it was a cruel quirk of Direct Interface, the method of connecting the brain to the virtual world, that the user did not choose his avatar. The subconscious mind generated the avatar, and the conscious mind just had to live with it.

With a little more prodding, he thought, *I can get these dupes to riot, and perhaps Mr Granger will finally promote me out of Anti-Virus.*

'That's right,' he yelled, 'let 'em know what we think of their Changsphere!'

But something was wrong. The crowd was actually growing *quieter*. Some of the demonstrators had clammed up completely and were staring at the sky. It was difficult for David, as a penguin, to look up, but he strained to follow their gazes.

Another group of avatars had arrived, about twenty of them. They were hovering above the demonstrators' heads, and they didn't look like they had come to join in. One of the newcomers, a zebra with neon-green and black stripes, looked down at David and spat, 'If you don't like it here, then waddle back to the Metasphere.'

A few of his demonstrators floated up to the newcomers' level, but David remained warily on the ground. He had lit the spark of protest and wanted to see how fast his fire would spread.

The hyena squared up to the zebra. 'We'll leave,' it hissed, 'as soon as Mr Chang gives back the quarter of the Metasphere his Guardian friends stole!'

'You'll leave now,' said the zebra, 'or we'll make you sorry!'

'Oh yeah? There are more of us than there are of you. Who are you, anyway? I'll bet you're Guardians yourselves.'

'Guardian terrorist scum!' cried David, and five more protesters took up the shout and lifted off to square up to the newcomers.

'The Guardians saved us,' said the zebra. 'They led us into the Changsphere when our Island was destroyed. So, we won't let you—'

The hyena suddenly turned from affronted to afraid. 'You're…Uploaded?'

It cowered away from the zebra, as a whisper of fear wove through the demonstrators: *'Uploaded!'*

David felt a shiver too. He thought it was unnatural, unholy. The dead shouldn't be allowed to roam among the living. *I can't even tell them apart from us*, he thought.

He knew he had to do something. His flash mob was on the verge of dissipating, losing its nerve. He yelled up at the newcomers, 'These are matters for the living, not the dead! You have no say! You have no rights!'

The blue hyena shrieked and clawed at the zebra as the standoff exploded into a brawl. A giant, fat leech – an Uploaded – sprang onto a protesting minotaur's head with an audible slurp.

This is golden, David told himself. *This'll get us on the big video blogs for sure, maybe even onto Bryony's vlog—*

A gasp went up from all around him. Half the

Uploaded avatars had broken away from the others and were dive-bombing the people on the ground.

A vampire bat swooped down on a slow-moving cow and sank its claws into its shoulders. At first, the cow was more irritated than afraid, but it kicked and thrashed as it was lifted into the air. It succeeded in breaking free, but only for a second. The bat was on the cow's back before it could fly away, and its mouth opened wide... and *kept* on opening...

David stared in horror at the bat. Its mouth was now as wide as its prey was big – even wider – and in a swift, angry motion, it jabbed its little head forward and gulped the startled cow down whole. The bovine avatar disappeared completely into the Uploaded bat.

David couldn't believe what he was seeing. It was impossible. He watched helplessly as his protesters scattered half blindly. The Uploaded stalked them with their mouths gaping open. David didn't wait to see if any more were caught and devoured.

He had to get out of here before the Uploaded came after him!

He turned and flew along the street. He beat his flippers as hard as he could, gaining height until he could see the shiny new shopping mall, where inside he had parked his exit halo. It wasn't far away. He was going to make it. But then David Foster made one fatal mistake.

He looked back.

A quick glance over his shoulder. It was enough. A hulking green caterpillar slammed into him, sending him reeling into the claws of a waiting kestrel that snatched him and dropped him onto a nearby rooftop. As David struggled in the bird's fierce grip, three more Uploaded landed around him: the caterpillar, the leech he had seen before and their leader, the zebra.

'Where are you waddling off to, little penguin-man?' the zebra sneered. 'We're just getting started.'

'Let me have him, Suki,' the leech pleaded in a sucking, slurping voice. 'I'm so hungry.'

'Please, leave me alone,' David cried. 'I was just passing by.'

'You're their ringleader,' said the zebra in an accusing tone.

'No, I'm not,' wailed David. 'I swear, I'm not. I was just—'

'You were right, what you said,' said the zebra. 'We are dead, but you, you have life.'

'Let me have him, Suki.' The leech was straining forward, saliva drooling from its mouth. 'I wouldn't waste his life like he has.'

The zebra shook its head. 'No.'

Thank God, thought David. 'Th-thank you,' he stammered. 'Thank you. I—'

'Joshua caught him,' said the zebra. 'He should have him.'

'No!' cried David. 'No, please, you can't! No, *please*!'

The kestrel had let go of him, but the Uploaded avatars had David surrounded. There was nothing he could do. Nothing but tremble as the bird of prey hovered over him, its beady eyes fixed upon him. It flexed its little sharp beak and, with a crack of bone, dislodged its jaw and opened its beak.

'I'm so hungry,' said the kestrel in an old man's voice.

David could feel the kestrel's hot breath on his face.

The kestrel lunged at him. David screamed as it opened its ever-expanding beak around him, and he found himself plunging into a deep, dark abyss.

High above the fray, Jonah looked down in confusion. An Uploaded bat had ingested a cow and then a kestrel had swallowed a penguin. He didn't understand what was happening. Where did they go?

The only way out of the virtual world was through a user's unique exit halo. *Perhaps the bat has also swallowed the cow's halo*, Jonah thought, hopefully. So far, none of the brawling avatars had taken any notice of him hovering high in the sky, but he knew he shouldn't stay, just in case things escalated.

As he flew on, he was torn about what to do. He knew he should reveal to the Guardians and Mr Chang what he had seen, but he didn't fully understand it himself. If the Uploaded were turning violent, Jonah worried that all of them could be banished. He couldn't take that risk. He'd just got his father back.

He would do anything not to lose him again.

2

Jonah soared towards the bright lights of the Chang Stadium. A giant red sign declared it to be the 'New Home of the GamesCon'. A clock counted down the hours until the opening of the biannual games competition, the biggest event in the virtual world, where every new immersive role-play game was launched and played by the world's top gamers. It read 52 HOURS, 16 MINUTES.

The giant arena surrounded a vast pitch and had the capacity for over a million avatars, including the hover space above the stands.

Right now, the sky above the stadium was perfectly clear, protected by a firewall program that prevented unauthorised access before the opening ceremonies. Jonah, however, flew straight through the firewall. He was invited.

Waiting for Jonah on the pitch was a sleek red dragon: his father. Jason Delacroix's avatar, with its huge wingspan, bright yellow eyes and three little horns along the flat of his snout, dwarfed Jonah's 'humatar' avatar.

The dragon opened his wings and Jonah flew at him for a hug. After what he'd seen, Jonah felt safe and secure wrapped in his dad's scaly wings.

Jonah knew his father wasn't really alive, that his avatar was an Uploaded composite of his father's digitised memories, but right now, held tight in his dead father's embrace, he didn't care.

An object appeared in Jason Delacroix's claw. He must have plucked it out of his personal inventory space. A football.

'Fancy a game?' asked Jason.

'You bet,' said Jonah.

They played the full length of the pitch, talking, laughing and teasing each other about their football skills.

Jason liked to reminisce about 'the old days', when he had been an RAF pilot protecting Britain's dwindling oil supplies. He had his fair share of 'war stories' to relate, and Jonah enjoyed hearing them as they kicked the ball.

Jonah had felt robbed of this, the normal father-son relationship that the other kids at school all took for granted. *School*, Jonah thought for a moment, *that feels like a million years ago.* The red dragon kicked the ball past him and Jonah realised that he had missed all this when he had been a kid, his dad off on long-haul flights, or Guardian missions, too absent to spend much time with him. And then...

Then, Jonah had lost him.

They had played a lot of football these past two months. Making up for lost time. Jonah was getting better at it too. The first few times they played, it had been a lot harder for his dad to let him win.

Jonah chased after his dad, tackled him on the halfway line and stole the ball from between his hind claws. But Jason kept pace with Jonah as he controlled the ball along the touchline.

Jonah shot for the open goalmouth. The ball described a perfect arc past Jason's red dragon avatar. It was headed for the back of the net.

Then, suddenly, Jason was between the ball and its target. He headed it clear. 'Hey!' cried Jonah. 'Not fair. The rules say no flying!'

'Who's flying?' said Jason. 'That was leaping! It only counts as flying if your feet leave the ground for longer than half a second.'

'Which yours did,' said Jonah.

'I don't think so,' said Jason.

'Replay!' they called together.

A window popped up between them. They watched the last ten seconds of their match replayed in slow-motion, along with scrolling statistics and analysis.

'There!' said Jonah. 'It says 0.83 seconds. You were in the air for 0.83 seconds!'

'I can't help it if my wings generate lift,' Jason protested.

They laughed together, Jonah moving into position to take his penalty kick. Jason's wings almost filled the goalmouth, but Jonah had learned that this could be a weakness as well as a strength.

Jonah aimed for the bottom-left corner of the net. Jason tried to get his claws to the ball, but his own wings got in his way. It was a goal!

Jonah heard someone clapping. A new avatar had appeared in the stands. Another dragon. This one was a golden treasure dragon. It had an elongated body, a pair of horns and a wispy white beard. It weaved and coiled its way through the fixed seating towards the pitch.

'This is what my Changsphere is all about, my friends,' said the dragon in a familiar voice, youthful but controlled. 'Bringing families, whole dynasties, together. Creating memories. Creating legacies. And you, Jonah, you made all of this possible.'

Jonah felt he would have blushed had he been in his real body.

The treasure dragon's name was Mr Chang. He was the genius creator of the Changsphere. Jonah had helped him by opening a portal between the Changsphere and the older Metasphere, so that people could travel between the two virtual worlds.

He hadn't actually meant to do this, but when the Metasphere's servers were failing, it was the only way to rescue the dead, including his father. Mr Chang didn't know that, though, and Jonah didn't feel inclined to tell him.

'I'm just glad we were able to give the Up…everyone a new start,' Jonah said, careful not to say the word 'Uploaded'. His father didn't know he was dead, and

Jonah didn't want to upset him by telling him. He'd heard that if the Uploaded knew how they reached the Metasphere, they would go mad. Judging from what he saw earlier, he worried that this was starting to happen.

'I am too,' said Mr Chang. 'Here in the Changsphere, we aim to give avatars the best of what digital life has to offer. Such as GamesCon. Are you excited, Jonah?'

'I can't believe I'm standing here,' enthused Jonah. 'Right where all the big RPGs are going to be played.'

'What are you most looking forward to?' asked Mr Chang.

'*Brain-Sucking Zombies 4*, of course,' said Jonah. He'd played and mastered all of the BSZ games since their debut online six years ago.

'Then you are in luck. Mr Wexler himself will also be a guest in my private box for the opening ceremonies.'

'It really is amazing,' said Jason, 'how much you've built in such a short time.'

Jonah nodded his agreement. 'I can't believe you lured the Con away from the Metasphere. Granger must've been furious.'

Mr Chang accepted the compliment with a bow. 'We had the support of the top developers, of course. For too long, the Metasphere has been allowed to decay for want of effective competition.'

'I remember when the Metasphere was brand new,' said Jason. 'I met my Miriam in there, you know. I was still in the Air Force at the time, but...'

He was doing it again. Jonah's dad was remembering – and not only that, but he was making connections between those memories. He was placing each memory in order, in its proper context. *The problem is,* Jonah worried, *he shouldn't be able to do that.*

Mr Chang drew Jonah aside.

'We have come a long way in a short time,' said Mr Chang, 'further even than I had hoped. Still, we could be doing more.'

'How?' asked Jonah.

'The Chang Bridge device,' said Mr Chang. 'Can you get it back for me?'

'I don't know. It's still in the real world, in Uluru. I don't know if I can get it.'

'Please try,' said Mr Chang. 'Now that a permanent connection has been made between our two virtual worlds, I can use the device to create many more. I can speed up the process of bringing families here, to be reunited with their ancestors. To build more memoirs, together.'

'About that,' said Jonah, hesitantly. 'My dad. He's becoming more...' He couldn't find the right words to express his concerns.

Mr Chang nodded sagely. 'Your father is more lucid than he was. He is able to reason now and to sort his memories into a linear timeline.'

'Yes.'

'You should understand, young Master Delacroix, that you have been lied to. Everyone has been lied to. Confusion is not the natural state of the Uploaded.'

'But I thought—'

'You believed, as you were told, that only a fraction of the human brain's contents could be digitally processed. The true figure is much higher. The Metasphere's overtaxed servers simply could not unpack and process the full data set of the human brain.'

'And your servers can?'

'Within my Changsphere,' said Mr Chang, 'the Uploaded can live as full a life as the rest of us.'

Jonah looked at his dad, who was practising keep-ups in the goalmouth.

'You're saying,' said Jonah, 'that you can truly bring the dead back to life?'

It seemed almost too good to be true. For three long years, Jonah had had nothing of his father left. Now, Jason was back. He was really back, playing football, talking, joking and being a dad.

'No, Master Delacroix,' replied Mr Chang. Jonah's hopes were at once dashed and then quickly raised again. 'I am saying that by bringing the dead here, Jonah, you have brought them back to life.'

Jonah had a feeling of foreboding in his stomach, an unshakeable sense of dread that this happy time was all about to come crashing down around him.

Mr Chang had to leave. 'I have many matters to

attend to,' he said. 'But you and your father may stay if you wish. Enjoy yourselves.'

They kicked the football back and forth, playing together now rather than against each other.

'Did I tell you,' said Jason, 'about the time Axel and I were attacked by a Millennial plane over the Atlantic?' Jonah grinned. He had heard the story before, but he didn't mind hearing it again.

'I think that was what made Axel's mind up for sure,' said Jason. 'That was why he joined the Guardians when they asked him.'

'Let's not talk about the Millennials and the Guardians,' said Jonah. Since that fateful day when Jonah discovered his father's Uploaded avatar hidden in a secret cellar of his family's digital gift shop, he'd been plunged into a violent metawar between these two factions. Jonah knew he couldn't push off the Guardians' cause forever, but for now, he just wanted to be a normal teenager. He just wanted to play football with his dad.

'I think I need to, Jonah,' said Jason. 'There's something I...I need to get straight in my head. You know that Axel recruited me too?'

Jonah nodded. 'Mum told me that all the time you were working as Matthew Granger's pilot, you were really—'

'I was a double agent,' confirmed Jason. 'I was secretly reporting to the Guardians.'

'But that's all in the past now.'

24

'I know, son. I know it is. The funny thing is...'

'What about this GamesCon, then? Have you ever been in a private box?' Jonah was trying to distract his dad. It wasn't working.

'I don't remember what happened,' said Jason. 'I don't know if I gave the Guardians the information they wanted or not. It's like...'

'You were a hero, Dad,' said Jonah. 'I was... I *am* so proud of you.'

'It's like there's a big hole in my memories,' said Jason. 'People here, sometimes they talk about the real world, only I can't remember the last time I was there.'

'You don't have to worry about the real world, Dad.'

'Someone said... They said there had been a terrorist attack. The airports had been bombed. They said no one was flying any more. And they said... Jonah, they said this all happened three years ago, but I had no idea. It's like someone stole three years out of my life.' Jason looked at Jonah, expectantly. 'I'm a pilot, son. How could I have missed something like that?'

Jonah swallowed. He didn't know what to say.

Jason trapped the football beneath a claw. He fixed his son with a piercing yellow stare. And then he asked the one question that Jonah had been dreading.

'Am I dead?'

3

Matthew Granger needed his brightest brains in one place.

His virtual conference room was packed with the avatars of his smartest staff and most loyal followers. He hovered before them in the form of a huge black spider.

These weren't just people who worked for Granger, these were people who shared his world-view. They pledged to fight for his vision for the future, and, if necessary, to die defending it. They were the senior members of a movement that Granger himself had founded: the Millennials. And, right now, he wasn't at all happy with them.

'The Changsphere has been in business for two months,' he said in a controlled rage, 'and Metasphere commerce is down by 4.2%.' At first, there was a quiet rumble of excuses and finger-pointing. 'I don't want excuses and I don't want scapegoats. I want solutions.'

The Millennials rushed to inform Granger that, in fact, they were doing the best they could. They had ideas for tempting users back to the Metasphere. They were sure that things would improve soon.

Granger barely heard their words. He knew that,

ultimately, there was little any of them could do. They could slow the rate of the Metasphere's decline. Reversing it, however, would require drastic action.

He broke up the meeting abruptly. He turned and flew through his hovering exit halo, and felt each of his five senses slipping away from him.

He woke up, semi-reclined, in the cockpit of a giant airship.

'I was about to send you a pop-up message, sir,' said the young man at the controls. Granger slowly readjusted to the real world and shook off the nausea as his inner ear recalibrated its understanding of real-world gravity. 'We're coming in to dock.'

Granger refocused his eyes and looked out through the windows of the airship to see the concrete and glass towers of an urban island, bathed in the morning sun, spread out beneath him. They were homing in on the southern tip of the island. Rising up to greet them was Manhattan's most iconic building: One World Trade Center. The glass and steel tower, the Freedom Tower as it was called, rose defiantly above lower Manhattan, looking down on the twin reflecting pools that commemorated the two towers that had once stood in their place. Granger had been born into a world without those twin towers, but their destruction was part of American history he learned in school. The terrorist attack, which had shocked the entire world back then, now felt quaint by comparison.

Granger picked up his titanium legs and snapped them onto his stumps.

He had lost his real legs in a car crash at the age of six. Granger didn't often miss them, though – and not just because of the cyber-kinetic walking system he had invented. Matthew Granger had created a world in which he didn't need to walk. A world in which he could fly. A virtual world. A better world. For everyone.

His Metasphere had become more than a phenomenon, it had become life as most people knew it. Until a few months ago, over 92% of all financial transactions took place inside the Metasphere, and Granger took his cut from each one.

Twenty years after his accident, after years of coding the first iteration of the Metasphere, which was hailed as Web 4.0, he became a billionaire and one of the most influential and celebrated people on the planet. But ever since then he felt as if he had been under attack. Everyone wanted a piece of his creation – from the faltering real-world governments desperate to shore up what little power they had left to those misguided anarchists the Guardians.

Now, a new breed of opportunist, the Chinese child prodigy, Mr Chang, had emerged – with the gall to compete with him. While Chang made Granger feel old at thirty-nine, Granger knew he was smarter than any competitor. Smarter and more determined.

He would never give up fighting. The Metasphere

was *his*. Only he had the vision to realise its true potential. Only Matthew Granger could safeguard the future. *Only Matthew Granger could save people from themselves.*

The airship docked with a tall, metal structure rising from the top of the Freedom Tower. Granger was the first to disembark.

He walked down a flight of twisting steel steps, his metallic feet clanking on each one. He was followed, as always, by a small army of bodyguards and flunkies. A similar army was waiting for him on the roof.

At the head of it was a young woman, polished and poised with tied-back, jet-black hair and a black power suit, whom Granger recognised immediately.

The woman stepped forward, her hand held out in greeting. 'Good evening, Mr Granger. It's good to meet you in person, at last. I'm Lori Weisberg. I'm—'

Granger took the woman's hand. He smiled, forcing himself to turn on the charm. 'I'm delighted to meet you, Madam President. You, but you alone, may call me Matthew. And, of course, I'm looking forward to doing business with you.'

'Welcome to the Republic of Manhattan, Matthew,' said the president, carrying herself with an air of authority that put ten years on her actual age of seventeen. 'I hope you will soon call it home.'

Jonah stared at his father. He moved his mouth, but no words came out. He didn't know how to answer Jason's

29

question. What could he possibly say to him?

Yes, Dad. Of course you're dead. Your real-world body has been dead for three years. You exist only as an Uploaded avatar now, a collection of digitised memories.

He was relieved when Jason looked away from him with a frown. Something had distracted him. 'Can you hear that noise?' he asked.

'What noise?' asked Jonah.

He could hear it too now. It sounded like voices – a chorus of chanting. They were outside the stadium, but calling loudly enough to be heard here on the pitch.

Jonah was afraid, at first. He thought back to the confrontation he'd witnessed earlier, and worried that mobs of settlers were clashing with anti-Chang protesters. But the voices didn't sound angry. They sounded excited. They had started to come together, to chant something in unison.

Jonah grinned. 'It must be one of the developers arriving. Maybe Luke Wexler is already here?'

'Hmmm,' said Jason. 'I'm not sure. It sounds to me like...'

And then Jonah heard it clearly, his own name.

'Jo-*nah*,' said Jason. 'They're shouting for you.'

Jonah floated up tentatively through the stands.

He wasn't sure he wanted to face what was outside, but he was certainly curious – and it provided a welcome distraction from his father's questions.

When he reached the edge of the massive Chang Stadium and cautiously raised his head up over the parapet, he was spotted immediately.

Outside, hundreds of avatars had gathered before the main doors – and they had gathered for Jonah. They flew towards him, chanting his name, holding up their hands to touch him. He was grateful for the stadium's invisible firewall, which held them back.

'They're all here for you, son,' said Jason, who had flown up to Jonah's side.

'I don't understand,' Jonah said.

'What's to understand?' asked Jason. He indicated a massive banner, which two avatars were flying: 'DELACROIX OUR SAVIOUR'.

'You're a hero!' said Jason.

'But I'm not a…'

'You led them to salvation,' said Jason.

'I did what I did to save you,' confessed Jonah.

'I know, I was there, remember,' said Jason.

Jonah looked at his dad. He wondered just how much he *did* remember.

'You saved the Uploaded, Jonah. When their island in the Metasphere was crumbling, when it looked like they would all be destroyed, you were the one who gave them an escape route. You led them here to safety. You're not just a hero, Jonah, you are their saviour.'

Jonah was overwhelmed by the idea, and by the attention. 'I don't know what to do,' he said.

'This is your moment, son,' said Jason. 'All these people are here for you. They love you. Go out there and feel loved.'

'But I do, Dad,' said Jonah. 'Now that you're back. That's all I wanted.'

'Go on!'

Jonah started forward, hesitantly. As soon as he slipped through the firewall, the crowd pounced.

It felt like everyone wanted a part of him. They pawed, tugged and screamed in his ear. He was glad he wasn't in his real-world body, or else he could have been badly hurt.

But Jonah listened to what the avatars around him were saying. They were thanking him for saving their digital souls.

'We would have depixelated if it hadn't been for you—'

'—finally someone to stand up to Granger!'

Most of the crowd were Uploaded. Of course, it made sense that they would be. Inside the Changsphere, the displaced Uploaded still outnumbered the living avatars. Jonah was shocked that he couldn't distinguish between the digital ghosts, who were usually disoriented and confused, and the avatars with living flesh-and-blood bodies behind them. Like Jason, the Uploaded had recently thrown off the confusion that had once clouded their minds. Many could think clearly, for the first time in their afterlife. They knew exactly where they were – and many of them, it seemed, knew *what* they were.

'*You gave us new life.*'

'*—freed us from confusion.*'

'*—helped us to live again!*'

They were coming alive – and that should have been wonderful, a miracle really, but Jonah had to suppress a little shiver at the thought: *The dead were coming back to life!*

And, his dad was right. Jonah was more than just their hero. He was their saviour.

Jonah thought he should get back inside the stadium, to his father. But when he turned to leave, he was blocked by a gigantic leech.

He fought the urge to recoil. It was rude to judge someone by their avatar. But it was also said that people's avatars reflected their true selves, far more so than their physical bodies did.

'You've done so much for us,' said the leech in a sucking, slurping voice. 'Can you do one more thing? Can you take us back?'

'Take you back?' asked Jonah. 'Where?'

The leech avatar drew closer to Jonah. It contorted its long, flat body to bring its mouth down to Jonah's ear. For an instant, Jonah looked into the leech's slimy mouth and saw hundreds of tiny, sharp teeth. Then, the leech whispered something to him.

Suddenly, a pair of hooves kicked the leech in the head and sent it flying. Jonah looked back at the newcomer, a pearly white unicorn with a striking red mane and tail hair, and the wings of a bird, and shouted, 'Sam, what are you doing?' He didn't understand why his friend was ruining his moment of fame.

'Saving you,' said Sam.

She took Jonah's arm between her front hooves and pulled him up after her. The crowd started shouting after him, begging him not to go. Jonah resented Sam's intrusion. He was enjoying the attention.

'Saving me from what?' he asked. 'I don't need saving!'

Sam pulled Jonah clear of the crowd. Jonah looked back over his shoulder. A few avatars had broken away from the rest to follow him. Within seconds, a hundred more had followed their lead. The crowd came streaming after him.

Sam kept the two of them ahead of it, her wings beating furiously. Floating in the sky before them were several golden rings of light.

'Which of those is your exit halo?' asked Sam.

One of the rings grew brighter at Jonah's approach, although the effect was only visible to his eyes. He pointed.

'Wait,' said Jonah, as Sam tried to push him through the light ring. 'What about my dad? I left him back at the stadium. I... I never said goodbye to him.'

'Don't you get it?' said Sam. 'I'm saving you from him!'

The crowd were almost upon them again.

Sam kicked Jonah hard with her hind hooves. He tumbled backwards through his exit halo, a protest still forming in his throat, and was enveloped by darkness.

4

When Jonah opened his eyes, he felt disoriented and nauseous.

He held his head, waiting for his senses to make the transition from the virtual world back to the real one. But he felt an unusual pang of motion sickness.

Then he realised that his whole body was moving.

He had connected to a computer terminal in the back of a land yacht, in a village called Woomera. But looking around at the barren Australian Outback, he wasn't in Woomera any more. The yacht – a wind-powered vehicle with four giant wheels and a fin-shaped sail – was gliding smoothly across the red desert sands and captained by a tall Aboriginal man Jonah recognised from the attack on the Southern Corner.

Slumped beside Jonah in the rear of the cockpit was Sam, her red hair matching the shade of the mane of her unicorn avatar. She was coming back to the real world and opened her eyes.

'What did you do that for?' cried Jonah. 'And where are we going?'

'Where do you think?' asked Sam, after she had taken a moment to let her stomach settle down. 'We're going back to Uluru.'

'I thought we weren't clearing out until Thursday.'

'It *is* Thursday. It's Thursday morning. You'd know that, Jonah, if you'd come back to reality every once in a while!'

Jonah liked Samantha Kavanaugh. He admired her self-confidence and her resourcefulness. On some days, he even caught himself thinking she was pretty. And she had been good to him, especially when the other Guardians had been mistrusting. Sometimes, however, she treated him like a kid.

Sam was only a year older than Jonah. But she was a warrior and had been a spy from a young age. Sam was brought up to be a freedom fighter, and she had been playing that role for some years already.

She was a Guardian.

The Guardians were the sworn enemies of Matthew Granger's Millennials.

They believed that the virtual world should be free, governed by its users, and not controlled by any one man. Until recently, Jonah had hated them. He believed they were anarchists, prepared to kill indiscriminately for their misguided agenda.

That was before he had learned that his dad had been one of them. That was the day that Jonah's life changed forever.

Pursued by the Millennials, Jonah allied himself with the Guardians, rejecting his previous beliefs about the importance of control and order in the Metasphere. But deep down, he still questioned whether he had chosen the right side.

Two months ago, Sam had led the Guardians to their first significant victory over Granger. With Jonah's help, they had captured the Southern Corner: one of the four secret server farms that powered Granger's Metasphere. It had been hidden here in the Australian desert, inside Uluru, the ancient and, to many people, sacred rock formation.

'*One down, three to go,*' had become the rallying cry of the emboldened Guardians.

'You still haven't told me,' said Jonah, 'what were you "saving" me from?'

'I'm not sure,' said Sam.

'What do you mean?'

'There's a meet-up,' said Sam, 'in the Metasphere, in twenty minutes. Dad wants you there. I was about to send you a pop-up about it, when I saw you…'

'What?' asked Jonah. 'What exactly did you see that got you so riled up?'

'You were completely surrounded by them, Jonah,' said Sam. 'You were being mobbed. It looked like they were attacking you.'

Jonah thought back to the mob he witnessed; wondering if he should confide in Sam. *No*, he told himself, *I can't risk them associating my dad with those monsters.*

'They were *thanking* me! They were thanking me for saving them from the Island and—'

'I was there too,' Sam pointed out. 'So don't you go getting a saviour complex, Jonah Delacroix.'

Jonah didn't answer her. Maybe it was vain of him, but he had enjoyed being a hero. It had made him feel good about himself for once. He was cross with Sam for tearing him away from that. Perhaps she was jealous. *That must be it. She was no longer the bright young star of the Guardian cause.*

'You've been logged on all night, Jonah,' said Sam.

'So?' said Jonah. 'Some people stay logged on for days!'

'And when I saw you were in the Changsphere... We've been getting reports that the Uploaded might be—'

'They're thinking more clearly, piecing together memories,' said Jonah, thinking back to the question his father had asked of him. 'Even starting to realise that they're dead. It's because of the—'

'I know. I know why it is, Jonah. The Changsphere is more powerful than we ever knew, powerful enough to give the Uploaded their consciousness again. I'm just not so sure if it's a good thing.'

'Why wouldn't it be?' asked Jonah. He didn't reveal that he had had the same doubts. He remembered the question his dad had asked him, and he shivered.

'The Uploaded were never meant to know the truth,'

said Sam. 'That was the deal. They could live forever, virtually, but they had to forget what it had cost them to get there. Each of them committed *suicide* to Upload. They're not supposed to know they're dead!'

'Most of them know, or are starting to realise,' said Jonah. 'It's like an awakening.'

'And that knowledge could drive them mad,' said Sam.

Jonah thought about his father, the way he was piecing together his memories, frustrated by the gaps, yearning to go back to the real world.

'Jonah, there have been rumours of attacks.'

'Attacks?'

'Uploaded avatars,' said Sam, 'attacking the living. Just rumours for now, but if the rumours are true…'

'My dad!' Jonah realised. 'You said you were saving me from him. You thought… You thought my own dad might hurt me?' Sam didn't answer him. 'Is that what this meet-up is about?' asked Jonah.

'I think it's about Uluru, and what happens once we hand it back,' said Sam. 'It's about planning our next move.'

She tossed a Pro-Meal pouch to Jonah. 'Here. You'd better eat this before you log on again.'

'I'm not hungry,' replied Jonah, looking at the cartoon chicken on the package.

'You haven't eaten since yesterday morning,' said Sam. 'I know it's easy to forget when you're online – but you have to look after your real-world self, Jonah. I'm worried about you.'

The next few minutes passed in silence.

Jonah peered into the Changsphere through his datapad. He saw the crowd of avatars outside the Chang Stadium breaking up, going their separate ways. Many of them were downcast, disappointed by their saviour's sudden disappearance.

He couldn't see his dad.

Jonah munched on his bland-tasting artificial protein mix. It wasn't pleasant, but Sam was right, it was necessary. Virtual food tasted better, but it couldn't sustain the eater. *If only it could*, thought Jonah. *If only I didn't have to keep coming back here!*

Sam turned to him. He knew what she was going to say. 'I suppose it's time?' said Jonah. Sam nodded.

Jonah was still plugged in from his visit to the Changsphere. An Ethernet wire, his tether to the virtual world, snaked from the computer terminal beneath his seat and went under his T-shirt. There, a plastic nozzle-like adaptor connected the wire with the opening in Jonah's lower back: the Direct Interface socket he had had fitted at birth.

The adaptor linked the computer to Jonah's brain, to his entire central nervous system, via his spinal fluid. Once connected, his brain would process the virtual world as a three-dimensional digital reality.

Sam gave Jonah a list of numbers, which he tapped

into the datapad: his Point of Origin co-ordinates. There were only eight numbers: a Metasphere grid reference. The new Changsphere co-ordinates were ten digits long.

'I think we should avoid the Changsphere for a while,' said Sam. She was telling, not asking. 'Just until we can find out more about what's happening in there.'

Sam had plugged herself back in too. Her body slumped in its seat as her consciousness transferred from the real world to the virtual world. Jonah leaned back. He looked up at the bright blue morning sky. He took one final breath of hot, dry desert air and snapped the adapter into place.

The nausea hit him again. Jonah felt his senses slipping away.

Even as they did, however, he remembered something. He remembered what the leech in the Changsphere had whispered to him. He hadn't taken it in at the time because he was distracted by Sam's unexpected arrival.

The leech had whispered just three words to Jonah, in that sucking, slurping voice. Three words that made little sense to him, if indeed he had heard them right.

'I'm so hungry!'

5

In a posh restaurant on Manhattan's Upper East Side, Matthew Granger was suffering through one of the finest meals he had ever tasted.

President Weisberg had reserved a semicircular booth for five, in the back corner, underneath the famous 'Manhattan Forever' painting, of a motorcycle-riding secessionist jumping over a US Army tank.

Granger didn't enjoy socialising, and he had deliberately taken a seat at one edge of the booth in case he lost his patience. He wasn't especially good at making small talk, least of all with people he hardly knew and respected less.

He knew the importance of having contacts in business, however – and especially now, when allies were scarcer than ever. And within the island enclave of Manhattan this was how such contacts were created and nurtured.

So Granger smiled and nodded as his four fellow diners talked to him about inane subjects like opera and a charity fundraiser for the children of Florida. He consoled himself with the fact that his honey-crusted gammon steak was perfectly prepared.

He knew that, across the world tonight, most people would be dining on Pro-Meal artificial-protein pouches.

Fine eating had become the exclusive province of the uber-rich and powerful. Manhattan, however, was the exclusive enclave of both.

And if Manhattan's president, Lori Weisberg, had her way, Granger would soon be joining them.

'You wouldn't regret buying into Manhattan, Matthew,' said Lori. 'Our community was built for people like you. When we seceded from the union, we fought for a place where the world's most important and influential people could feel at home. Of course, we also have the lowest tax rates in the Western world, and virtually no crime.'

The Manhattan revolution had been a bloody one, but Granger couldn't argue with its success. The island was a rock of stability and security in a tumultuous world. It was run as one massive housing co-operative overseen by a board of directors. The more shares a person bought in the island, the more seats he had on the co-op board. And the board appointed the president.

'She may be young, but she ain't wrong, Matty,' said Luke Wexler in a Texan drawl that grated on Granger's nerves.

Once a coder for Granger's Millennial Corporation, Wexler was now the world's number one games developer. He had a movie star's profile and a rock star's ego. And Granger despised him.

'You know I'm a Texan at heart, *Matty*, but moving here was the best decision I ever made,' said Wexler. He doffed his trademark black cowboy hat in the direction of their young host. 'Well, except for leavin' the Millennial Corp.'

'That's not exactly how I recall it,' said Granger, remembering how he'd fired Luke for stealing Metasphere code and repurposing it for an immersive role-playing game. 'Leaving and being escorted out by the police for data theft are two different things.'

'Well, history is a funny thing, *Matty*. And the important thing is that we're both sitting here as, what did you call us, Madam President? As "the world's most important and influential people"? I kinda like the sound of that.'

'Mr Wexler had some trouble with some overly passionate fans,' said Lori, sensing the tension. 'I assured him we could provide him with all the security he needed. Mr Castle relocated here two months ago, for similar reasons.'

Ellias Castle, who was already tilting slightly from three martinis, sat opposite Granger on the other edge of the booth, and nodded in agreement. Granger hadn't met him before, but he knew him by reputation. Castle was a young hotshot financier. He had operated out of the City Tower in London – until it had been destroyed in a terrorist bombing. The truth was, Granger himself had ordered the building's destruction to kill Jason Delacroix, a traitor he believed he had tracked to the skyscraper.

Granger smiled at Lori. 'I have my own army.'

'You must need it,' said Bryony, fifth and final diner,

who lounged at Granger's immediate right. Bryony – no surname – was a striking woman, tall and statuesque with a polished bald head that reflected the restaurant's tiny spotlights. Looking closer, Granger noticed the telltale scars of too many cosmetic operations on the edges of her beautiful face.

She was the world's most followed and most indiscreet video blogger. Millions of people hung on her every word. They let her tell them which games to buy, which movies to see and which celebrities were important.

'Of course, I have detractors,' said Granger. 'A man in my position—'

'You have been called the most hated man in the world,' said Bryony.

'Yes, by you,' snapped Granger. 'I did see that particular vlog. Thank you.'

'You should try working for Matty,' joked Wexler. 'Nah, I'm only kiddin'. You shouldn't.'

Granger hated it when Wexler called him 'Matty', and he was pretty sure that Wexler knew it.

'Matthew didn't come here to discuss work. I'm sure he'd rather talk about—'

'No,' said Granger, setting down his knife and fork. 'No, it's OK, Lori. It's hardly a secret that the Metasphere is in a time of transition.'

'Try a full-scale meltdown!' boomed Wexler.

'Losing GamesCon,' said Bryony, 'that must've been a big blow.'

'I have to admit,' began Ellias, waving his empty martini glass in the air to signal for another, 'that I just moved my entire virtual property portfolio to the Changsphere. Get in early is my MO.'

'The Changsphere is a nothing but a passing fad,' said Granger. 'Its novelty will wear off and people will return to one virtual world they know and trust.'

He had no doubt that Bryony was recording his every word.

'Nice PR pitch, Matty,' said Wexler. 'But I don't reckon we should believe the hype. The Metasphere's yesterday's software. While you were locked up in jail, young Chang got the jump on your tech!'

'Technology moves very fast, Luke,' said Granger. 'And you have to be a lot more than *lucky* to stay on top. That's why I'm working on an upgrade to the Metasphere's operating system, which will—'

'But what about those Guardians?' asked Castle. 'They pulled a hostile takeover on your Southern Corner. They've taken a quarter of the Metasphere from you!'

'And they murdered a lot of hard-working, innocent people in the process! The Guardians are a clueless but very dangerous rabble of anarchists,' said Granger. 'They say they want freedom, but they don't know what real freedom means. They don't understand that a society needs structures, institutions, laws and leadership. I'm not worried about the Guardians. They'll soon go the way of the real-world governments.'

'This government,' Lori interjected, 'is perfectly stable. And fully capitalised.'

'Of course, Madam President,' said Granger. 'That's very clear.'

'Well, I'll take luck where I can get it. And right now, that's in the Changsphere. You may want to vlog this, Bryony, cuz I'm sayin' it for the first time. Lucky Luke Wexler's gonna launch *Brain-Sucking Zombies 4* at GamesCon in the Changsphere.'

'Luke Wexler abandoning the Metasphere,' said Bryony. 'Now that's a story.'

Lori leaned over to Bryony with an intense stare. 'Now, Bryony, you know this dinner is strictly off the record.' She then leaned back, placed her white linen napkin over her empty plate and pushed it away from her. 'Why don't we take this upstairs?' she suggested. 'I have reserved a private bar for the five of us. And, Mr Granger, perhaps I could tell you more about our social calendar here?'

Granger nodded, grateful for the diplomatic intervention.

'One of your army brats is trying to get your attention, Matty,' said Wexler, pointing at the door.

Granger craned his neck to see one of his Millennials, a wiry young man in black fatigues with a scar on his concerned face. Granger was part relieved, part apprehensive.

Dinner was over. So much, Granger thought, for nurturing contacts.

*

'We've found one, sir,' said the young Millennial man.

'Already?' said Granger. They climbed into a yellow auto-cab: an automated vehicle that ran on an electrical smart grid. The door slid shut behind them with a soft hiss. The Millennial handed Granger a datapad.

'Stuart,' he said. 'My name's Stuart, from the rapid response cell.'

'I didn't ask,' confirmed Granger.

'Right, yes, sorry, sir. But it looks like your suspicions were correct.'

'And that's a surprise to you?'

The Millennial froze under Granger's glare. He wasn't as tough as he looked.

'There are two sets of code here,' observed Granger.

'You can see the parasite code has overwritten the user's avatar code sequence.'

'Yes, yes,' said Granger, 'I can see. And you've tracked this user's Real World Location? How soon can you get him here?'

The driverless cab pulled away. It glided past Central Park, headed downtown. The pavements around them were empty but for an occasional security patrol: a far cry from the crowded thoroughfares of other major world cities.

'That's just it, sir. He's already here. It's David. David Foster.'

Granger had no idea who 'David Foster' was. He was

beginning to work it out, however, when his Millennial follower saw his confusion and explained:

'From the anti-virus division. David's one of us, sir. He's a Millennial. He plugged in at the Freedom Tower, went into the Changsphere, and when he logged off...'

'What?'

'He was someone else.'

'You look surprised to see me, David,' said Granger. It was an understatement.

David Foster sat on the floor of a tiny cleaner's cupboard, handcuffed to a shelving rack. His jaw had dropped open as Granger had walked in.

He closed it now. 'N-no, sir,' he said. 'Well, a little, maybe. I don't understand what's happening. Why am I chained up?'

Granger set up a folding chair and sat down on it. He *did* remember David now. He was one of Granger's programmers: an overweight kid with chalk-white, greasy skin.

'How long have you worked for me, David?' he asked.

'I don't know. A couple of years, maybe.'

'Do you know where you are?'

'Yeah, of course I know. What... What do you mean?'

'Tell me,' demanded Granger. 'Tell me where we are.'

David looked at Granger, then at the Millennials

standing guard over him, as if he thought this might be a trick. 'One World Trade Center. In New York… Manhattan, I mean. The Republic of Manhattan.'

Granger clicked his fingers over his shoulder. A flunky handed him a datapad, containing the information he had asked for: David Foster's records.

Granger thumbed through the data. 'It says here you started working for the Millennial Corporation over three years ago.'

'A couple of years. Three.' David shrugged. 'Whatever.'

'And before that, you were…?'

'Nothing,' said David. 'This is my first… Unless you count the money I made role-playing online. This is my first job. It's the only job I ever wanted. My brother—'

'Yes, your brother works for me too, doesn't he? His name?'

'His name is Gareth. But why—?'

'And your mother's maiden name?' Apparently, this was a tougher question, because David hesitated. After Granger prompted him, however, he answered correctly – as he did to the next three questions too. Still, Granger wasn't satisfied.

'Please, sir,' said David, 'if I've done something wrong—'

'You were in the Changsphere,' said Granger.

'Yes, sir. You sent me in there.'

'Do you remember why?'

'As a spy. To find out more – about the Changsphere itself, and about the Uploaded, and to stir things up if I could.'

'And what did you learn?'

'I tried, sir,' said David. 'I tried my best. It's hard in there. It's hard to tell the Uploaded from the living avatars. They aren't different like they used to be.'

'Nevertheless,' said Granger, 'I think you did encounter at least one Uploaded avatar. And I think it did something to you.'

David shook his head. 'No, sir.'

'You're a programmer, David. Tell me, what do you make of this?' Granger showed his pad to David. He had called up the data he had been shown in the cab. The data that suggested that, while David Foster had been in the Changsphere, his brainwave patterns had suddenly, massively changed.

'I don't know, sir,' said David. 'I don't know what to make of it. Maybe it's a bug. The Changsphere is still new, after all, and Mr Chang... Well, he isn't as smart as you are, sir. I expect his software is probably full of glitches.'

Granger smiled at the compliment, despite himself. 'You're good,' he said. 'You're very good. And you certainly have access to David Foster's surface memories. I wonder what we might find, however, if we were to scratch beneath that surface?'

Granger leaned back in his folding chair. It creaked under his weight. 'Plug Mr Foster in,' he instructed his minders, 'and bring me a handheld monitor.'

David looked startled. 'What are you doing?'

'Tell me about your avatar, David,' said Granger. 'Tell me what shape you take in the Metasphere.'

Two Millennials grabbed David by his shoulders. They yanked him forward and pulled up his shirt, revealing the plastic ring that guarded the socket in his back. One of them had an Ethernet wire, which snaked out of the storeroom to a terminal outside. The other unwrapped a new, sterile DI adaptor pack.

'You haven't answered me, David,' said Granger. 'According to your file, your avatar is a penguin. Isn't that cute? But I don't think that's what we'll see when we plug you in.'

David maintained a sullen silence. Granger could see the sweat forming on his brow.

'No, I thought not,' said Granger. He gestured to his Millennials to stop what they were doing. There was no need now.

He leaned forward. He was smiling again – but this time, it was the smile of a predator that had cornered its prey.

'Who are you? And what have you done with David Foster?'

6

A victory concert was rocking Guardian Island, once the Island of the Uploaded.

Jonah had to shout to make himself heard by Sam. 'This is where the Guardians are holding the meet-up?'

Avatars descended from all directions. They touched down on the sun-kissed beaches and threaded their way through the forests inland. The first band, a girl group called Crush, was already onstage and the whole island throbbed with their bass vibrations.

'Where better?' asked Sam. She tossed her unicorn's head, flicking her red mane out of her eyes.

Jonah knew the Guardians had no formal headquarters; it was part of their ethos to remain a network, not a hierarchy. Each time they assembled in a different part of the Metasphere. This way, they could keep one step ahead of the law, and the Millennials.

'Hey, you kids!' A winged creature, a gryphon, floated down to greet them. Jonah knew this gryphon well, with its body of a lion and head and wings of an eagle. His name was Axel Kavanaugh. He was Jason Delacroix's oldest friend, and Sam's dad.

'How about all this, then?' Axel grinned broadly. 'Isn't this just brilliant? The biggest gig the Metasphere has ever seen – and it's all free! This is what the Guardians are all about. This is what we've been fighting for. This is freedom!'

Axel led Jonah and Sam towards the music. The closer they got, the more crowded the Island became. Soon they were elbow to elbow – in some cases, flank to flank or wing to wing – with other avatars. Axel continued to press forward doggedly, clearing a path for the others to follow.

Jonah knew this island well – parts of it, at least. It had had another name once: the Island of the Uploaded. This was where the living had come to visit the dead. The last time he had been here, the Island had been destroyed and Jonah had only narrowly escaped. Now the Guardians had rebooted the Island, creating a stable landmass with a huge, open space at its centre.

The portal to the Changsphere still hovered above the Island: a square window of pure, bright light. Jonah watched as a small flock of avatars flew into that light – another family, he guessed, emigrating to a better life.

A stage had been erected in the new central clearing. Axel pushed his way up to it. A hulking gorilla stepped in front of him, barring his way.

'We're with the band,' said Axel, and the gorilla stepped aside.

The Guardians assembled beneath the stage, in what looked like a medieval cellar, dark with vaulted ceilings. The meet-up hadn't started yet. For now, an eclectic mixture of avatars stood in small groups, debating, arguing or just catching up with each other. As Jonah floated between them, he heard clips of their conversations:

'—lost a lot of good people that night, but it was worth it to—'

'We need to strike first before—'

'—Granger's going to want revenge.'

'—it's creepy, the Uploaded mixing with the living like they're—'

Across the crowded room, Jonah spotted a familiar chestnut-brown Clydesdale horse. Jonah stepped back to avoid the gruff avatar.

'Over here, Bradbury!' Axel shouted. 'You old warhorse! What are you doing here? We haven't seen you in weeks!'

'I couldn't miss the victory celebrations, could I?' said Bradbury.

'Where are you these days?' asked Axel. 'Maybe we could get together for—'

'I'm on assignment, Axel,' said Bradbury, 'and you know I can't give away my RWL, not even to you.' Bradbury laughed, but fell silent when he noticed Jonah's small humatar avatar. 'What's the kid doing here?'

Jonah had been hanging back, hoping to remain inconspicuous. He didn't like Bradbury much. Now, however, he found himself the centre of attention.

'He's earned the right to be here,' said Sam.

'Has he found us the three other Corners yet?' asked Bradbury.

The question had been directed at Axel, but everyone looked to Jonah for the answer. He shifted awkwardly. 'I...well, no, I haven't, but...'

Axel's eyes narrowed. 'I thought you spent last night with Jason.'

'I did,' said Jonah.

'Then what's the problem?' asked Axel. 'Jason must know where they are. That's why he went undercover as Granger's pilot in the first place.'

'I haven't asked him yet,' said Jonah. 'Dad's still confused.'

'Now *I'm* confused,' said Axel. 'I heard the Uploaded were thinking more clearly by the day, getting their memories back in order.'

Bradbury glared at Jonah. 'We need to find those other three server farms,' he growled. 'We hold the Southern Corner, but that's little use to us if the Millennials still control the other three.'

'I know,' said Jonah.

Bradbury turned to Axel. 'Maybe you should talk to Jason yourself. You were his friend, after all. He might—'

'No,' said Jonah. 'I'll do it. I'll ask him. Next time I see him. I promise.'

They were interrupted by an angry shout: 'What's

that traitor doing here?'

Another humatar, gnarly-looking with dreadlocks, pushed his way towards them. He jabbed an angry finger at Jonah. At the moment he had spoken, the band above had fallen silent. The humatar's raised voice, therefore, had carried to everyone down here.

A hush fell over the assembled Guardians. They all turned to stare at Jonah.

'I called this meet-up,' snapped the angry humatar, 'and he isn't on the guest list.'

Sam leapt to Jonah's defence. 'What do you mean, "guest list"? Jonah proved himself on the field of battle.'

'By letting Granger live?'

'I didn't see you at the Southern Corner,' shot back Jonah.

The humatar's skin was literally crawling with animated tattoos. A helicopter circled his neck while a spider spun its web beneath his left ear. Jonah recognised the tattoos – and the humatar now, too. He had seen him before, at another Guardian meet-up. The humatar's name was Jez, and he was not a leader, exactly, but one of their founders, and as such possessed a great deal of influence that he wasn't afraid to wield.

'I'm right, aren't I?' Jez snarled, right up in Jonah's face. 'You had that creep at your mercy and you let him walk away!'

'I let him fly away, actually,' said Jonah. 'Because I'm not a murderer.'

'Then you're not one of us,' Jez shot back. 'Freedom comes at a price that a true Guardian isn't afraid to pay.'

'He might be a spy!' The accusation came from a female mantis avatar scuttling to Jez's side. She held her forelegs out before her, clasping them menacingly.

'Liv's right,' said Jez. 'What do any of us really know about this kid, except that he came from nowhere and suddenly he's planning missions and eavesdropping on our meet-ups. He could be working for Granger!'

Jonah couldn't believe these people; after all he'd done for the Guardians at Uluru…

'That's ridiculous!' Sam protested.

'I vouch for Jonah,' said Axel. 'He saved my life and Bradbury's. And he's Jason's kid. If you have a problem with him, you have a problem with me.'

'I don't mean to disrespect you, Kavanaugh,' said Jez. 'But when it's your meet-up, you can set the guest list. He ain't welcome at mine!'

Sam opened her mouth to argue further. Jonah stopped her. 'It's OK,' he said. 'I don't want to be the cause of any trouble. I'll see you back in the real world later.' He glanced over at Axel. Axel nodded.

The band had started up again. Jonah turned and walked away, determined to keep his head held high. He could feel forty pairs of eyes burning into his back.

Funny how things change, he thought. Less than an hour ago, Jonah had been called a saviour by the

Uploaded. But here, among his supposed allies, he was called a traitor.

At least Jonah's association with the Guardians had been good for one thing. It had got him to the front of the crowd.

Crush had finished its set, and a new band took the stage. They called themselves the Beetles – though only one of their avatars was an actual beetle. The lead singer looked more like a giant ant, and the drummer was a green pyramid. *The Beetles*, Jonah thought, *stupid name for a rock band*.

Their music wasn't very good, but it was passionate. The lyrics were all about freedom and fighting the system, and the crowd lapped them up, roaring their approval. Many of them waved Guardian banners, which would have been illegal two months ago. In the Millennial-controlled quarters of the Metasphere, they still were.

The best thing about the band was its sheer volume. The music filled Jonah's head and drove out all other thoughts – for a short time, at least. He couldn't help but look at the stage, though, and wonder what might be happening underneath it.

It's not fair, he thought. He felt an ache of frustration in his stomach, and he balled his fists so tightly that his fingernails cut into his palms. After everything he'd done for the Guardians. But still not on the guest list!

He heard a ping-ping sound, even over the pounding music. A red dialogue balloon appeared by Jonah's head. A message from Sam or Axel, he guessed, apologising for the way he had been treated. Perhaps they had talked Jez and the others round, and were asking Jonah back to the meeting.

Well, maybe I won't go, he thought. *Maybe I'll just stay and watch the concert.*

He pulled the pop-up around to read it:

I NEED YOUR HELP.

It wasn't from Sam or Axel. It was from the last person Jonah ever expected to hear from.

Its digital signature read simply: MG.

7

Jonah stared at the pop-up, unable to move.

It floated beside him, invisible to the huge crowd around him. He tried to concentrate on the music, but again and again he found himself staring at the pop-up.

He remembered what Matthew Granger had said to him, the last time they had met: *You are Millennial material, Jonah. Leadership material. We would make an excellent team, the two of us.* He had also promised that they would meet again.

With Matthew Granger, a promise could also be a threat.

Jonah knew he should swipe away the pop-up, but the message intrigued him: I NEED YOUR HELP. Jonah knew, from Granger's autobiography, that he wasn't the kind of man who liked to ask for help from anyone.

Jonah looked at the pop-up again – and, this time, he noticed something new about it. In its bottom-right corner, there was a small black arrow – and suddenly, as if it could somehow sense Jonah's eyes upon it, the arrow began to blink yellow.

A shortcut icon.

He reached out to touch the arrow, but stopped himself. He remembered where he was. He remembered the accusation laid against him: that he might be a spy. And here he was, thinking about making contact with the Guardians' worst enemy. Wouldn't that just prove Jez and the others right?

So what if it does? thought Jonah, with a surge of bitterness. *So what if I do talk to Granger, hear his side of the story? At least he thinks I'm worth talking to!*

He reached for the arrow again. His fingers brushed against it, and before he knew what was happening the pop-up expanded to the height and shape of a doorway. And sucked him in.

A red light enveloped Jonah, and the sounds of the Guardians' concert were cut dead. His leading foot touched down on a concrete floor, and a cool air-conditioning breeze brushed his face. The doorway sealed behind him.

He was in an enormous hangar. *No*, he thought, *it looks like* twenty *enormous hangars knocked together.* There were scores of avatars floating and flying around, busying themselves with all manner of digital contraptions.

Jonah's gaze, however, was drawn to one avatar in particular: an enormous black, hairy spider, with eight glistening black eyes and prominent fangs. Matthew Granger! He was squatting on all eight legs, waiting for Jonah – and suddenly Jonah's curiosity was replaced by fear.

'Do you like it?' asked Granger.

Jonah didn't know how to answer him. He couldn't begin to take in all he could see. In one part of the hangar, work was progressing on what looked like a vertical bullet train. In another, a group of avatars experimented with pop-up houses.

'This is our virtual lab,' said Granger, 'where we test new code and programs before we roll them out. Not many people know this building even exists. So I'm trusting you, Jonah, to keep this place a secret.'

Jonah was looking over Granger's shoulder, to where an owl and a rocking horse were stacking up glowing white rings.

'Disposable exit halos,' said Granger. 'We want to make it possible for each avatar to have as many exit points from the Metasphere as he or she likes, perhaps even carry one in their inventory space. Imagine, not being anchored to your Point of Origin!'

'It's incredible,' said Jonah.

'This is what the Millennial Corporation is all about, Jonah,' said Granger. 'Programming the future, improving the Metasphere for its users – no matter who might try to stop us.'

'You're trying to compete with the Changsphere,' Jonah realised. 'Upgrades to lure users back.'

Granger's eight eyes narrowed. 'Mr Chang is not as clever as he pretends to be. I invented Web 4.0. He simply copied my code and revved it up with more servers.

That's not innovation, that's theft.' While Granger was in prison, Mr Chang had had three years to program a sharper, more powerful virtual world and Jonah could sense the anger in Granger's arachnid avatar. 'Now that I am in control of the Metasphere once again – most of it – I will make his Changsphere look like a 2D simulation.'

Granger led Jonah through the huge hangar.

Jonah watched in awe as the programmers worked with embedded shortcuts, such as the one that had brought him here. He marvelled at the sight of experimental pop-up windows that looked out onto the real world.

Jonah made himself focus. 'You said you needed my help,' he said.

'I did,' confirmed Granger.

'I don't know if I can... What I mean to say is...'

'You are still with the Guardians,' said Granger. 'I understand that, you are still confused. You're young, and it goes with the territory. But you need to grow up soon, Jonah.'

Jonah thought back to his confrontation with Granger on the top of Ayers Rock. He felt like he'd already grown up a lot since that night, but he was still confused about his place in the world – both worlds.

'I asked you to think again about the choices you have made,' said Granger, 'and I'm sure you have been doing that. I wouldn't have contacted you so soon, except that a...situation has arisen.'

'What kind of situation?'

'The kind that is bigger than either the Millennials or the Guardians. A situation that pertains to the very survival of the virtual worlds.'

Jonah had a sinking feeling in his stomach. 'The Uploaded?'

Granger nodded. 'You're perceptive, Jonah. You understand far more than you think you do. And I'm willing to bet, far more than those Guardians give you credit for.'

Jonah tried hard not to agree with Granger, but he was right. 'The Uploaded are changing,' he said. 'They can think more clearly in the Changsphere than ever before.'

'Yes,' said Granger. 'Mr Chang has given them that facility – without once pausing to think about the consequences. And I believe the consequences will be dire.'

'Can you help them? The Uploaded?'

'Yes,' said Granger. 'If you help me. What do you know?'

'I saw it happen, in the Changsphere. A mob of avatars, Uploaded, attacked a group of live ones, and...' Jonah paused. Not only did he not know how to describe what he'd seen, he realised he shouldn't have been telling Granger this much at all. 'I've spent some time with... some of the Uploaded lately,' Jonah added, defending them. 'And not all of them are—'

'I heard rumours of these attacks,' said Granger. 'So I sent some people to investigate. One came back... changed.'

'Changed how?'

'I could show you better in the RW. What part of the world are you in? I could send a jet to collect you.'

Jonah kept his mouth shut. He knew better than to tell Granger his Real World Location. The black spider smiled. 'Never mind,' he said. 'You will have to take me at my word instead.'

He showed Jonah to a small door at the end of the hangar. Inside, in an expansive office, Jonah sat down in a plush chair while Granger hovered above a mahogany desk.

'This employee of mine – his name was David Foster – he had his whole life ahead of him, like you. But when he logged off, he was someone else altogether.'

'He was changed?'

'This madness affecting the Uploaded... It is more than just grief over the lives they have lost. It is a more primal urge than that.'

Jonah swallowed. 'One of them, the Uploaded, he whispered something in my ear.'

'What was it?'

'"I'm so hungry."'

Granger nodded. 'We detected a rewriting of David's avatar code sequence. We brought him back to the real world, where I questioned him myself. The person

I spoke to looked exactly like David. He had much of David's knowledge. Even some of his mannerisms were the same. That person, however, was not David.'

'I don't understand,' said Jonah.

'The Uploaded *are* hungry, Jonah,' said Granger. 'Hungry for life itself. And they have found a way to take it from the living, and escape the virtual world to be reborn in the real world.'

Jonah froze at the suggestion. 'Dead people coming back to life?'

'That's right, Jonah. The dead are rising.'

It took at least ten seconds for Granger's words to sink in, another ten for Jonah to formulate a response. Even then, he could only manage a feeble, 'How?'

'The Uploaded can *usurp* a living user's avatar.'

'Usurp?' echoed Jonah.

'You once held two avatars in your brain,' said Granger, 'yours and your father's. This is a similar state, but far less stable. The avatar of the Uploaded merges with the live user's, only in this case it subsumes it. The Uploaded gains access to the user's DNA-based code – and thus to his exit halo. Once the Uploaded avatar flies through that halo—'

'He'd wake up in the user's body. But... Can that really happen?'

'Ask David Foster! Except you can't. Because a digital parasite inhabits his brain, a once dead man called Joshua,' explained Granger. 'And Joshua's last memory of the real world is of his eighty-sixth birthday, twenty years ago.'

'So what happened to David? The real David?'

'To all intents and purposes, he no longer exists. Joshua's personality and his memories have overwritten those of the host brain. He now has full control of David's brain and his body.'

'And any of the Uploaded can do this? They can all be…born again?'

'I have been able to verify four cases of usurping so far. I know that doesn't sound like many – but, by its very nature, this transgression is difficult to detect.'

'You think there could be more victims?'

'At this point, there could be hundreds, thousands. Hundreds of thousands. We have no way to know for sure, but every reason to expect that, whatever the number, it's only going to rise exponentially.'

Jonah was overwhelmed. He had no idea that the violent attack he witnessed was the start of something so fundamental. 'We have to tell people,' he said, starting to panic. 'Warn them of the danger!'

'And that, Jonah, is where you come in.'

'How? You want me to…what? Warn the Guardians?'

'I doubt that would make much of a difference,' said Granger. 'But the Uploaded, they see you as their saviour. They respect you, and they'll listen to you.'

'I don't know…'

'You might be able to persuade them to curb their appetites. You might be able to buy some time for me to develop a final solution.'

'Why?' asked Jonah, suspiciously. 'I mean, why do you care about what's happening in the Changsphere? I thought you'd be glad that it's...'

'This is bigger than any rivalry between us. Chang created this situation – with your help, I might add – but all I care about is containing this new threat before it destroys everything you and I love about the virtual world.'

Now, Jonah understood. The Uploaded may have migrated to the Changsphere, but the portal between the Changsphere and the Metasphere was still open.

'The virtual world,' said Granger, 'is supposed to provide a haven from the real world. Should that ever cease to be the case, it...'

'It would be the end,' said Jonah.

'Yes,' agreed Granger. 'The end of both the Changsphere *and* the Metasphere.'

'I'll think about it,' said Jonah.

'That's all I ask,' said Granger. 'For now.'

Granger opened another pop-up with an embedded shortcut that Jonah stepped through to arrive back at Guardian Island. He reappeared at the concert, right at the front, blocking the view of a group of annoyed avatars.

'Where'd he come from?' barked a sausage-shaped dog.

'This is our spot,' protested a bright red fire hydrant, the dog's dancing partner.

Jonah was in no mood to enjoy the music, however, and he wove through the crowd to find his way back to the Island's shore. He lay down on the beach where he had once visited his Uploaded grandmother. He stared up at the clear blue sky with a heavy burden on his mind.

It seemed like everyone wanted something from him.

Mr Chang wanted his Chang Bridge device back. The Guardians wanted the locations of the rest of the Four Corners. Granger still wanted Jonah to join his Millennials. And now... Now, he would have to face the Uploaded. He had so many questions, but one rang out in his head louder than the metal clash music from the stage.

Why me?

8

The Australian desert sky was darkening, and Jonah could see the broad, flat-topped shape of Uluru ahead of him.

The great rock glowed a fierce shade of red in the rays of the setting sun. Jonah had been travelling all day, and his muscles felt stiff.

He hated the fact that it took so long – and was so difficult – to get anywhere in the real world. He couldn't imagine what it was like in his father's time, when people flew in aeroplanes to take holidays in faraway places. Sam had told him that the prop plane they had flown from Sydney to Woomera was recently destroyed by a *GuerreVert* attack on the private airfield. He was just glad that these land yachts had internet access, so at least while his body was stuck in one, his mind could roam free.

Sam had beaten him back from the Metasphere.

'How was your secret meeting?' asked Jonah. He was annoyed, but sounded more bitter than he had intended.

'Look,' said Sam, 'I'm sorry about Jez. He doesn't speak for all of us.'

'Well, you should definitely tell him that, because he seems to think he does.'

'I think he's actually a bit jealous of you.'

'He's got a funny way of showing it. You'd think he'd be happy that we took the Southern Corner.'

'Well, you *did* let Granger go.'

'That wasn't—'

'I know. I know what happened, and I don't blame you for it. But the thing about Jez is, he's been a fighter all his life. Like most of us have. You're different, Jonah.'

'Um, thanks. I think.'

'What I mean is, you weren't trained for this. No one ever prepared you for...for what we do. You just sort of stumbled into all of this.'

'Yeah,' said Jonah. 'I suppose.' *So what you're saying is,* he thought, *if I want to earn the Guardians' respect, I have to become like Jez?*

The electric fences around Uluru had been dismantled. The land yacht sailed right up to the base of the rock. It was starting to get cold, so Jonah pulled on the black hoodie that Sam had packed in Woomera.

They parked alongside five other land yachts, returning them to the tribe, and climbed out of the cockpit to join a busy throng of Guardians and Aboriginal Australians. They were loading up six large trucks with equipment salvaged from inside the rock.

The Guardians greeted Sam warmly, but mostly ignored Jonah. Some of them would have been at the meet-up, of course, and would have seen Jez's dismissal of him.

The Aborigines, in contrast, were glad to see Jonah and Sam both. They gathered around them, thanking them for all they had done. It wasn't quite the mobbing that Jonah had had in the Changsphere; still, it felt good to be appreciated again.

Another land yacht pulled up, and Axel Kavanaugh leapt out of the driver's seat. In the real world, he was wiry with intense eyes, flowing grey hair and a close grey beard.

'I never thought I'd see this day,' he whooped. 'The Southern Corner, gone.'

'Not exactly gone,' Sam reminded her father.

'No,' said Axel with a grin, 'not exactly gone.'

The Southern Corner – the installation that Granger had built inside Uluru – had powered a quarter of the Metasphere. Now, that job was being done by small server farms across the world. Server farms that belonged to Guardian loyalists. Thousands of Guardian sympathisers were helping out too. Their personal computers were running fragments of Metasphere code with their spare processing power.

'The Southern Corner is ours now,' crowed Axel, 'and no one will ever be able to take it back from us, because we each have a part of it.'

Four more Guardians emerged from a cave opening in Uluru's side. They were struggling to carry a huge server out between them, manhandling it down the treacherous slope. As Jonah watched them, he remembered Mr Chang's request.

'Do you think anyone would mind,' he asked, 'if I went in there? Just for one last look at the place?'

Axel shrugged. 'Go ahead, kid!'

Jonah climbed up into the cave. He followed a bright light, through a once-secret door into a network of manmade service tunnels.

He got lost in the maze, his mind drifting back to that fateful night. The night of the Guardians' attack on this hidden installation. He hadn't taken much part in the fighting himself, but he had seen the terrible consequences of it. He felt as if these tunnels must be haunted by the ghosts of those – Guardians and Millennials both – who had died for the causes they believed in.

He thought about Kala, an Aboriginal girl whom he had got to know a little. She had given her life to remove the servers from the sacred interior of Uluru. Jonah couldn't imagine being that certain of anything.

'Is that him?' said a voice.

Jonah turned to see three young Guardian technicians at the other end of the long tunnel.

'That's Jonah Delacroix,' said another.

They congratulated him on the victory and Jonah asked them for directions to the control room.

'I thought you'd know your way around here,' joked the only girl in the group.

'There was a lot going on that night,' said Jonah. 'I was just glad to get out alive.'

She pointed to a cluster of pipes and cables that ran along the walls. 'Follow the yellow cable and it'll take you right there,' she said.

Jonah thanked her, and followed the cable to the empty control room. The once bustling room was stripped almost bare; even the operators' chairs were gone. Jonah feared for a moment that the object he had come for might have been taken too.

He found the Chang Bridge device, however, right where he had left it, plugged into a dead server panel. Etched into its silver top was a hologram of a golden treasure dragon, like Mr Chang's own avatar. It had a row of LEDs along its leading edge, but they were dark now. Its code had become part of Metasphere source code, and the device itself, which resembled a personal hard drive, was dormant.

That was probably why no one had taken it yet, he thought. It didn't look like anything useful. But it was useful to its creator.

Jonah slipped the device into his hoodie pocket. He paused to take one last look around the control room. Then he left to rejoin the group outside.

The Guardians had made a deal with the local

Aboriginal tribe. In exchange for their help in capturing the Southern Corner, Uluru would be returned to them, its original owners.

And now was the handover ceremony. At the base of Uluru, Jonah joined about fifty Guardians and as many Aborigines sitting in the red dust. An Aboriginal elder spoke solemnly about Uluru's importance to them. He recounted ancient tales of giant serpents and lizard men, and even referred to Matthew Granger as the reincarnation of *Lungkata*, a deceitful lizard man of legend.

He expressed his hopes that with the 'infection' at Uluru's heart cleansed, the spirits of their ancestors could return to reside within the sacred rock.

Jonah marvelled at how all cultures seemed to want to keep their dead alive in one form or another. He thought about his father, dead but still alive in digital form. Then his thoughts turned to his mother, whom he missed every day, and he despaired at the thought that he'd never be able to see her. Jonah didn't know if he believed in spirits or Heaven, but looking up at the great rock Uluru, for a moment he allowed himself to believe that the spirit of his mother, lost to this world, would find a peaceful resting place in another.

Axel spoke next, on behalf of the Guardians. He was more succinct, but respectful. He thanked the Aborigines for their friendship and sacrifice and promised never to return to this sacred place.

Jonah didn't think he had ever seen Axel so serious.

With the formalities over, Guardians and Aborigines shook hands and embraced, and went their separate ways by moonlight.

The Guardians climbed into their loaded trucks, and Axel found a space for himself, Sam and Jonah in the back of one of them. They struggled to make themselves comfortable between two teetering mounds of computer equipment.

'Where to next?' asked Jonah, as they set off.

'Back to Sydney,' said Axel. 'We'll hole up in a safe house there while we plan out our next mission. We're gonna hit a Millennial payment-processing facility. Small change, of course, compared to what we could be doing, but...'

Jonah took the hint. 'I'll be seeing my dad soon,' he mumbled, 'very soon. But...don't be too surprised if he can't tell us anything yet.'

'You keep saying that, Jonah. Is he getting back his memories, or not?'

'He is,' said Jonah, 'but he still doesn't like...*I* don't like him talking about that time, about those days leading up to when he...'

'You know,' said Axel, 'when we saw Bradbury at the concert, he said—'

'Dad!' said Sam, warning him to stop.

'Bradbury has a theory. He thinks you know more than you've been telling. He thinks you know where the rest of the Four Corners are, and he thinks you've known it all along. Now I'd like to prove him wrong.'

'I... I...' Jonah stammered.

'But is he right?' demanded Axel. 'Have you been holding out on us?'

'Dad!' protested Sam again. 'You're starting to sound like Jez!'

'Well, maybe Jez has a point!' snapped Axel.

'I said I'd talk to my dad,' said Jonah, sullenly, 'and I will.'

'When?' demanded Axel.

'GamesCon,' said Jonah. 'We're going to—'

'In the Changsphere?' Sam cried. 'Jonah, no! I told you, it's not safe in there.'

'But my dad—'

'You can talk to your dad from the real world, can't you? Send him a pop-up. Or...or just wait until we've found out more about these rumours, about—'

'I don't want to just talk to my dad,' insisted Jonah. 'I want to *be* with him! Can't you just give me that? For one more day!'

His outburst was met by an awkward silence. It was a silence that suited Jonah just fine.

Axel leaned back against the side of the van, using a spare pair of overalls as a pillow. He closed his eyes. 'Sounds to me like the kid's made up his mind,' he said. He opened one eye to glare at Jonah. 'Now, you just have to decide about that other thing, Jonah. You have to pick a side.'

Sam made herself comfortable too, and soon she and Axel were both asleep. Jonah was relieved not to be under their scrutiny any more. He hated keeping secrets from them, but the secrets were piling up. He hadn't told them about the Uploaded attack he'd witnessed, and he couldn't tell them about his meeting with Granger. And he couldn't admit that, yes, he knew the whereabouts of all of the Four Corners, he just wasn't sure he wanted the Guardians to find them.

He knew that more people would die if they did.

All the same, he felt ungrateful. The Guardians – Axel and Sam, really – had been sheltering him, feeding him, clothing him, for months now. He didn't know how he would have survived without them. He *couldn't* survive without them. Unless...

Unless he took Granger up on his offer.

Axel had been right. It was long past time that Jonah made some hard decisions. *And I will*, he swore to himself. *I'll talk to Dad at GamesCon, maybe after the opening ceremony, and we'll work it all out together. We'll work out what to do. Just...*

Just let me have a little extra time with him, before I have to start fighting again!

9

After a long day of travel across the Australian outback, Jonah, Sam and Axel finally reached an abandoned warehouse in Sydney, their temporary safe house. It was a step down from even the rough accommodation in Woomera, with thin mattresses spread out on frayed carpet over a concrete floor. *It may not have running water,* thought Jonah, *but at least it has internet access.* Jonah wasted no time logging on; his father was expecting him.

He had set his co-ordinates for the inside of the Chang Stadium. He was redirected automatically, and materialised in the huge parking lot outside.

It was evening in the Changsphere, but the bright lights of the stadium lit up the virtual world like daytime.

Thousands of other avatars pixelated to life around Jonah, with their exit halos automatically redirected and filed in neat rows in the parking lot. The avatars were buzzing about the spectacles to come. Jonah looked up to see a massive swarm of avatars hovering over the stadium (*the cheap seats*, Jonah remembered) but looked down quickly to hide his face from the crowd. He didn't want to be recognised and mobbed again.

He had to enter the stadium through the main gates

today. He walked past the ticket touts, the bookies and the merchandise vendors. Security scanners confirmed that Jonah carried no viruses or Trojans with him. His avatar code sequence was recognised, and a pop-up balloon directed him to his seat.

Mr Chang had been as good as his word. Following the arrows in the pop-up, Jonah came to a flight of stairs, alongside the VIP entrance he should have used. He climbed up to a luxurious private box, where his dad was waiting for him.

'I was starting to think you weren't coming,' said Jason Delacroix.

'I haven't missed anything, have I?'

A long-toothed walrus offered Jonah a glass of virtual champagne. Jonah clinked his glass with his father's and took a sip. But the liquid inside tasted like lemonade and Jonah realised it had an age-check subroutine embedded into its coding.

'I was worried about you, son,' said Jason. 'After Sam dragged you away the night before last... That was Samantha, wasn't it? Axel's little girl?'

'Yeah, it was. But she's not a little girl any more.'

'She should have come over and said hello.'

'She... We were in a hurry,' said Jonah. 'There was a meet-up and—'

'A Guardian meet-up?' asked Jason. 'You should have said. I could have come with you. Was Axel there?'

'Um,' said Jonah.

'I think it's time I checked in with the Guardians,' said Jason. 'They must be wondering where I've got to.'

'Um, yeah. We need to talk about that, Dad. But not today, OK?'

The other avatars in the private box were moving to their seats.

Jonah hadn't paid them all that much attention before, other than to check if Mr Chang was among them, which he wasn't. Now, however, he noticed a black-clad humatar, a cowboy, who caught Jonah's gaze and doffed his Stetson hat in his direction. Jonah would have recognised it anywhere. His jaw dropped open.

'You...you're Lucky Luke!' he gasped. 'I mean... you're Mr Wexler!'

'Guilty as charged, pardner,' said the cowboy in a Texan drawl.

'I love your games, Mr Wexler,' said Jonah.

'Call me Luke.'

'I bought him that *Brain-Sucking Zombies* for Christmas one year,' said Jason, 'and he played that game into the ground.'

'That was a long time ago! You know, Jonah, I'm launching *BSZ4* at the Con. I could put y'all on the guest list to play a preliminary round.'

'That would be amazing,' said Jonah.

The stadium darkened and the music started with a long drum roll.

Jason led Jonah to a soft red leather chair, and sat down in the seat to his right. The seat wasn't quite wide enough to hold Jason's huge dragon avatar, but it seemed to make him comfortable all the same.

To Jonah's left sat an overly coiffured white poodle with a pair of opera glasses. 'It's all frightfully exciting, isn't it?' said the poodle in a posh accent. Jonah wondered if she was someone famous too.

'Let the games begin,' chuckled Jason as he stretched to put one wing around Jonah.

Jonah gaped as hundreds of performers in colourful costumes trooped out onto the pitch below him. They juggled and sang and performed elaborate flying somersaults, with digital pyrotechnics exploding around them. The combined effect was a choreographed explosion of colours, lights and sounds, and Jonah cheered along with the rest of the million-strong crowd.

He remembered the last GamesCon, two years ago. Jonah hadn't been able to afford a ticket, then, even in the hover space above the stadium. He had watched on a portable monitor at home, alone because his mum had had to go out to work and his dad...

He tried not to think about those days. He concentrated on the colours, lights and sounds, and lost himself in the moment.

Then his dad leaned over and whispered to Jonah, 'I remember.'

And Jonah felt the weight of his past – and his future – settling on him again.

'It's all been coming back to me,' said Jason, 'everything I'd forgotten. I just need you to fill in a few gaps for me. Please, Jonah. I know I said I could wait, but…'

Jonah swallowed, and turned to him. He had been dreading what was coming, but he couldn't put it off any longer.

'I was working with the Guardians,' said Jason. 'We discussed that, right?'

'Yes,' said Jonah. 'But you never told me.'

'You were too young to know the truth. But what I was doing, it was dangerous. I knew that, one day, I might…'

'It's OK, Dad,' said Jonah. 'I know.'

'Do you remember when your grandmother died?' asked Jason.

'Not really. I was only a baby.'

'We knew it was coming. We talked about it, and Mum decided she wanted to be Uploaded. She wanted to leave a part of herself behind. For all of us.

'I can't tell you how much of a comfort that was, Jonah, to be able to visit her when I liked, on the Island, to be able to talk to her. I wanted that for you too. If I… If I ever had to go away, I wanted you to be able to find me again, so I could explain…

'But I knew, if I died, it was likely to be sudden, violent

85

even. I wouldn't see it coming. I wouldn't get the chance to Upload myself for you. So I found someone. One of Granger's original programmers. He had dropped out. He was living in a farming commune in the Canadian Rockies. I persuaded him to help me. He showed me how to create a copy of myself, of my avatar. It was like Uploading, only this wouldn't kill me. It was a gruelling, painful process, and I trained for months to be mentally fit for it. One day, I was in the gift shop, in the cellar under the gift shop. I ran the program and then…after that, there's nothing. My memories end right there, like I just left them in that dusty cellar. Which is why I have to ask you again… Jonah…'

Jonah swallowed back tears. 'Yes,' he whispered. 'Yes, Dad. The "you" I'm talking to now is… You're the copy. I filtered your avatar and later, when I had to get to the Island, I Uploaded you.'

Jason nodded, quite calmly. 'So that's it? I am dead.'

'You're also alive, in here, Dad. Alive and talking to me.'

'How did I die, Jonah?'

'The airport bombings,' said Jonah. 'You'd just landed at Heathrow, in Mr Granger's private plane. You rushed into the burning terminal. You were trying to save lives. It's like I told you before, Dad, you were a hero. Everyone said so.'

'But I left you behind, Jonah,' said Jason. 'I'm sorry. I didn't want to do that. How long has it been?'

'Three years,' said Jonah. 'But you're here now. That's what matters.'

'That makes it all the harder, son,' said Jason. 'Why I can never see you again.'

Jonah looked at his father, saw the sadness in his yellow dragon eyes. 'No!' he whispered. 'Why?'

'I think you know why, Jonah,' said Jason. 'I think Sam knows it too; that's why she dragged you out of here like she did.'

'I don't care what Sam or anyone says. I won't—'

'I'm trying so hard to resist, to control it. But your grandmother was right. She tried to warn me.'

'Dad, you're scaring me,' said Jonah. 'What is it? What's wrong? I'm sure, whatever it is, we can fix it between us.'

'Your grandmother chose to hide in a far corner of the Changsphere, to remove herself from temptation. She said she couldn't trust herself around the living. I didn't understand, but now... Being here, around all of these people, all of this life... And you... I can't help it, Jonah. I'm so...'

'No, Dad, don't say it.'

'I'm so hungry!'

10

The opening ceremony concluded with a frenzy of fireworks.

The crowd leapt to their feet and applauded wildly. The sound crashed over Jonah like a tidal wave. He was staring at his dad in mounting horror.

It was only as the applause died down that Jonah became aware of another sound. A new sound. Like a rumble of thunder, but growing louder and louder.

At first, Jonah assumed it was all part of the first game, *Alien Attack 7*. The pitch below had been reconfigured into a dusty, grey moonscape and the first players were taking their positions outside a crashed spaceship, ready to defend the moon against an alien onslaught. They heard the rumbling sound from above, and outside of the stadium, and realised one by one that it came from outside the game. *Not a rumble,* Jonah thought, *but a roar.*

A roar of voices!

Suddenly, a swarm of avatars, thousands strong, every one screaming, descended into the stadium. Mass panic erupted.

'Get out of here, Jonah,' said Jason. 'It's begun!'

'What?'

'The uprising.'

A ferocious rhinoceros avatar dropped down through the mass of spectators above them and flew straight for the VIP box. By the time Jonah realised that its great horn was poised to skewer him, it was too late for him to dodge it.

But the rhino slammed into an invisible barrier and fell back, dazed but undeterred. The walrus waiter had activated a firewall program, visualised as a glass shield over the front of the private box.

The rhino was shaking off its dizziness, coming around again – and several more avatars were hammering and scratching on the glass, desperate to break through it. The barrier wouldn't hold for long.

The private box was emptying fast. Lucky Luke was organising the evacuation, taking charge by dint of his booming voice and larger-than-life presence.

'They can't help it,' said Jason. 'The Uploaded sense life and they hunger for it.' He spoke through gritted teeth. He was hunched over as if in pain.

'And...and you?' asked Jonah, nervously. 'What about you, Dad?'

'I'm in no danger, son. Not from them. I don't have what they need.'

'That's not what I meant,' said Jonah.

Jason looked at his son, and there was something new in his yellow eyes now. Something that Jonah couldn't quite identify, but it made him afraid all the same.

Jason sprang up and unfurled his great dragon wings, so suddenly that even Jonah recoiled from him.

The poodle woman shrieked again: 'He's one of them too! There's one of them in here with us!'

'Run, Jonah,' said Jason again. 'I mean it. Dive through your exit halo and never come back to the Changsphere. I can't... I don't think I can protect you if you stay!'

And, at that moment, the glass shield exploded inwards.

Jonah ran to the door, out of the private box and down the stairs. He faltered between flights, only too aware of what – or rather, who – he was leaving behind. A group of four Uploaded avatars, the rhino, a snake, a rhombus and a flower, flew around the corner behind him and Jonah set off again. He finally reached the main concourse level of the stadium, at the VIP entrance, and realised too late it was a bottleneck. In front of him, scores of avatars were fighting, blocking the VIP entrance. Behind him, the Uploaded avatars were closing in fast. They screamed a horrible screech.

Jonah pushed forward and threw himself into the fray. He found himself face to face with a slimy alien-looking being, with slick black eyes. Jonah thought it was attacking him. He raised his arms to protect himself – but the alien was only trying to get away from him, terrified of Jonah.

In the chaos, it was impossible to tell which avatars were Uploaded and which were their living prey. Jonah stumbled into a purple sheep and mistook it for harmless – until the sheep's mouth opened to twice the size of its head and roared at him.

He back-pedalled away, and saw the coiffured poodle from the private box fending off a larger brown-and-white dog. It kept flying at her, snapping at her throat. Jonah grabbed the attacking dog from behind and threw it hard into the wall. The poodle didn't stop to thank him. She saw a clear route to the door and scrambled for it.

A crocodile swooped out of nowhere and snatched the poodle in its jaws, swallowing her whole. *Gone*. The crocodile broke free from the fray, and flew out of the door.

It was just as Granger had warned. The crocodile had *usurped* the poodle's avatar, and now it had gone in search of the poodle's exit halo, its gateway to the real world.

He had to get out of here.

But the avatars that had invaded the private box – and chased Jonah down the stairs – had caught up with him at last. They joined their Uploaded fellows in the concourse, surrounding Jonah and the rest of the living. One of the living avatars, a frightened squirrel, tried to break through the cordon, but was rebuffed by the angry rhinoceros's horn.

The dead closed in around the living, and opened their mouths wide to feed.

Jonah was trapped.

Granger was back at the Freedom Tower, inside his new operations room.

He was surrounded – as was so often the case – by computer screens, each of them showing the same scene from different angles. Granger looked from one to another of those screens, and even *he* felt a chill in his blood.

His Millennial followers – there were at least twenty of them in the room – were watching the screens too, and a dreadful hush had descended upon them all.

They were bearing silent witness to a massacre.

Spectators were fleeing from the stadium in droves. They were being picked off in mid-air by the Uploaded, devoured and usurped. Even as Granger watched, a bluebird was gulped down by a ravening leopard, and a cat by a giant mouse.

Hundreds of thousands of avatars were crowding into the parking lot, rushing for their exit halos. Granger couldn't tell who was alive, looking for their own exit halos – and who was Uploaded, looking for someone else's.

Sam couldn't believe what she was seeing. She didn't want to. But it was happening in the Changsphere, and Jonah was trapped inside.

She couldn't get the DI adaptor pack open. In her haste, she resorted to pulling at it with her teeth. The foil stretched and finally tore, and the adaptor fell out.

It landed on the dirty warehouse floor.

She snatched up the adaptor, sucked on it to clean off the carpet hairs, and then spat them out. She knew she shouldn't use a non-sterile adaptor, but there was no time to find another.

Jonah's body lay on his mattress, eyes closed. Beside him, a handheld monitor plugged into his terminal showed the plight of his virtual self. Sam lay down on the mattress next to his and plugged herself in.

Axel came racing around a plasterboard partition and snatched the Ethernet wire from Sam's hand. He gave it a firm yank, and pulled it from its wall socket.

'Dad,' cried Sam, 'what are you doing? I was just—'

'Just putting yourself in danger,' Axel snapped. 'Logging in to the Changsphere?

After everything you said to Jonah!'

'He's trapped!'

'And so will you be,' Axel said. Then he followed Sam's eyes to the monitor and his face paled. 'You warned him,' he said quietly. 'And he still went in. I'm sorry, kiddo, you're not going in. I forbid it!'

Sam gaped at him. 'Since when did you forbid anything?'

'Since you stopped thinking! I'm your father, Samantha, and I—'

'Then you should act like one!'

Axel winced. 'I know you're upset, kiddo, but—'

'Jonah risked his life to save you and Bradbury!'

'And I'd do the same for him if I thought there was a chance, even a slim one. But look, Sam. Just look at what's happening in there!'

Sam looked at the monitor and watched helplessly as Jonah tried to escape the mob of avatars. All around him, the Uploaded attacked, widening their mouths and ingesting the helpless living avatars.

'It's too late for Jonah,' said Axel.

11

Twenty ravenous Uploaded avatars surrounded Jonah and the six other living avatars.

He wondered what it would feel like to be usurped. Perhaps it would be like sleeping, he thought. Or perhaps he would be awake, aware, in the back of his own brain, a passenger in his own body. He closed his eyes and waited to find out.

'*Wait!*'

The caution came from one of the Uploaded: the brown-and-white dog that Jonah had fought before. It was staring at Jonah, wide-eyed.

'I can't wait,' the rhinoceros moaned. 'I'm so hungry!'

'Don't you see who this is?' said the brown-and-white dog. And the other Uploaded stared at Jonah too – and they *did* see.

Awe-filled whispers rippled through them:

'*It's the humatar.*'

'*The saviour.*'

'*The boy who led us into the light.*'

The Uploaded started to back away from Jonah. The other living avatars stared at him, amazed by this power he appeared to wield, their eyes beseeching him to use it to help them. He didn't know if he could, but he opened his mouth to try.

'Let… Let them go,' he said, trying to sound brave. 'These people have lives, like you once had. I… I'm asking you as your saviour to let my people go.'

He didn't know if any of the Uploaded would heed his request, but he had to try.

'I led you into the light so you could live on. And now, you have a new life in the Changsphere. You don't need to take it from these people. You don't need their life, you have your own. In here.'

The rhino looked unconvinced and stomped the ground menacingly. But he didn't advance. Jonah figured the rhino was waiting for someone else to make the first move.

Finally, after a silent standoff, one of them did. But it wasn't the move that Jonah had expected.

The brown-and-white dog turned and flew away – and the rest of the Uploaded followed him one by one, the rhino last of all.

The living avatars seized their chance. They rushed for the exit door, and Jonah was about to follow them when something stopped him. An idea. An idea that he wanted to ignore, but couldn't.

He remembered what Granger had said to him: *The Uploaded, they see you as their saviour… They respect you… You might be able to persuade them…*

Granger had been right. Jonah knew that now. The

Uploaded would listen to him – just him, no one else. His words had persuaded this group of hungry Uploaded, but what about the rest of the swarm? He had to stop them too. He was the only one who could. He wished that it wasn't the case. He wished he didn't have that responsibility. His stomach was sick with fear.

But Jonah knew what he had to do.

Granger reached for a datapad. He tapped in the co-ordinates of his R&D lab in the Metasphere, one particular corner of it.

An image appeared on the nearest monitor to him: a fat raccoon in a lab coat, a pair of pince-nez spectacles perched on its nose. The raccoon was surrounded by spirals of 3D programming code. It pawed at the symbols thoughtfully, sometimes deleting or amending one or flipping it into a different spiral.

Granger typed another command, and a real-time video window appeared beside the raccoon. Granger could see his own youthful-looking face staring out of the pop-up.

'Mr Harrison,' he said curtly, 'we have run out of time. I need that code now.'

'But, Mr Granger,' wailed the raccoon, 'we're still in beta testing. We need—'

'Now, Mr Harrison!' Granger snapped. 'Things have progressed more suddenly than we anticipated. The Metasphere must be protected. If you value your online existence, Mr Harrison, you will upload that code to the servers immediately!'

'What's he doing?' cried Axel, watching Jonah on the monitor. 'He had a chance to escape and now he's blown it!'

Jonah had taken to the air and was flying deeper into the Chang Stadium.

He soared out over the stands, deftly weaving his way between brawling avatars, avoiding the grasping hands and talons of the life-hungry Uploaded.

'He's doing what Jonah does,' said Sam, 'putting himself in danger to help others.'

She reached for the trailing Ethernet wire, but Axel saw what she was doing and snapped it from her hands. 'I said no, Samantha, and I meant it.'

'I have to get him out of there,' she argued. 'If I'd gone in right away, I could have stopped things from going this far. I could have—'

Axel shook his head. He had pulled a datapad out of his overalls – and Sam realised as he did so that it was chirruping an alarm.

'You'd better see this first, kiddo.'

'What is it?' asked Sam.

'We've been expecting something like this for weeks,' said Axel. 'I had one of the tech guys set up this alert, so I'd know when it happened.'

'When what happened?'

Axel thrust the datapad under Sam's nose, so she could see for herself. 'Matthew Granger,' he said. 'Ever since the portal to the Changsphere became permanent, he's been attempting to hack it, close it down. It looks like he's finally doing it!'

'But that would mean...'

Axel nodded grimly. 'The Changsphere is still new,' he said. 'It still runs on the Metasphere backbone built by Granger. It's only because of the portal between those two worlds that we can access it at all. Once that portal has been closed...'

'There'll be no way into the Changsphere,' breathed Sam.

'Or out of it,' confirmed Axel. 'Any avatar still in there – alive or dead – will be stuck in there forever. Including you, Sam, if you go in there.'

'And...and Jonah!'

'Yeah,' said Axel, 'and Jonah. He'll be trapped inside.'

Jonah was almost there: the centre of the Chang Stadium.

He could see the raised platform where the singers had stood before. Their microphones had been discarded. If Jonah could only reach them...

An urgent red pop-up appeared in front of him. He braked in mid-air, suddenly unable to see where he was going.

GRANGER CUTTING OFF CHANGSPHERE, said the pop-up. GET OUT!!! SAM.

Jonah floated, uncertainly, as living and dead avatars brawled around him. *What do I do?* he asked himself. He was the only one who could bring an end to this chaos. Jonah had convinced himself. But now… Now that he was out here in the very thick of it…

A claw came swiping through the intangible pop-up. It almost tore the flesh from Jonah's virtual face. The claw was followed an instant later by a winged lion, its roar like thunder. It didn't seem to have recognised Jonah.

'Wait! I'm…the…saviour,' he stammered in terror. 'I mean…' He swallowed and tried again. 'I'm Jonah. Jonah Delacroix. I led you into the light. You must remember.'

'The little humatar's right. I recognise him. It is him!'

The deep voice came from right behind Jonah. He whirled around. He was horrified to see that, while he had been backing away from the lion, three more Uploaded had come up behind him. For the second time, he found himself surrounded.

'Listen to me,' he said. 'This isn't right. You must see that. I didn't bring you here so that you could…you…'

'If you really are the saviour,' the lion growled, 'then save us. Save us from the hunger that burns in our souls!'

'I…can't,' confessed Jonah. 'I don't know how… But I know people who can. They'll find a way to—'

The lion roared, 'We can't wait! We need to feed!'

The others agreed.

'So hungry…'

'…can't bear it…'

'…need life.'

More and more avatars were forming up around him. Like the Uploaded in the hallway, they were keeping their distance – all but one.

The winged lion strained forward. He was making little motions with his claws towards Jonah, as if it was all he could do to keep from ripping him apart. As if the lion saw no reason see why he shouldn't do just that.

And, because the lion refused to be cowed, his fellows were emboldened too – and, although they drew no closer to Jonah, nor did they back away from him.

'What good is a saviour,' snarled the lion, 'who cannot save us?'

He sprang at Jonah.

Jonah dived for the ground, tried to duck beneath the lion's pounce. He was too slow. The lion landed on his back, sank his claws into his shoulders. Jonah winced with pain. He hit the ground hard, and threw up a cloud of moon dust.

He rolled and pinned down his attacker. Jonah felt the lion's grip loosening and tore himself free. He tried to fly away but the rest of the Uploaded penned him in.

He appealed to them again: 'I know how hard this is for you, but you… You must have loved ones in the real world. Think about them! How would you feel if one of them was usurped, if they had their lives stolen by one of you?'

'My family haven't visited me in years,' said the lion. 'They sent me to the Island, then forgot all about me. They abandoned me! Why should I care about them?' The lion climbed to his four feet. 'They're out there living their lives,' he continued, 'but what about me? What about us? We deserve life too!'

The other Uploaded murmured their agreement. They didn't want to listen to reason, Jonah realised. Their cravings had grown too strong.

The lion came at him again. Jonah made a break for it. He hoped to take the Uploaded around him by surprise, burst through their ranks before they knew he was coming. Once again, he was frustrated. He found himself caught and held by a muscular dwarf and a red snake, which coiled around his legs.

Either one of them could have usurped him. Instead, they waited for their de facto leader, the lion, to claim his kill. They were starting to work together!

Jonah struggled as hard as he could, to no avail. The lion loomed over him, opening his mouth wide. Jonah could see the creature's sharp, glistening fangs, his rough tongue, his deep red tonsils…

The red dragon came from nowhere, swooping down on the lion. It snatched the lion in its mouth, thrashed it about and finally hurled it away into the distant stands.

'Dad!' cried Jonah.

A couple of the Uploaded rushed gamely at the dragon. Jason tore at them with his claws, thrashed them with his wings. 'I thought I told you to run!' he yelled at Jonah.

'I thought I could reason with them, make them—'

'It isn't safe for you here!' roared Jason. 'You aren't safe around *me*! I can't control my hunger, Jonah, any more than the rest of them can. Every second I'm near you, I just want to… I can't help myself, I…'

The lion flew at Jason again, spitting with fury. The two Uploaded avatars were locked in savage combat. Jonah wanted to help his dad, but he couldn't get near him. Every time he tried, he was kept at bay by slashing claws or snapping teeth.

He saw the microphones beneath him. He had a clear path to them now. He swooped, grabbed hold of the nearest of them, put it to his lips.

'Stop! I brought you here to live life, not to take it!'

But it was too late. The stadium was emptying fast, anyway. The remaining living avatars had mostly fled for their halos, and the dead were chasing after them.

Jonah put down the microphone. He looked back at his dad. Jason had got the lion's head between his claws and was breathing fire on him, singeing the fur on his face.

With the lion brawling with Jason, the snake and the dwarf closed in on Jonah. It was now or never. He knew he had to get out of there. He felt a wrench in his stomach as he flew, evading his stalker and leaving his dad behind. The sky was swarming with Uploaded – but Jonah knew of a way past them.

He remembered seeing something, the last time he was here, when he and his dad had played football. A tunnel opening beneath the stands. He flew down into it.

The tunnel sloped downwards, running underneath the stadium. It was deserted – and, from the angle of it, Jonah guessed it would take him right into the halo parking lot. He only hoped he hadn't waited too long to use it.

He remembered Sam's urgent warning: GRANGER CUTTING OFF CHANGSPHERE. He prayed his exit halo would still be waiting for him outside.

12

Mr Chang paced his command floor, high above Hong Kong's Victoria Harbour.

A few hours ago, the night sky through the picture window behind him had been filled with fireworks and holograms: a treat for the thousands of real-world workers at this facility, to mirror the celebrations in the virtual Chang Stadium.

Now, the sky was empty, as a hundred computer operators frantically tapped at their datapads and spoke to each other in concerned whispers.

There was nothing they could do. Mr Chang had known as much for some minutes now. He looked at each monitor as he passed it, his windows into his virtual world. He watched helplessly as the live avatars still trapped in his Changsphere were hunted down by gangs of rabid, ravenous Uploaded.

They couldn't get through their exit halos. Mr Chang watched as one of them tried, diving into the ring of light and rebounding as if from a solid wall.

'It's Millennial code, sir,' reported one of the operators.

'Granger,' sighed Mr Chang. 'It is the way of the *wangbadan* to sign his work for all to see.'

Mr Chang's voice radiated calm authority and

wisdom. That much, he had in common with his avatar, the golden treasure dragon. Most people who met him in the real world were surprised by his young age. Mr Chang was sixteen years old.

He took a deep breath before issuing his next command. 'We must evacuate.'

Before Mr Chang had finished speaking, he had turned his back on the room. He ignored the shocked intakes of breath from behind him. He knew he would be obeyed without question; his employees respected him too much to do otherwise.

He stood and gazed out through his picture window. Hong Kong Island had been his first acquisition as CEO of the Chang Corporation. He had evicted the sitting tenants, over seven million people, and filled the towers with computer equipment. He had turned the island into a gigantic server farm – the engine of his new world.

And now, his new world lay in ruins.

He knew only too well what Granger's next move would be – because it was what he would have done in his place. It was the art of war.

Jonah awoke to find Sam kneeling over him.

She looked shocked but overjoyed as he opened his eyes. She was talking, asking questions. Her tone was urgent, but Jonah couldn't make out her words. His ears felt full of cotton wool. His head was spinning and he wanted to be sick. This was more than the usual transitional nausea. What was wrong with him?

He closed his eyes, breathed deeply, waited for the floor to stop spinning.

'—remember who I am?' Axel's voice. Jonah opened his eyes to see Sam's father hovering over Sam, nervously stroking his grey beard.

'What? Yeah. Yeah, of course I do. Why wouldn't I…?'

Jonah tried to sit up. 'Take it easy,' said Sam. 'You've had a rough ride. Your brain needs time to adjust to your body.' He didn't know what she was talking about.

He reoriented himself with the real world. He was in the Sydney safe house, the warehouse. He pushed himself up onto his elbows. He could feel the hard floor through his thin mattress and the frayed carpet.

'I'm OK,' said Jonah. 'Really, I'm OK. And I'm still… I haven't been usurped, if that's what you were thinking. I'm still me. I'm still Jonah.'

'Never said you weren't,' said Axel.

'We saw everything,' said Sam. 'But, Jonah… It's been almost fifteen minutes since you dived into your exit halo.'

'What? It can't be! I…'

Sam showed Jonah a handheld monitor. It was set to the co-ordinates of Guardian Island. A giant safe, enwrapped in thick steel chains, hovered over the island where the opening to the Changsphere had once been.

'Mr Chang's anti-viral software put up a good fight,'

said Axel. 'It took almost half an hour for the portal to be sealed completely – and during that time, data transfer rates to and from the Changsphere were slowed to a trickle.'

'I was worried you might not make it back,' said Sam.

'Or that you might not be whole when you did,' said Axel. 'What do you remember?'

'I remember…' began Jonah, trying to remember the chaos of the Changsphere. It felt like he had just woken from a terrible nightmare. But the true terror was that he knew it had all been real. 'I remember the tunnel underneath the Chang Stadium and the parking lot, and all those people fighting to get to their exit halos, and… Dad! He saved my life! He fought off that lion so I could—'

'We saw,' said Sam. 'It's OK. Jason beat that lion.'

'But he's still in there – trapped inside.'

'Along with any living avatars who didn't make it out in time,' added Axel.

'The Changsphere is completely cut off,' said Sam. 'No one can get out now.'

'But I only just found him again,' cried Jonah. 'We have to reopen the portal or…'

Axel shook his head. 'There's no way, kid. Even if we could, the Uploaded are a threat to us all. We got the low-down on them while you were online.'

'When they swallow a living avatar,' explained Sam, 'they can use its exit halo as a gateway to a real-world body. We're getting reports in from all over the world, people logging off from the virtual world with a new personality.'

'Completely *usurped*,' said Axel, looking at Jonah. 'That's what you called it? That's a good word for it.'

'There must be a way we can...do something for them,' said Jonah. 'Help them with their hunger, so they don't have to...'

'Maybe so,' said Axel, 'but until someone works out what it is, it's best they stay contained in the Changsphere.'

Jonah gaped at Axel.

Sam saw his expression and added kindly, 'At least you got a second chance with your dad, Jonah.'

'Yeah,' said Axel, 'you got to spend a little more time with him. You should be grateful for that, kid. It's more than some people ever get.'

Jonah noticed Sam and Axel share a brief but mournful look. Sam reached up and squeezed her father's hand.

'We did it, sir!' crowed one of Granger's Millennial operators. She saw the look on Granger's face and corrected herself. 'I mean, *you* did it.'

Granger nodded. He looked at the image that dominated all his screens: the floating safe above the former Island of the Uploaded. 'Not quite yet,' he said.

He knew that what had been done could still be undone. A bridge had been built once between the

Metasphere and the Changsphere. It could be built again.

Granger's datapad beeped. He transferred the incoming image of a bald eagle to a monitor. He recognised the avatar of President Lori Weisberg.

'If you'll pardon my abruptness, Madam President… Lori,' said Granger, 'I do have something of an emergency—'

'I'm aware of the situation, Mr Granger,' said Lori. 'And I need your help. One of our own is trapped in the Changsphere.'

'Who?'

'Luke Wexler. His cleaner found him plugged in, but his monitor was filled with gibberish. I hoped maybe you could—'

Granger could hardly have cared less about Luke Wexler, but he affected concern to placate the president. 'I will do all I can for an old colleague,' he lied.

An icon popped up on his datapad, a grey shark.

'Thank you,' she said. 'It's good to have someone of your calibre here on the—'

'If you'll excuse me,' Granger interrupted Lori. He didn't wait for an answer from the president. He tapped the shark icon and Lori's image was replaced by the tiger-shark avatar of one of his lieutenants.

'Tibur,' snapped Granger. 'Have you made the preparations?'

'Yes, sir,' said the shark. 'I'm in Manila now, fully

crewed, and we are ready to sail.'

'The next time I hear from you, it had better be to report that Hong Kong Island has been destroyed.'

Tibur opened his mouth to speak again, but Granger flicked his image away before he could. The room around him had fallen silent, as his operators stared at him.

'There is no other way,' he assured them. The servers that powered the Changsphere, and the emboldened Uploaded, resided in the towers of Hong Kong. They would have to be destroyed. 'The Uploaded are beyond saving, as are those who are trapped with them. We have to think of the living now. We have to keep the Uploaded from ever returning to the Metasphere. Containment is the only cure!'

Jonah felt better after some sleep. He sat up on his mattress and slurped down a chocolate Pro-Meal pouch.

Something was bothering him, though. 'Why didn't you help me?' he asked Sam. 'If you were watching me all that time, why didn't you—?'

'I'm so sorry, Jonah. I wanted to,' said Sam. 'Dad stopped me.'

Jonah felt a flush of anger. *Of course he did*, he thought. *Axel doesn't care about me, only about what I can do for him!*

Out loud, he said, 'Axel never wanted to use the Chang Bridge device. He hated the idea of the Changsphere.

He said it would just be another dictatorship.'

'I remember,' said Sam.

'He's probably glad that things turned out this way.'

'That's a horrible thing to say!'

'But he doesn't care about the Uploaded! He's supposed to be Dad's oldest friend, but he hasn't asked to see him once since he…came back.'

'People don't get to come back from the dead, Jonah!'

Jonah froze, sensing that he'd hit a nerve.

'It's not fair,' she said solemnly.

'But my dad came back to me,' said Jonah, 'and now he's locked away with the others, just like Axel wanted in the first place.'

'My dad can be single-minded sometimes, but he'd never have wanted that!'

'I don't know.'

'I do. Listen, I know he's been cross with you,' said Sam. 'But you did promise him the locations of the Four Corners, and now it seems like you—'

'I still need more time,' mumbled Jonah.

'How much more?' Sam pressed him. 'Honestly, Jonah, I wonder if my dad's right. You need to make up your mind about whether you're with the Guardians or not.'

Jonah didn't say anything.

'Can I ask you something?' she said. 'As a friend, not as a Guardian. Jonah, do you already know where the Four Corners are?'

Jonah didn't want to lie to Sam. 'I just need more time,' he said.

'You've been spending so much time in the Changsphere,' said Sam, 'you've hardly set foot in the Guardian-controlled quarter of the Metasphere. Why don't we go there now? You'll be amazed at the upgrades.'

He couldn't think about the Four Corners now, though. He couldn't think about the Guardians or the Metasphere.

'Will you do something for me first?' he asked. 'As a friend, not as a Guardian — then I'll tell you anything you want, I promise. I need your help, Sam.'

'To do what?' Sam asked. She saw the answer in Jonah's eyes, and groaned. 'Jonah, we've been through this.'

'You don't understand. When I saw Dad at the games, he was like he used to be. He didn't get confused. He knew who he was and where he was. It was like... He's alive, Sam. My dad's alive again. And I can't just leave him to rot inside the Changsphere!'

'But what can we do? I don't know how we can even—'

'I do. I know how.' Jonah reached into his pocket, felt the shape of the slender Chang Bridge device in there. 'But I can't do it alone,' he said. 'Will you come with me, Sam — to Hong Kong?'

'There's no way... Jonah, there's no way the Guardians

will let us have a plane. Not for something like this. That's even if we could persuade my dad to—'

'We don't need Axel,' declared Jonah, 'and we don't need the Guardians. We just need a plane. And I know where we can get one.'

13

Jonah flew over a sunny cornfield. For as far as his eyes could see, there was nothing and no one else around him. But this was an illusion.

He didn't see the wall in front of him until he had flown through it. He had known it was coming, however.

Jonah found himself inside a walled castle courtyard. Black and green flags fluttered from the towers above him. He had reached a corner of the Metasphere that few people knew existed. The virtual base of a group he despised but now needed, *GuerreVert*.

He set down on the flagstones and waited for the castle guards to come to him. It wasn't long before they did.

Some of the guards – not all of them, but plenty – looked like guards should. Their avatars had helmets and pikestaffs, as if they had been born to this role. They pressed the points of those pikestaffs into Jonah's throat. He stood his ground.

'I'm a friend of Delphine's,' he announced.

'Delphine has no friends,' one of the guards grunted.

Jonah wanted to say, *Yeah, I can believe that.* Instead, he said, 'I'm Jonah Delacroix and I'm here to collect.'

It made no difference to them. They took Jonah

by the arms and propelled him roughly across the courtyard, towards a raised portcullis. 'I know the way,' he protested, but his captors ignored him.

They dragged Jonah under the portcullis, into the castle itself. They crossed an expansive hallway. Then, to Jonah's alarm, he was bundled through a narrow doorway and down a flight of uneven stone steps into darkness.

At the bottom of the steps, a tiny natural cave had been blocked off by iron bars. The guards pushed Jonah into the cave and swung a barred door shut behind him. A heavy lock clunked into place at the wave of one guard's hand.

Then the guards turned and left. They climbed back up the steps, and Jonah was alone, imprisoned. He groaned and slumped down onto the cold, damp stone floor. A set of manacles hung from the wall beside him. From somewhere, he could hear an echoing drip of water. This wasn't exactly the welcome he had hoped for.

He had been there for at least an hour before Jonah heard a heavy metal footfall on the steps. He climbed to his feet, waited for his visitor to come into view. It was a knight in literal shining armour. The knight's helmet visor was closed, hiding its face, and it wore a black and green feather as a crest. A sword was holstered at the knight's hip.

'Hello, Delphine,' said Jonah.

The knight inclined her head, perhaps in confirmation, perhaps not.

'It's me,' said Jonah. 'Jonah Delacroix. And you owe me a favour.'

The knight fixed Jonah with a suspicious stare.

'I have never seen this avatar before.'

'The last time I was wearing my father's avatar. A red dragon.'

'A disguise?'

'A *necessity*. Delphine, you met me in the real world, along with Sam and Axel and—'

The knight nodded curtly, and spoke in Delphine's French-accented voice. 'I know who you are, *mon frère*. We had your avatar verified as soon as you stepped across our boundary.'

'Then why—?'

'Nobody flies into my castle and makes demands of me.'

'You owe me,' said Jonah.

'I owe you nothing,' she hissed. 'But if you have a proposition, I will listen.'

She waved a hand, and Jonah heard the door of his cell unlocking.

Delphine took Jonah on a stroll around the castle hallways. The sound of their footsteps echoed from the stone walls, even when their feet didn't quite touch the floor.

Jonah was just glad to be out of the dungeon. Now, however, he had to carry out the most difficult and dangerous part of his plan.

'I need to get to Hong Kong,' he said. 'From Sydney.'

Delphine reacted exactly as he had expected. 'And this is my problem how?'

'I know *GuerreVert* has an Australian branch. I know they have a plane. A floatplane. I've seen it. I need… What I mean is, if I could—'

Delphine laughed at Jonah. It was a nasty, scornful laugh, and it made Jonah's cheeks hot with anger. 'I want to borrow your plane for a few days,' he said, 'that's all. I think you owe me that much.'

'I owe you nothing,' repeated Delphine.

'Sydney Harbour,' said Jonah. 'Two months ago. I was on board that freighter your people sank and I almost drowned. And not just me. Sam, too. And Axel and Bradbury—'

'Then it was your misfortune,' said Delphine, 'to be in the wrong place at the wrong time, *non*? Shipping freighters pollute our air and heat our planet. They are legitimate targets.'

'We were supposed to be allies! You said—'

'Allies of convenience, that was all. An arrangement that has now expired.'

'I thought you, your people, you supported the idea of a free Metasphere. We're still fighting for that – the Guardians are, I mean.'

'I am sure your Monsieur Kavanaugh has Australian contacts,' said Delphine. 'I am surprised he sent you to see me at all, in fact, when—'

'This has nothing to do with Axel.'

'*Non*? Now I am intrigued.'

Jonah squirmed under Delphine's blank stare and finally confessed, 'I wasn't sent by the Guardians. This is personal.'

'*Finalement*,' said Delphine, 'we get the truth.'

Jonah looked at her in surprise.

She came to a halt. As she turned to face Jonah, the orange light from a nearby brazier lit one side of her closed visor. The other half was cast in shadow.

She was about to tell him to leave, he knew she was. Before she could, he blurted out: 'I recorded a message before I came here. To Mr Chang in Shanghai.'

Delphine didn't react at all, not visibly. Jonah wished he could see her expression behind that armour, get an idea of what she was thinking. He suspected, however, that her avatar had no face at all, that the armour was all there was.

'*GuerreVert* has caused a lot of problems for Mr Chang, for his business. I know he'd be very interested in what I know about you. The RWL of your French safe house, for example. The co-ordinates of this castle. And…and I know your name and the names of your friends, and what you really look like.'

'You have sent this message?' Delphine asked, quietly.

'I put it on a two-hour delay,' said Jonah. 'But you kept me locked up for at least an hour, so—'

'Then there is still time. You can stop it.'

'I will. If you give me what I want.'

'I cannot get you that plane,' said Delphine. 'I have no influence in Australia, they are an autonomous cell.'

'But you're the leader, aren't you?'

'We are united in cause, not controlled by commands. Like you and the Guardians.' Jonah didn't like the comparison, but didn't have time to argue the differences between freedom fighters and terrorists. 'There must be something you can do, with less than an hour left.'

Delphine sighed, exasperated.

She thought about it for an agonising few seconds. Then she said, 'Perhaps I *can* be of some small assistance to you. There might be a way...'

Jonah hadn't seen much of Sydney during his short stay.

His impression was that it was a newer version of London, sunnier, but just as overcrowded and poverty-stricken. Most real world cities were the same, it seemed, the world over. And Jonah had seen more of them in the past two months than in his entire life.

Even at night, like now, there were vagrants slumped in every boarded-up doorway, under every graffitied bridge.

The streetlights were solar-powered, but most of them were out. So it was just as well that Jonah had Sam with him, lighting their way by torchlight.

She had spent all day trying to talk him out of this – but when it came to the crunch, she had been waiting at the back door of the safe house at the agreed time. Jonah had known she would be. He could rely on Sam. They had snuck out without telling Axel, although Sam had left a pop-up message on a time delay for him, telling him not to worry.

'I still can't believe you talked Delphine into this,' she said. 'Into lending us a plane... I mean, Delphine of all people!'

'I can be persuasive,' boasted Jonah. 'When I need to be.'

They were crouched on an oily beach, beside a sign warning that the water was unsafe for swimming. An old warehouse building stood against the sky, facing out to sea. Its wooden timbers were ancient and rotting, and Jonah could see moonlight through them. The warehouse was surrounded by a rusty chain-link fence.

'Are you sure this is it?' Sam whispered.

'It's exactly as Delphine described it.'

'So what do we now? Did Delphine give you a password or a contact?'

'Not exactly,' confessed Jonah.

'What does "not exactly" mean?'

'It means that...' *OK*, thought Jonah. *Time to come clean*. 'It means that, well, no one knows we're coming. Delphine gave me the RWL of this place, but she said that was all she could do. She said the rest was up to us.'

Sam looked at Jonah in horror. 'So, you're saying…?'

'There shouldn't be much security,' said Jonah. 'The main *GuerreVert* compound is far away from here. This is just where they keep the floatplane moored.'

'You said we were borrowing that plane,' hissed Sam, 'not stealing it. You said Delphine had arranged it.'

'She did,' said Jonah, 'in a way. It's just that, well…'

'It's just that no one told the owners,' said Sam, 'No, Jonah, I'm sorry. This… We can't do this. I would never have come this far with you if you'd told me the truth.'

'You can turn back if you want to,' said Jonah. 'But I'm going on.'

'You don't mess with *GuerreVert*, Jonah.'

'They messed with us,' Jonah said. 'With you! And they nearly killed Axel. So I say they owe us.' He knew the risks he was taking, he just couldn't let that stop him. There was too much at stake.

He had been watching the warehouse. He had seen no sign of light or movement, no indication that anyone was inside or patrolling outside. He ran forward, keeping low and to the shadows where he could. He half expected to be blinded by searchlights, to hear shouting and maybe even gunfire. He breathed a sigh of relief as he made it to the fence. He crept around it until he found a dark spot with no windows overlooking it. Jonah heard footsteps crunching on the sand behind him, and Sam joined him. As he hoped she would.

'Thank you,' he whispered.

'Let me get one thing straight,' said Sam. 'I'm not doing this because I think it's right. I'm not doing it because it's a good idea. I'm doing it because without someone at your back, you don't stand the slightest chance of getting out of this alive!'

14

The warehouse had a small back door, but it was heavily padlocked.

Jonah searched for a better access point, and soon found one. A broken window had been boarded up from this side, but the planks had started to come loose.

Sam rummaged through her rucksack for a crowbar. She began to wrench the nails out of the rotten planks. She was as careful as she could be, but still the harsh sound of splintering wood made Jonah wince. Sam was soon done, however. She had cleared a gap through which they could both fit.

'You're good at this,' Jonah whispered.

'I should be,' replied Sam. 'I used to do this with Dad all the time – breaking into Millennial installations in the middle of the night. It's how we first met, remember?' She handed her rucksack to Jonah and wriggled through the dark window. She dropped out of sight.

Jonah held his breath until Sam's face reappeared. She beckoned to Jonah to pass her rucksack through the window, then to follow it.

It didn't take them long to find what they were looking for. Jonah and Sam crept out of a dusty, disused office to find the *GuerreVert* floatplane right in front of them. Jonah had seen the floatplane once before, as he had entered Sydney Harbour on a Chang Corp freighter. It looked bigger up close – a lot bigger.

He had only flown one aeroplane before, and it had been half the size of this one. This plane floated on twin pontoons on a rectangular pool of water, which stretched all the way to the big warehouse doors. Its tail fin was painted black and green.

'Don't you find it suspicious,' whispered Sam, 'that we haven't seen anyone yet?'

Jonah shrugged. The same thought had occurred to him, but he preferred not to question their luck.

He studied the fuselage and giant propellers, conjuring up his father's memories. He declared the plane flight-worthy, climbed onto the portside wing and clambered in through the hatch. He found the flight deck and dropped into the pilot's seat, and ran through a mental list of pre-flight checks, hesitantly at first.

'Are you sure you know what you're doing?' asked Sam, sitting down beside him. 'I know you could fly before – but you had your father's avatar in your brain then.'

'I still have an imprint of his memories. They're my memories now. I remember flying planes like this one, even though I never have.'

'That must be so weird,' said Sam.

Jonah didn't answer her. He didn't want to think

about it, because he knew he would only end up second-guessing himself. 'We need to get those doors open,' he said. 'And it may not be quiet. If there *is* anyone around…'

Sam nodded. 'I'll do it,' she said. 'You start up the plane at the same time. That way, with any luck, we can be out of here before…'

Her voice tailed off. She froze, halfway out of her seat – just as Jonah became aware of a movement behind him. He half turned too, and was shocked to find himself looking down a gun barrel.

There were two men behind him. They must have been hiding, waiting in the passenger compartment. They were dressed in combat fatigues and carrying pistols, which were levelled at Jonah and Sam's heads.

'We've been sent by Delphine,' said Jonah.

The nearer of the two men, the terrorists – the one who was holding his gun on Jonah – smiled at him, exposing the gaps in his uneven yellow teeth.

'We know all about it, mate,' he said in a broad Australian twang. 'Delphine says *bonjour*.' Jonah let out a sigh of relief.

'And *au revoir*.'

The gunman tightened his finger around the trigger.

'I'm sorry, Sam,' Jonah said. 'I should have listened to you. I should have—'

Sam lashed out with her foot. She kicked Jonah's captor in the knee. He howled in pain and Sam snatched the gun from his hand.

The other terrorist was too slow to react. He brought up his own weapon, but hesitated to fire it in case he hit his own ally in the confined space. Sam pushed him backwards, out of the floatplane's door.

The eco-terrorist pedalled the air helplessly for a second, then he splashed into the water below.

Sam turned on the first terrorist, raised the gun she had taken from him. Outnumbered now, the terrorist grabbed Jonah for a human shield. 'Gotcha, mate.'

But Jonah was more wiry than he had anticipated and scrambled free. Sam took aim at the terrorist's head with his own pistol.

'I'm going to blow that smile off your face, mate,' said Sam.

The terrorist put his hands up. 'I surrender,' he pleaded. 'Take the plane. Just don't… Don't shoot, OK? I've got me a wife and kids about your age. I—'

'You should have thought about that,' said Sam, 'before you threatened my friend.'

Jonah had never seen Sam so angry before. He was worried she might actually pull the trigger. 'No, Sam, you can't,' he breathed.

'Can't I? He'd have done it to you in a heartbeat. He's *GuerreVert*, Jonah. That's what they do. They're killers. Remember the freighter? Remember what they did to us? Remember what they did to my dad?'

'That wasn't me!' cried the terrorist. 'Honest, it was—'

She pressed the gun barrel into the man's mouth, muzzling his protest.

'I remember,' said Jonah. 'But you don't need to take his life.' Sam didn't answer him for a long moment. 'Sam, listen to me please. You're a fighter and a warrior, but you don't have to be a cold-blooded murderer.'

She trembled, and the gun rattled against the man's shivering teeth. Then, her eyes seemed to clear, and to Jonah's relief she said, 'I know. You're right. But I really, really want to.'

She slowly pulled the gun from the terrified man's mouth and motioned with it, driving her captive across the cockpit to the open door. 'Jump,' instructed Sam – and the terrorist was so grateful to be alive that he obeyed her without question.

Before he had even hit the water, Jonah was back in the pilot's seat, starting up the twin engines. Sam leaned out of the cockpit window and cut the mooring ropes with her knife. 'The warehouse doors,' said Jonah.

'I'm on it,' said Sam – and, suddenly, she was gone. She had swung herself out of the plane and landed at the waterside.

Jonah heard a spluttered cry from one of the terrorists, still in the water. A moment later, there were three gunshots. His heart leapt into his mouth. He tried to follow Sam's movements through the shadows of the warehouse, but she was too fast.

Then a terrible racket struck up: a rumbling,

screeching sound. Jonah couldn't imagine what it was at first – until a crack of light appeared between the warehouse doors and began to widen. Sam had done it!

The only problem was, the terrorists had to know where the door control lever was. Which meant they would know where Sam was, now. And it seemed they had made it to dry land too. A gun muzzle flashed three more times in the darkness.

Jonah pushed in the throttle all the way, and the floatplane surged forward. It was between Sam and the gunman now – so the gunman switched targets.

Bullets thudded into the side of the floatplane. If one of them hit the fuel tank, Jonah and Sam's escape would be over before it had begun. There was nothing Jonah could do, however, but keep his head down and keep going.

I can do this, he told himself. *I can! My dad was the best pilot I know, and I have his instincts to guide me. I just have to trust them.*

He nudged the left rudder pedal, inched the floatplane closer to the platform dock. He felt its pontoon scraping wood.

'C'mon, Sam!' he yelled.

A heavy weight hit the port side of the plane, rocking it. Sam had leapt for the flapping door, and made it.

She pulled herself inside. The warehouse doors were fully open now and all Jonah could see ahead of them were the stars twinkling in the clear night sky.

The floatplane burst out of the warehouse at speed, throwing up two great plumes of foam in front of its pontoons.

'Thank you, Sam,' said Jonah.

'You sure you can fly this?'

'They're my memories now,' he repeated as he eased back on the control stick and lifted the plane expertly into the air.

15

'Where is she?' yelled Axel. 'Where is my daughter?'

Sam's mattress had not been slept on. Her clothes and her rucksack with all her tools were gone, and no one had seen her since last night.

A thin man charged with guarding the safe house came running to answer Axel's call.

'They snuck out, in the middle of the night,' he said. 'They didn't come back?'

'You were supposed to be on guard!' Axel shouted.

'From people getting in, not from people getting out,' he protested.

Axel was furious, and since Sam wasn't here to be furious with, he would have to settle for this incompetent watchman.

'I thought it was, you know,' the man protested when Axel grabbed him by the collar, 'just teenagers being teenagers.'

'Not Sam,' said Axel, gravely. 'If anyone's the teenager in our relationship, it's me. I'm the one who does things on wild impulse, without thinking about the consequences. Things like breaking your legs.'

He threw the man down. He wasn't worth it. He had to find Sam. If she'd snuck out with Jonah, it was for something serious – and probably very dangerous.

Matthew Granger woke up screaming. He sat up in his bed, sweating cold, his silk pyjamas clinging to his damp skin. He felt for his legs, but of course, there was nothing there but stumps.

The nightmare had come back. The one where Granger was six years old again, back home in Marin County, California. Lying in the wreckage of his parents' people carrier. Something jagged digging into his back. The smell of burning metal in his nostrils from the firemen's oxyacetylene torches. Helpless.

The lowest point of Granger's life.

Fate had dealt him a shattering blow that day. It had taken his parents and his legs. But Granger had vowed to fight it. He had refused to be a victim.

He hadn't had the nightmare in a long time. More than once, he had fooled himself into thinking it had haunted him for the last time. He had thought he had left that tragic day behind him. It always came back, though – and usually at times like these. At times when Granger felt helpless, trapped.

He reached for his cyber-kinetic legs. It would do him good to walk with them for a while – just to remind himself that any difficulty could be overcome, that *he* could overcome it. He paced his room: a presidential suite of Manhattan's Three Seasons hotel, furnished in bronze and bone. He reached for his datapad. He was hoping for a report from Tibur, but he knew it wasn't due for some hours yet.

He was hungry for information – and he knew where to find it. Granger called up Bryony's latest vlog.

He was looking at video footage of the vlogger, captured in the real world. If Bryony even had an avatar, she was careful not to show it. She might have been in the business of revealing people's secrets, but she was sure to keep her own.

Her words came out in a breathless barrage:

'—*been saying for months, of course, that the Changsphere was just*—'

'—*only person to blame for this disaster is Mr Chang himself. The reclusive entrepreneur has been keeping a low profile since*—'

'—*real winner today is Matthew Granger, who has always maintained that*—'

Granger sat on the edge of his bed, leaning over his datapad eagerly. He wanted to hear this part.

'—*mentioned before, I enjoyed a private dinner with Matthew this week, and*—'

OK, maybe not *that* part. Granger thumbed the 'skip' icon.

'—*promised improvements to the Metasphere's coding – although, of course, with the Changsphere now out of the picture, who's to say if*—'

Skip!

'—*concern now is how many Uploaded might have*

come through the Changsphere portal before it was sealed off. I hear tell from a friend of a friend of a very reliable source that there has already been a sighting of—'

Skip!

'—with zombie avatars prowling the virtual streets. It's like the plot of a Luke Wexler immersive role-playing game. Not-So-Lucky Luke, by the way, is currently—'

Skip! Skip! Skip!

'—if they should find another way out? No, my followers, I'm sorry, but the only way to protect ourselves is to shut down the Changsphere altogether. I know that losing the Uploaded will be distressing for many of us, but the dead are just that – dead. And for the sake of the rest of us, it's finally time to let them go!'

Granger clicked off his datapad, removed his mechanical legs, got back into bed.

He knew it shouldn't matter to him what a gossip like Bryony thought. But it mattered to a lot of other people. Granger had learned, in the past, that just one word from her could reduce his net worth by billions of meta-dollars.

It was good, then, that Bryony agreed with him about what needed to be done.

Still, Granger couldn't get back to sleep. He told himself he just wasn't tired, but that wasn't the truth. The truth was, he was afraid. Afraid that, if he closed his eyes, he might find himself in the wreckage of a Marin County car crash again.

*

The calm waters of the South China Sea sparkled in the morning sun.

Jonah had slept for a few hours while Sam watched over the plane on autopilot. But he didn't feel rested.

They were skirting the Philippines: a thousand islands remaining, a handful of which hadn't yet been deforested. Jonah had never seen so much green in the real world.

He'd sent Mr Chang unanswered pop-up messages and had even tried to raise him on the floatplane's radio. He hadn't yet received a reply.

'What's the plan?' asked Sam.

'I need to get back into the Changsphere,' said Jonah. 'I can't do that from the Metasphere any more, but—'

'Yeah, that much I figured,' said Sam. 'You can log in from the local servers in Hong Kong – if Mr Chang agrees. But what then?'

'I can get my dad out of there.'

'You can't. There's no way—'

'I'm going to build a bridge.'

Sam looked at Jonah, astonished. 'You mean a Chang Bridge? The one that opened the portal between—?'

'Mr Chang wants it back,' said Jonah, 'so I'm bringing it to him. In return…'

'I'm not sure it's a good idea, Jonah. If you open another portal, you'll be allowing the Uploaded to—'

'Not all of the Uploaded. Just one of them. I'm going to find my dad, Sam. I'm going to get him back into the Metasphere. Then, once he's out, we can shut the portal again behind him. I'll log off, and we can fly back to Sydney.'

He cast a sidelong glance at Sam. He had expected more of an argument – at the very least, a reminder that the Changsphere was dangerous. Sam, however, said nothing. She knew how much this meant to him.

Jonah tried the radio again. 'Calling Mr Chang,' he said into the handset, 'this is Jonah Delacroix. I've got the...equipment you wanted. Do you read me? Mr Chang?' They had to be in radio range by now. Why wasn't he answering?

'Jonah...' said Sam. She was gazing out of her side of the cockpit.

Jonah followed her eyes. He saw a massive grey boat, ploughing through the waves, belching out thick, black smoke in its wake. *Chang Corp?* he wondered. *No...* Even from up here, he could see that this boat was heavily armoured, bristling with gun emplacements. A warship!

'What do you think it's doing out here?' he asked.

'I don't know,' said Sam. 'Nothing good, I'll bet. And, to judge from its heading—'

Jonah could see it too. 'It's heading to Hong Kong.'

'I suggest,' said Sam, 'we get there before it does.'

'There's, um, something else too,' said Jonah. He

indicated the fuel gauge. It was showing more than half empty.

'I knew it,' groaned Sam. 'I knew the fuel tanks on this thing weren't big enough for the round trip.' Jonah had known it too. He just hadn't wanted to say anything. They had only got this far at all because the *GuerreVert* plane ran on an efficient biofuel mix. *Fuel like the airlines experimented with back in the day*, said a voice in his head, his father's voice, *until the food riots began and biofuel became even more expensive than the petrol.*

'So we don't have enough fuel to make it back to Sydney,' sighed Sam. 'That's great. That's just great!'

Jonah looked at the warship below them. 'Getting back might turn out to be the least of our problems,' he said glumly.

16

Hong Kong had been described as the real world's most vertical city. As the *GuerreVert* floatplane swooped towards its tightly clustered steel and glass towers, Jonah could see why.

The towers of Hong Kong Island, however, were dark, cold, lifeless. Jonah felt an icy knot forming in his chest. He still hadn't heard back from Mr Chang. Or from anyone in Hong Kong.

His father's piloting instincts took over, and he guided the plane down gently into a southern-facing bay. The first thing he noticed was that there were no boats here, either out on the water or tied up. Jonah skimmed across the waterfront, craning for a sign of human life.

'I don't see a single person,' he said.

'Maybe everyone's inside,' Sam said doubtfully.

He guided the floatplane to a dock that abutted the row of skyscrapers, and he and Sam climbed out onto a long wooden jetty. Sam found some rope in her rucksack to replace the one she had cut in the *GuerreVert* warehouse back in Sydney, and she tied the plane up securely.

They headed inland. The streets, too, were empty, and the sky seemed a long way away. Jonah felt hemmed in, like a rat in a maze. His footsteps echoed off the surrounding skyscrapers, returning as eerie echoes to his ears. Every city he had been to before in the real world had been teeming with people, filled with the sounds of voices, the thrum of rickshaws, and the wails of sirens. Jonah found the silence of Hong Kong unsettling.

'I knew ChangCorp had cleared out the residents a few years ago,' said Sam. 'But I didn't expect it to be fully deserted.'

A sudden fear gripped Jonah. 'Not deserted,' he said, thinking back to the gunboat they had spotted heading this way. 'Evacuated.'

'Let's find your father and get out of here fast.'

They chose a nearby skyscraper. Although its glass doors were locked, Sam wasted no time. She produced her crowbar again, and told Jonah to stand back as she smashed through the glass. She set off a screeching alarm, but no one came to investigate it.

They hurried across the empty lobby to the lifts and rose four storeys to emerge onto a floor filled with computer servers.

The alarm had given up by now, falling silent, so all they could hear was the humming and ticking of the cold, green server towers and their own nervous breaths. The air had a faint metallic scent to it, with perhaps a hint of burning.

Jonah had brought an Ethernet cable and DI adaptor

pack. As he unwrapped them, Sam found a chair to support him.

He connected the lead to a server, fastened the adaptor to its end. He sat down and felt for the socket in his back. As he twisted the cold adaptor into place, he shuddered, feeling it click twice as it connected with his nervous system.

Sam wired her datapad into the same server. 'Do you know where you're going?' she asked. Jonah did. He had memorised the co-ordinates for the Chang Stadium. He amended them a little, however. After his recent experience there, he felt it safest to arrive a few streets away.

He took the Chang Bridge device from his pocket, gave it to Sam. 'Here,' he said. 'You know what to do with it?'

Sam nodded. 'I'll be watching you on this,' she said, tapping her datapad. 'Once you find your dad, I'll install the Chang Bridge and open a portal next to you.'

'And as soon as he's through...' began Jonah.

'I'll close it again,' Sam confirmed, 'before the program can be finalised and the opening made permanent.' Jonah felt reassured that Sam would be there in the real world, watching over him.

He confirmed his co-ordinates and felt his head do a somersault as he lost sight of Sam and was sucked into the Changsphere.

*

He materialised at ground level, so as not to draw too much attention to himself. His exit halo bobbed beside him and Jonah passed his hand through it to make sure that it hadn't become solid.

He was standing on an abandoned Changhai street corner in the shadow of the massive stadium. Above him, billboards boasted new 'dream homes', urged settlers to 'live the Chang dream!' and wished them 'good fortune in Changhai'. It was as empty as the streets of Hong Kong and just as eerily quiet. Jonah shivered. When he had last flown above this area, just a few days ago, it had been bustling with activity. Now, that dream had become a nightmare.

He saw a shadow gliding along the street: an avatar was flying overhead. Quickly, Jonah crouched under the billboard until it had passed.

'You down there!'

Jonah flinched at the sound of the voice. It had come from an apartment window above him. The window had been boarded up, so Jonah couldn't see the speaker. His first instinct was to run, but the voice hadn't sounded threatening. A pair of bright eyes peered out from between the wooden boards.

'Are the exit halos working again?'

'I'm sorry,' said Jonah. The avatar behind the window must have seen him arriving.

'Have you come to save us?' asked a trembling voice. 'It's been nearly two days!'

Jonah thought about his new moniker, *the saviour*, and felt overwhelmed with guilt that he had returned only for his father, and not for this poor, trapped avatar.

'There's no escape from them,' the man behind the window whispered. 'The Uploaded. They roam the streets day and night. They tried to break down my door last night. I fended them off with a virus code, but they'll be back!'

Jonah wondered how many live avatars, like this man, were stuck in the Changsphere, barricaded inside their brand-new homes and businesses. And how many had been usurped. 'I'm sorry. I'm here...I'm here for someone else.'

'I have no one in the real world,' said the man behind the window. 'I'm alone in my flat. My real-world body will starve and waste away. Please save me!'

'Get out of there, Jonah,' muttered Sam through clenched teeth. She hurriedly tapped out a pop-up message to Jonah: GET OUT OF THERE. U CAN'T RESCUE THEM ALL.

She was watching Jonah on her datapad, as promised. Her heart leapt into her mouth as she saw a shape behind him: a grey wolf avatar, swooping silently out of the sky towards Jonah.

Sam cried out Jonah's name, although she knew he couldn't hear her. She tapped in a two-word warning: BEHIND U.

Jonah read the first pop-up from Sam and swiped it

away, resigned to the fact that she was right. When the second pop-up chimed, he thought at first that she was simply hammering home the point. But then he read it and turned around.

Jonah came face to snout with a drooling, crazy-eyed werewolf.

He whipped around and flew for his life.

Jonah darted along the street, took a sharp corner, came up short to find more avatars hammering on a boarded-up door ahead of him. He doubled back before they could see him. The wolf slashed at Jonah as he swooped under it. The wolf howled as it missed him and chased after him.

Jonah flew around the block, the slavering wolf snapping at his heels. But Jonah was outpacing the hungry avatar. As he rounded another corner and started looking for a hiding place, Jonah spotted an open door swaying on broken hinges, and swooped through it.

He found himself in an emptied-out roadside café. Plates of virtual fried eggs and bacon had been abandoned on the red-and-white checked tablecloths.

Jonah ducked down behind the grease-streaked window as his pursuer alighted outside. The wolf sniffed the air, and – too late – Jonah realised that the Uploaded could *sense* life. He just hoped he was too far away from this particular Uploaded avatar for it to sense him…

Luck was with him. A tense minute passed and the werewolf gave up and slunk away, hungry. Jonah left the café and struggled to get his bearings. He was used to flying above this city, not walking through it, and he didn't know which way to go.

Sam came to his rescue. She must have seen he was disoriented, because she sent him another pop-up: STADIUM THIS WAY —>.

Jonah followed Sam's directions, hurrying through the empty streets, finding cover where he could. He approached the Chang Stadium from the rear, and soon came in sight of its giant parking lot.

The lot was swarming with avatars. They had to be Uploaded, all of them, lurking here because they knew the exit halos in the lot were the only possible escape for their living prey.

There were thousands of abandoned exit halos. Jonah knew that for each of them a living soul was still trapped in the Changsphere. He didn't doubt that, in time, more and more of those souls would return to this spot. They would be worried about their real-world bodies, or just weary of the constant battle to survive here.

They would be driven, in desperation, to try their useless exit halos again. And the Uploaded would be waiting for them when they did.

Jonah could see the mouth of the tunnel he had used before, the one that led to the heart of the stadium. There were no Uploaded near it, but he couldn't reach the tunnel without crossing open ground. He would be seen for sure.

Perhaps that wouldn't be a problem, he thought. He looked no different to the Uploaded, after all. So long as they didn't get close enough to him to sense the life force behind his avatar...

The plan was risky, but it was all Jonah had. He took a deep breath and stepped out of hiding. He flew up to the edge of the parking lot, trying to look super-confident, as if he belonged there. A few of the Uploaded cast suspicious glances at him, but he kept his cool and his distance from them.

He caught his breath as he recognised one of them: the brown-and-white dog that had let him go before. Jonah turned his face away from it, without making the movement too obvious. He kept his sights firmly on the tunnel ahead of him. He was close now.

Not close enough!

Out of the corner of his eye, Jonah saw the dog staring at him. It wrinkled its nose as it sniffed for his scent. 'Life!' it cried out.

Jonah flew for the tunnel, the Uploaded streaming after him like a swarm of enraged wasps. A collective moan went up from them: a haunting sound of longing, which made Jonah wish he could close his ears. He glanced over his shoulder to see how close they were – and wished he hadn't, because that act only slowed him down and the fastest of the Uploaded were gaining on him.

There was a glowing blue firewall barrier blocking his way.

Jonah was flying at it full tilt. He closed his eyes and hoped that his VIP pass to the Chang Stadium was still valid, allowing him to go places that others could not. He was lucky.

Jonah flew straight through the barrier into the sterile white light of the tunnel beyond. Behind him, his frustrated pursuers reached between the iron bars with wings and claws, straining for their quarry, and their moans were louder and more dreadful than ever. Jonah thought he'd better get out of their sight before it occurred to them to fly over the top of the stadium and ambush him at the tunnel's far end.

He had made it barely a third of the way down the tunnel when another pack of Uploaded sprang out in front of him.

They had come from a side passageway, which was marked as leading to the locker rooms. Six of them in all, led by the winged lion avatar that had attacked him before. The lion's eyes lit up with malice at the sight of him.

'No dragon daddy to save you this time, little humatar,' he snarled.

He backed away, but there was nowhere he could go.

For the second time, the lion pounced on Jonah. It opened his mouth impossibly wide, and Jonah felt himself being sucked into a dark, endless abyss.

17

Jonah felt himself falling.

But his body – his virtual body – hadn't moved. It was as if...as if...

His thoughts, his feelings, his memories, everything that made him Jonah Delacroix... It was as if all that was shrinking away, being crushed into a tiny little corner of his brain by an influx of *new* thoughts and feelings and memories.

Images of a life not his own flashed before Jonah's mind's eye – accompanied by overwhelming, almost unbearable, raw emotion.

He was a young man, playing guitar on stage, feeling pride in his work. He felt a surge of bitterness that no one wanted to pay for music. He saw his three children and could almost have cried with the love he felt for them. Then he saw those same faces, older, and that love gave way to resentment.

Jonah saw an old man in a mirror, and he wondered where all the years had gone.

He felt an unbearable hunger, and for an instant he saw himself – his gawky-looking humatar – from the outside. And then...then, Jonah remembered:

Finding his father's avatar. Reaching out to touch it.

Being almost overwhelmed by his father's memories as they rushed into his head…but remaining in control…

Then Jonah fought back.

'Get out… Get out of…' He heard the words coming out of his mouth, although he hadn't been aware of speaking them. He sliced through the foreign memories with a sword of consciousness and fended off every encroaching thought and image with memories of his own.

'Get out!' screamed Jonah. It was guerrilla war inside his head. All at once, a million Jonahs were fighting a million invaders, memory versus memory, brain cell by brain cell.

The war dragged on for what felt like an eternity.

To Sam, watching from the server room, it was all over in a second.

To her horror, she saw Jonah disappear into the winged lion's mouth – and then the lion doubling over as if with stomach pain before spitting him out again.

Both of them collapsed, but Jonah caught himself with his hands. The lion hit the tunnel floor with a resounding smack and lay on his side, trembling, white-eyed. His avatar was depixelating, merging into blocks of corrupted code.

Jonah was on his knees, his senses reeling from the battle. But he was still himself. He hadn't been usurped.

The rest of the Uploaded – both in front of Jonah and behind him, at the tunnel gate – were staring at him in awe. Some of them turned and fled, while a couple actually fell to their knees out of worship or fear.

'The saviour is the destroyer,' Jonah heard one avatar whisper.

Jonah looked at the lion splayed out alongside him. His avatar was almost whole again – refreshed by the Changsphere's servers – but he was still shaking.

Mr Chang had once told Jonah he was special, because his brain could store two avatars at once. His father's and his own, for example. Jonah struggled to understand what he had just done. When the lion had tried to usurp him, Jonah's brain had fought back like a real-world body fighting off infection. It seemed incredible, but...

Jonah stood. He felt a little unsteady himself, but he had no time to waste.

The Uploaded pack, now leaderless, parted as he approached them. Jonah walked through them, half expecting them to strike as soon as he turned his back. They didn't, of course, too afraid of sharing the winged lion's fate.

Jonah was safe, he realised. The Uploaded couldn't hurt him. Soon, word would spread of what had just happened here, and then they wouldn't dare try.

All he had to do now was find his dad.

*

The embattled red dragon knew he couldn't last much longer.

Jason was mentally exhausted from fighting off the other Uploaded, protecting the living from being usurped. But even worse was the *hunger*.

He had gained a brief respite by barricading himself inside a conference room on the stadium's top level. His barricade had just come crashing down. Four Uploaded avatars burst into the room. Jason was waiting for them, filling the doorway with his massive dragon form. The invaders thudded into him, scratching and biting at him – but it wasn't Jason they were after.

He had found Lucky Luke hiding in one of the private boxes. The cowboy's chivalrous streak had backfired on him. In helping others escape, he had missed his own chance. Jason had sensed his presence and taken Luke under his leathery wing – the least he could do for one of his son's heroes.

Jason braced himself against a charge from an angry rhino – one he had encountered before. They butted horns and, although the rhino came off the worse for the impact, Jason was forced onto his back claws.

A purple parakeet, spry and cunning, seized its chance to dart past him. Jason snapped his head around and breathed fire after it, setting its feathers alight. The bird squawked and nosedived into the carpet, rolling to extinguish the flames.

While Jason was distracted, an orang-utan leapt onto

his shoulders and a playing-card figure – the Jack of Spades – tried to run him through from behind with a rapier. He swatted the Jack away with his wings, but the ape was more tenacious. Hairy hands covered Jason's eyes, half blinding him. His arms were too short to reach his attacker, to pry it from his head.

Through the orang-utan's fingers, Jason saw a dark, human shape, bearing down upon him. He thought it was another Uploaded, until he heard a familiar voice:

'*Yeee-haa!*'

Lucky Luke broke a chair over the orang-utan's head. It slid off Jason's shoulders to land at his feet, dazed. As Jason fought off another two-pronged attack from the rhino and the Jack, Luke picked up the orang-utan and drop-kicked it through the door.

'Hit the road, you varmint. You ain't welcome round these parts!'

'Get under cover, Luke!' snapped Jason. 'You know what these things can do to you if you get too close.' *And not just them...* Luke was so energetic, so vital, so full of irresistible, wonderful *life...*

The desire to take Luke's life was almost unbearable, but Jason fought against the instinct with all of his will power. He didn't want to become a monster.

The rhino caught Jason off-guard. Its horn gouged him in the gut, drove him backwards. He stumbled into a conference table, which until a minute ago had been bolstering the door. It collapsed under his weight, and

Jason only just caught himself before he hit the floor.

He was floating on his back, and before he could right himself the parakeet came screeching for his throat, a ball of seething feathered fury. The Jack of Spades vaulted over the prone red dragon and went for the greater prize: the cowboy.

Lucky Luke drew a pair of pistols and levelled them at the Jack. 'I'm the world's top game designer, boy,' he said in a warning growl. 'Wanna bet I couldn't have reprogrammed these here six-shooters to fire a virus that'll take your code sequence apart?'

The Jack didn't look too game to take that bet – but just then the rhino pushed it aside. 'We agreed this one was mine,' it snarled.

To judge by Lucky Luke's expression, his threat had been a bluff. He backed into a corner and cowered as the rhino advanced upon him, stretching its mouth wide open.

Jason clawed his way through the parakeet, threw himself at the rhino. As they wrestled, the Jack stabbed at Jason with its rapier and the parakeet flapped about his head. Even the orang-utan had recovered its senses and flew in to rejoin the fray.

Jason's avatar was strong, but he couldn't fight all four of them at once.

'Looking for life?'

Suddenly, the Uploaded stopped and turned to see who had entered the room. Jason used the distraction to pounce on the rhino. He wrapped his wings around the rhino and ground its face into the carpet. He looked up at his saviour, and saw the very last person he had expected to see.

It was Jonah.

Jonah had been on the verge of giving up his search.

His dad hadn't been on the pitch or in any of the private boxes. Jason might have fled the stadium and could have been anywhere in the Changsphere by now. He might even have gone to join Jonah's grandmother in isolation.

But Jonah spotted a commotion in the glass boxes overlooking the pitch and had gone to investigate.

As he stepped into the conference room, four Uploaded avatars looked at him with a mixture of awe and uncertainty. Lucky Luke took advantage of their hesitation to sidle his way around them. He had almost reached the door when the orang-utan got in his way. 'You're mine!' it said, obstinately.

Quickly, Jonah flew between the cowboy and the ape. 'Then you're mine,' he said.

'Jonah, no!' cried Jason.

The orang-utan opened its jaws and swallowed Jonah whole. This time, Jonah knew what to do. The orang-utan's consciousness tried to cloud over Jonah's mind, but he fought back on all fronts. As the usurping avatar attempted to imprint its own memories onto Jonah's mind, he destroyed each image, exploding a life once lived and expelled the Uploaded avatar from his brain, dumping it back on the ground in a semi-pixelated mess.

'Who's next?' threatened Jonah, staring down the rhino.

But the rhino scurried out of the box and into the corridor, followed by the Jack of Spades and the terrified parakeet.

Jonah rushed to his father and reached around his scaly neck in a tight hug. But their reunion was short-lived. Jonah led his dad and Luke out of the box through the window. They flew out onto the pitch, Jonah and his dad flanking Lucky Luke like bodyguards. Jason was full of questions, but Jonah said he would explain everything to him later. 'I'm going to get you out of here,' he promised.

'I'd be mighty grateful if you could do that, son,' said Luke.

There were plenty of Uploaded circling above the stadium, but they gave the escaping trio a wide berth. Word of Jonah's immunity to usurping had spread fast.

They flew up and over the stadium, out into central Changhai. Once they had flown a few blocks, Jonah halted in mid-air and called out, 'Now, Sam! Open the portal now!'

And they waited.

They waited for what felt like an eternity. Jonah

eyed a few Uploaded who had followed them from the stadium and were keeping their distance, hovering and watching.

Then, a bright pinpoint of light flared a few metres away from them, and the pinpoint grew into a blinding white square.

Lucky Luke gaped at it, and held onto his cowboy hat. 'What in tarnation…?'

'A bridge back to the Metasphere,' said Jonah, 'but we can only keep it open for a few seconds before…' He glanced back at the Uploaded, nervously. They were as dumbfounded as Luke and Jason were, but Jonah knew that wouldn't last.

'Go!' he said. 'Both of you, go!'

Lucky Luke didn't need telling twice. With a tip of his hat to Jonah, he dived through the window of light. Jason, however, hesitated.

'Jonah, I'm not sure this is a good—'

'Please, Dad. I can't… I won't leave you trapped in here. I won't lose you again.'

'OK,' said Jason. 'OK. If it's what you want.'

'Message me on the other side,' said Jonah. 'I'll find you in the Metasphere.'

Jason nodded. He beat his wings and followed Luke to safety.

Alone now, Jonah allowed himself a moment of pure relief. Then he turned, and saw that the Uploaded onlookers had begun to approach.

'Sam, they're through,' he called. 'Close the Bridge now!'

But the portal remained open, beckoning the Uploaded to fly through as Jonah had once taught them to do.

The Uploaded picked up speed as they rose. They were close enough now that Jonah could see the eagerness in their eyes. They remembered the last time they had seen a light like this one. They knew what it meant, where it would take them: to a new hunting ground with enough living avatars to feed their hunger.

Jonah tried to ward them off. He hovered between them and the portal. 'No, please,' he cried, 'you mustn't go through!' But the Uploaded weren't listening.

They overwhelmed him with their numbers, and Jonah heard their excited whispers as they barged past him:

'So hungry...'

'...saved us again, shown us the way...'

'...new life.'

'Thank you, my saviour. Thank you!'

'Sam,' he cried, 'where are you? Sam, close the Bridge!'

But, even if Sam could have answered him, it was already too late. The first swarm of Uploaded avatars had just flown into the bright white light and disappeared.

The Uploaded were swarming from across the Changsphere. Jonah couldn't stop them. But he kept trying. Surely Sam would close the portal soon, he thought.

Then he glanced to his right and saw something that chilled him to the bone.

Another portal, like the first. It was hovering in mid-air, about four hundred metres away from him. And, when Jonah looked left, he saw a third portal…and a fourth and a fifth behind him, each one attracting a fresh stream of Uploaded avatars.

He felt numb inside. *How could this have happened? What did I do wrong?*

18

'This can't be happening,' moaned Sam to herself.

She ran her hands through her hair. The Chang Bridge had done what it was supposed to do. It had opened a portal between the virtual worlds.

But then, it had kept on going.

Pop-up after pop-up was appearing on Sam's datapad, each one a notification that a new portal had been created. In the time it took her to shut one down, three more had appeared to replace it. They were appearing over Changhai and across the entire Changsphere.

The Chang Bridge, thought Sam. It was humming and flickering to itself in its server panel slot. She reached for it, closed her hand around it.

'Allow the device to do its good work, Miss Kavanaugh.'

Sam turned. There were three men behind her.

All three of the men were Chinese. Two of them were muscular, fierce-eyed and wearing flak jackets. The third – the one who had spoken – was barely a man at all, but a boy, younger than Sam herself.

'Please, Mr Chang!' she exclaimed. 'The dead are—'

'We will leave the portals open,' said Mr Chang, his voice barely registering above a whisper. 'All of them.'

Sam looked from the boy to his henchmen. She thought she could have taken them with her combat training – had they not been training their guns at her head.

She felt the Chang Bridge device thrumming between her fingers. One tug was all it would take to yank it out of its server panel.

'But they're escaping into the Metasphere. We can't let them—'

'Who are you to deny our honoured ancestors a chance at resurrection?'

'By stealing life from the living?'

'Is it not simply a continuation of the circle of life?' asked Mr Chang. 'Life to death to life again.'

'That's not resurrection, that's body theft!'

'I believe I can cure the Uploaded of their hunger. I may even be able to restore their victims to their own minds and bodies. Those portals will buy me that time. You came to Hong Kong by air from the south, I presume?'

Mr Chang took Sam's silence as a yes.

'Then no doubt you saw the Millennial warship approaching this island.'

'Millennial?' echoed Sam.

'Granger wishes the Uploaded destroyed. It is what he has always wanted – and now he has the excuse he needs. His ship will be in firing range within minutes and the dead will be gone, forever.'

Sam looked nervously at Jonah's lifeless body.

'Maybe…' she ventured. 'Maybe it's for the best. I mean, maybe we should have let the dead go instead of clinging onto them. Maybe…'

'I doubt young Master Delacroix would agree with you,' said Mr Chang. 'He's brought you a long way, and risked much, to save just one of the Uploaded. Do the rest not deserve equal consideration?'

He was right, of course. Every one of the Uploaded was loved by someone. Once.

'And what about the living, Miss Kavanaugh? What about those poor, unfortunate souls that Granger sealed inside my Changsphere? Are we to abandon them too?'

She shook her head and said, 'This will change everything.'

'Then that shall be my legacy,' Mr Chang replied.

Sam sighed and took her hand off the Chang Bridge. 'I need to warn Jonah.'

At Sam's urging, Jonah flew back to his exit halo, still hovering alone on the abandoned street corner. He didn't know what else to do.

He stopped on his way at the boarded-up window through which he had spoken to the trapped survivor earlier. At least he could help him now, direct him to a way out of here. But the boards had been torn down and there was no one around.

Perhaps the avatar had heard about the portals already

and made it through one of them. Jonah certainly hoped so. He took one last look at the Changsphere, once a land of hope and promise, now a scene of mass carnage, and dived through his exit halo.

As Jonah opened his eyes in the real world, he saw an unexpected face.

'Master Delacroix.'

'Mr Chang?' Jonah blinked as if he thought he might be seeing things. 'What are you doing here? We thought you'd... Where's Sam? I have to tell her...'

He refocused his eyes and saw Sam too – and two other men, with guns. He sat up, too fast. He hadn't quite readjusted to the real world yet and the movement made him feel sick.

'The portals,' gasped Jonah. 'There are hundreds of them. The Uploaded...'

'Yes,' said Mr Chang. 'We know.'

Jonah looked at Sam. She returned his gaze with a helpless shrug.

'You...' He addressed Mr Chang. 'It was you who opened those portals?'

'No, Jonah, it was you,' replied the billionaire. Suddenly Jonah realised that he'd been used by Mr Chang, again.

'You knew what was happening with the Uploaded all along, and you knew that once the rest of the world found out... That's why you really wanted the Chang

Bridge back so badly. You couldn't bear to see the Changsphere quarantined.'

'I had feared you wouldn't bring me the device in time,' said Mr Chang. 'I was attempting to code a new bridge when I was informed of your arrival.'

'The alarm we set off,' Sam realised.

Jonah felt sicker than ever. This wasn't the first time Mr Chang had kept something from him. It wasn't the first time he had used Jonah to get something he wanted. Jonah gripped the arms of his chair in frustration.

'Why?' he asked. 'Why would you inflict the Uploaded on the Metasphere? Why would you—?' He never finished the question.

Suddenly, there was a tremendous explosion, and the building shook.

At first, Jonah thought it was falling down; he had been in a building that had done that once. He fell off his chair and flailed for something to hold onto, although he knew it wouldn't save him.

It took him a moment to realise that the shaking had stopped. The floor beneath his hands and feet was still intact, and Sam had run to the nearest window. 'I can't see anything,' she reported. 'Just dust and smoke.'

They heard another explosion, then another – more distant, this time.

'Make your exit,' said Mr Chang. 'Both of you.'

'What about you?' asked Jonah. 'Aren't you...?

Mr Chang shook his head. 'I will stay and keep the

servers running. For as long as I can.'

'Don't you see what's happening?' cried Sam. 'The warship is here. You said yourself, Granger wants the Uploaded destroyed! I think... I think some towers have already fallen, and this one could be next.'

'The Changsphere is – it *was* – my world,' said Mr Chang. 'I owe it to the people who came here, who trusted in me, to do all I can for them.'

Sam took Jonah by the hand. 'Come on,' she said as she pulled him to the stairwell.

Jonah looked back at Mr Chang, flanked by his bodyguards. 'Goodbye,' he said.

Mr Chang smiled back at him, and made a formal little bow.

They raced out onto the stairs, Jonah and Sam, just the two of them again now. They had barely begun to descend when the next explosion came: the closest one yet. The steps below them crumbled and fell away.

Jonah found himself engulfed in a cloud of brick dust and plaster. Sam grabbed him by the arms and dragged him onto the landing, coughing and spluttering. Below them, where the stairs had been, was a swirl of dusk and smoke.

'Any ideas?' gasped Jonah between coughs.

Sam shook her head. 'Even if the lifts are working, we can't risk them.' She shrugged off her rucksack and opened it. She groaned. 'The windows are out too. We're

163

too high up to jump, and I used all my rope to moor the floatplane.'

'Up,' coughed Jonah. 'We have to…go up.'

'Up where?'

'To the executive offices. They'll have gliders up there.'

'Jonah, you'd better be right.'

They were halfway up the next flight of stairs, Jonah's lungs burning from the dust, when he remembered Mr Chang.

'He'll be trapped down there,' Jonah called.

'We don't have time,' insisted Sam. 'I'm sure Mr Chang knows what he's doing.'

They climbed to the fifty-fourth floor, the fifth from the top. Exhausted and panting, Jonah ran past all of the glass-fronted offices until he found what he was looking for, the biggest office with a familiar metal cabinet standing in the corner.

'There!' he shouted, pointing to the Pegasus logo stamped into the steel cabinet. He yanked open the cabinet door. The escape glider hung inside. Jonah grabbed it by its aluminium frame, located the canvas straps, and turned as Sam appeared behind him.

'It looks like that's the only one on this floor,' said Sam.

'Take it,' said Jonah. 'You put these straps over—'

'No. No, Jonah, you go. I'll—'

Jonah shook his head firmly. 'It's my fault you're here, Sam. You go first.'

'Jonah!'

'I'm not arguing! There are five more floors to search. I'll find another one.' He almost choked on his words – not because he didn't believe them, but because Jonah remembered the last time he had been in a situation like this one.

The City Tower in London. The day he had lost his mother, because there had been only one glider and not enough time. She had given her life to save him. He wasn't going to ask Sam, his best friend, to make the same sacrifice.

Jonah strapped Sam into the glider harness and pulled her to the shattered window. He remembered his mum's hands pressing down on his shoulders.

'No, Mum, don't!'

'It's the only way. I love you, Jonah.'

Sam hesitated, one foot on the window sill. 'I'll come and look with you. If there isn't another glider, we can try to share this one. It might take our weight—'

Jonah pressed the red toggle of the ripcord into her hand. 'Go,' he said. 'It's the only way, Sam.' And he pushed her out into the dust-filled sky.

Jonah's push took Sam by surprise.

She fell out of the window, pulled her ripcord almost reflexively. Two black canvas wings sprang out of Sam's harness around a lightweight aluminium frame, and she was no longer falling, but flying.

She saw Jonah's face at the window, watching her until she was safe. He was mouthing something at her: '*I'll meet you at the plane!*' She gestured to him to go, save himself, and Jonah seemed to get the message because his face disappeared.

Sam glided between the towers of Hong Kong – the remaining towers. All across the island, she could see the flashes of more explosions. She saw more burning towers crumbling or toppling like dominoes. To her right, a glass tower sank into a cloud of dust before her. Sam quickly worked out how to steer her glider wings, twisting them now to avoid being sucked down into a whirlwind of debris.

She was choking, her eyes streaming. She glided out over the harbour, where at least the air was clearer. She saw the floatplane in dock where they had left it, and she began to spiral down towards it. She saw the gunship anchored at the mouth of the harbour, spitting missiles at the once tall cityscape.

One whirling missile struck a skyscraper close behind Sam and she felt the heat of the explosion washing over her back. When she turned, when she looked, her heart leapt into her mouth. She saw three more buildings falling; right next to the one she had just left. Through a dust haze, she saw Jonah's building teetering. Its top section dislodged and, as if on a hinge, slammed into the skyscraper beside it.

The dust haze thickened, and Sam could see no more. The only thing she knew for certain was that there hadn't been enough time for Jonah to get to another floor, to locate another escape glider. He had still been inside.

'*Jonah!*' yelled Sam, panic-stricken, angry at her friend for pushing her out of the window first. She thought back to what she had said to her father. *He's doing what Jonah does. Putting himself in danger to help others.*

She loved him for it and she hated him for it.

19

Jonah was halfway up the next flight of stairs when the missile hit.

He heard the whistle of its approach, knew what was about to happen. He braced himself for the explosion but was still deafened by it, and blinded by a flash all around him. He was thrown against the wall and showered with chunks of concrete.

His stomach dropped into his shoes. There was no doubt about it, this time. The skyscraper was falling.

But it didn't fall far.

Jonah picked himself up gingerly, onto his hands and knees. He was still in one piece, though he couldn't understand why.

The staircase was almost horizontal. Jonah crawled forward, felt the building swaying with his shifting weight. He stopped. He lay still for a minute, terrified. He couldn't stay here. He had to move.

Jonah pulled himself up – along – the stairs and out of the stairwell and onto the fifty-fifth floor. He looked across the floor and out of the window. He couldn't see much through the dust, just the silhouettes of a few surviving neighbouring buildings. They appeared to be listing at a forty-five degree angle – but, of course, it was

Jonah's building that was askew.

It must have crashed into an adjacent skyscraper. And that skyscraper, held fast, was supporting Jonah's building. But for how much longer?

He had been given another chance. If he could get to the roof of this building, maybe there would be a way across to its still-vertical neighbour. Then, assuming that its staircase wasn't blocked too, he could take it down to street level.

That's a lot of ifs, thought Jonah.

The stricken tower creaked and groaned around him, and he realised that speed was more important now than stealth. The leaning tower was going to collapse soon, whatever he did.

He developed an awkward rhythm across the stairs, soon hardly banging his shins on them at all. When the staircase turned, Jonah had to scramble along the wall to reach the next flight, fearful that the bricks beneath him would give way.

He nearly made it up to the fifty-sixth floor in this fashion, before the stairwell above him was too mangled to pass.

There was nothing he could do but lower himself back to the fifty-fifth floor. Crouching at a steep angle to it, he had to reach to open the door, then wriggle up behind it and haul himself up over the frame.

Jonah found himself on another server floor with no

executive offices – so no escape gliders. He just hoped he had made it high enough to cross over into the adjacent building, which was still vertical.

He slid down the tilting floor on his back. Fortunately, it was clad with protective black plastic, and the rough surface slowed his barely-controlled descent. A few of the green servers had broken free of their moorings, and were piled against the outer wall.

He collided with the building's outside wall, and thought he might lose his step and fall through a glassless window. Jonah flattened himself into the angle where floor and wall met and peered outside. He was met by another crushing disappointment.

The skyscraper had indeed fallen into the next building, and the uppermost floors of both were hopelessly ensnarled. Jonah might well have been able to crawl from one to the other – had he only been able to reach the floor above this one.

As it was, he found himself staring at a sheer drop, that other tower a tantalising few metres away from him. Close, but nowhere near close enough.

Jonah couldn't jump the gap. For an insane moment, he considered scaling the outside of his tower – but there were no real handholds, and the angle of the wall would have worked against him. It would have been suicide to attempt it.

Suicide.

The very thought cut across his mind like a dull

knife. Jonah realised he was in a tower of powerful computer servers, and if he acted quickly, he might be able to Upload himself. At least that way, he could live on digitally, like his father, instead of perishing in a burning building like his mother.

Most people who Uploaded themselves grappled with the choice for months, sometimes years. Jonah's nan had even sought counselling before making that final decision. Jonah didn't have the luxury of time. It was now or never. He imagined his new afterlife, confined to the virtual world, and wondered if he too would succumb to the hunger for life and find an unsuspecting victim to usurp. What would it be like to take over someone's body? These questions rang through Jonah's mind as missiles dismantled the city around him. Was Uploading just the easy way out?

Jonah chose to fight.

He chose to fight for his life. He wanted to live, even if it killed him.

Suddenly, an almighty din struck up behind him: metal clashing against metal. Jonah whirled around. A server was hurtling down the slope of the room towards him.

He leapt away from the window just in time. The heavy server came within a hair's breadth of breaking his trailing foot. It toppled over the low windowsill and was gone. Jonah watched through the broken window as it plummeted away from him.

The server shattered against the adjacent building and fell to the distant street in pieces. But it had given Jonah an idea. A desperate idea.

He wasn't going to jump across to the adjacent building, he was going to fly.

He spent the next few minutes in a frenzy of activity, working for his life.

He ripped up the server room's protective plastic flooring. He pulled it up and set it against the window sill, creating a ramp, perfectly horizontal, from the sloping floor to the open window.

Next, Jonah located a small mobile server, upturned and battered. He pushed it off its base: a steel rectangle on four wheels, like a massive skateboard.

He dragged the wheeled server base up to the far wall, its highest point. He positioned it carefully in a straight line from the window. He checked that there were no obstacles in its path.

Then Jonah lay down on his stomach on the server base.

He ignored the hammering beat of his heart, and the panicking voice in the back of his head that told him he couldn't do this. He thought about his father, and Sam. He had promised them both he would see them again. He had no choice but to try. He hoped he wouldn't die trying.

He braced his feet against the wall, held himself in

place with his hands on the floor. And pushed off with all the strength he could muster.

His makeshift roller-luge zoomed down and across the room. The base tilted too far to the right. He was going to miss the ramp and slam into the brick wall below the window. He leaned left with all of his body weight, almost tipping over, and steered the server base back towards his intended trajectory.

He hit the ramp, gained lift, and burst up and out of the leaning skyscraper. The wind was in his face, his stomach was in his mouth, and there was nothing beneath his wheels. He was flying.

Jonah let the makeshift skateboard fall out from under him. Its weight would only drag him down now. He saw the face of the adjacent skyscraper rushing to meet him. He was falling a little way short of a window. He flailed for it, caught the sill with his hands as his body slammed painfully into the building.

Gravity reasserted its hold on Jonah, and he felt as if his arms were being pulled out of their sockets. He gritted his teeth, hauled himself painfully up. The windows of this building, like the other, had been blown out. He flopped over the window frame and collapsed onto another floor filled with ChangCorp computer servers.

He lay on the ground and listened for a moment as the whirl of servers was drowned out by the sounds of creaking metal and crumbling concrete. Panting for breath, he was more grateful than he could ever have imagined that the floor beneath his back was flat and level.

He stood slowly up to look back at the fallen tower he'd just escaped from and suddenly a tremendous explosion blasted debris through the window. Jonah took cover and crawled away from the window, careful not to cut himself on shards of glass and burning metal. Finally, he scrambled to his feet, struggling to breathe. Through stinging tears, he could see that a great hole had been punched through the leaning skyscraper he had just fled. It must have taken a direct missile hit!

The tower was disintegrating, turning to dust. Jonah had escaped in the nick of time. But he knew that his new haven could be hit next and he darted for the stairs.

Sam landed in the water and desperately unhooked the glider to keep from drowning. As she bobbed in Hong Kong's harbour, all around her the towers burned and collapsed. The entire city was covered in smoke and ash. She swam to the plane, untied it from the dock and climbed aboard.

She knew she should get out of the harbour as fast as possible. But she had never executed a solo take-off, and she wanted to wait, however foolishly, for Jonah.

Another nearby blast threw up choppy waves around her, rocking the plane. Cold water seeped into the cockpit and wet Sam's feet.

Jonah isn't coming, she tried to tell herself. Even if, by some miracle, he had escaped from the falling tower, Hong Kong Island was a raging inferno now. And the longer Sam waited for her missing friend, the greater the chance she would burn along with him.

She started the floatplane's engines. She pulled out the choke. She couldn't bring herself to do it. She waited a little longer.

She thought she heard Jonah's voice, calling out her name. She thought she must be imagining things. Perhaps the guilt of leaving her friend was playing tricks on her mind. But then the voice grew louder: '*Sam! Sam!*'

And Sam turned and she looked and, through the cockpit window, she couldn't believe what her eyes were seeing.

Jonah was racing along the jetty towards her, covered in dust and ash.

The plane had drifted a little from its moorings, but Jonah didn't wait for Sam to bring it back. He ran full-tilt off the edge of the jetty, dropped like a stone and, for a heart-stopping second, disappeared beneath the waves.

He re-emerged, thrashing his arms and legs in an uncoordinated swimming stroke that was somewhere between breaststroke and doggy paddle but that nonetheless propelled him forward. Sam ran to the door, leaned out of the plane and snagged Jonah as he swam up to her.

'Thank God!' she cried, as she helped Jonah into the plane. 'Thank God you're OK. How did you…? I thought I'd never see you again!'

He collapsed into his seat. 'Thank you for waiting,' he gasped. 'This time I was worried that I might not make it back.'

Sam was already taxiing the plane away from the burning cityscape. She pulled back on the throttle, but Jonah placed his hand on hers, and eased it forward again. 'Not yet,' he said. 'Wait till…further out.' Sam understood. The curve of the bay was shielding them from sight of the Millennial boat.

They took to the air, at last, although Sam remained tense until she judged they were out of range of the warship's missiles. She looked back with regret at the Hong Kong skyline, now brutally decimated. Even as Sam watched, she saw more towers collapsing. The sky above the island was a glowering red, choked with smoke.

It was a long time before either Sam or Jonah spoke again.

20

Jason Delacroix flew out of the white light. He was greeted by the odd sight of a giant black safe, wrapped in chains.

There was no sign now of the sprawling city he had just left. He was hovering over a crystal-blue ocean, above a solitary island, with clean white beaches and lush green forests. Jason grinned as he recognised it as the Island of the Uploaded. He had made it back to the Metasphere.

Lucky Luke was waiting for him. 'What kept you, pardner?' he asked.

'A word with my son,' said Jason. He couldn't tell the cowboy the whole truth.

'I thought you were a goner. Good to see you safe and sound. I owe you my life, hombre, and Lucky Luke don't weasel on a debt.'

'Where to now?' asked Jason.

'I guess it's back to the RW for me.'

Jason raised his eyebrows. 'The real world? But isn't your exit halo in the Changsphere?'

'Nope. I parked it this side of the portal; I had business in the Metasphere on my way through. Good thing I did, too. Lucky by name, I guess...'

Jason felt a surge of jealousy towards Luke. After all they had both been through, at least he got to go home. Jason would never see the real world again.

Unless...

The thought grew in Jason's head as the hunger grew in his soul.

'Darn it!' groaned Luke. He struck his forehead with the palm of his hand.

'What's wrong?'

'I only just remembered, I got a game launch to reorganise. Well, I can't hardly launch *Brain-Sucking Zombies* in a Changsphere full of roving zombies, now can I? I'm gonna have to set up shop back in the Metasphere, and won't Granger just love that!'

But Jason wasn't listening to Luke Wexler's petty problems. He was distracted by the sight of the portal.

'It's still here,' he said. 'Shouldn't Sam have closed it by now?'

And, almost on cue, the Uploaded began to arrive.

The portal spat them out, one by one at first and then in tens and hundreds. They fanned out across the blue sky, whooping in delight to see their old home below them.

'Oh, Jonah,' breathed Jason in dismay, 'what have you done?'

Lucky Luke shrank behind him, nervously. 'Um, I don't know about you, pardner, but I figure I'd best vamoose before—'

'Yeah,' said Jason. 'You best had.'

*

Jason flew to the mainland with Luke.

He thought he might keep going: follow his mother's example and find a place to hide himself. Somewhere he wouldn't be exposed to temptation and he might not ache with so much hunger. The Metasphere was smaller than the Changsphere, however, and more densely populated. Jason doubted that any part of it could be remote enough. And, anyway, Lucky Luke was coming in to land on a virtual city street, and Jason couldn't help himself, he was following his new friend, stalking him.

The hunger grew as he descended through layers of flying avatars.

He closed his eyes, swallowed hard. He thought about his son. Jonah had done so much, risked so much, for him. So how could he let Jonah down?

He had thought he could be strong, stronger than the usurpers, but instead he felt weak. There was so much life here – too much to resist – and Jason knew he couldn't trust himself around it. He should have stayed in the Changsphere.

Lucky Luke had drawn a crowd. Excited avatars were falling upon him, asking if it was really him.

'We heard you were trapped with…'

'…knew if anyone could make it out…'

Jason suspected that, normally, Luke would have enjoyed the attention. Not right now, though.

Luke appealed to his adoring fans to listen to him.

'You have to hightail it outta here,' he warned them. 'The Metasphere ain't safe for the living no more! The dead are rising.'

'It's a publicity stunt,' scoffed one avatar, a porcupine, 'for the new game. Come on, Mr Wexler, fess up – this is the plot of *BSZ4*!'

'No, seriously, friend,' urged Luke. 'Dive into your halo if you want to survive this here uprising!'

'I love this game already!' shouted the porcupine to the other fascinated avatars.

Luke turned to Jason. 'They don't believe me.'

'People believe what they want to believe,' said Jason.

'I guess you're right,' Luke sighed. 'I'd better mosey on back to the real world.'

'Give my regards to Texas,' said Jason, quoting a song he'd once heard.

'I park my boots in the big city now, pardner,' said Luke. 'Manhattan. I'll give your regards to Broadway!'

As Luke turned, his exit halo glowed with anticipation. Jason knew this was his chance. The hunger burned so hot, but it wasn't just the pull of life. Luke was going to slip through his exit halo and wake up in Manhattan, the most secure nation in the world, and the home of the Western Corner servers.

Luke turned back to tip his hat. That was when Jason pounced. He opened his great dragon jaws and swallowed Luke in a single, violent gulp.

*

A woman's voice was screaming beside Jason's head. He wished the screamer would stop, because the sound echoed in his brain, making it impossible to think.

He felt nauseous. It reminded him of the airsickness he suffered every time he had to fly. *No, wait*, he thought, *that can't be right. I love flying...don't I?*

He had been a...*games designer? No, a pilot. I am – I was – an Air Force pilot, and then...* Why was it so hard to remember his own name?

Jason. My name is Jason. Jason Delacroix!

He surfaced as if from a deep, dark dream. *Someone else's dream.* He was crouched in the middle of a road – *a virtual road, it has to be, because I'm in my virtual self, my dragon avatar –* and the screamer was actually right beside him, but someone else was hushing her, pulling her away from Jason. *Luke's fans*, he remembered.

What...what did I just do? Where's Luke? Where's Lucky Luke?

There was no sign of the black-clad cowboy, as Jason had known there wouldn't be. He thought he could hear Luke's voice, though, hear it in the back of his own head – and he thought Luke was screaming too.

Jason felt different. As the full realisation of what he had done crept over him, he felt guilty, ashamed. But there was something else too. He felt...fulfilled, *content*. For the first time in what seemed like forever to him, Jason didn't feel hungry.

Something caught his eye, something he hadn't seen

in a long time: an exit halo, glowing brighter than all the others. Lucky Luke's exit halo. No, now it was Jason's. It was glowing for him, beckoning him back to the real world.

On the other side of that hovering ring of light was everything he had been hungering for: *real life*.

Jason Delacroix dived through the pulsing exit halo and for the first time in over three years, awoke in the real world.

Sam had offered to stay at the floatplane controls for a while. Jonah was grateful to her. Every muscle in his body was aching. He just wanted to sleep. But, when he closed his eyes, all he could see was smoke and flames.

'How many do you think made it through?' Jonah asked. 'How many Uploaded...?'

'How many died because they *couldn't* leave the Changsphere?' she shot back. 'How many did Granger kill today?'

'Granger? What does he have to do with—?'

'He sent that warship,' said Sam. 'At least, Mr Chang believed he did, and it makes sense to me that it would have been him. Who else?'

Jonah didn't answer that. He *couldn't* answer that. *First Axel,* he thought, *then Mr Chang. Now Granger too, saying one thing to my face, trying to make me believe in him, then...this. Is there no one I can trust in any world?*

No one but Sam.

'Do you think… Do you think we did the right thing?' he asked.

'I don't know,' said Sam. 'I can guess what Dad will have to say on the subject. But then, Mr Chang said… I don't know, Jonah. I just don't any more.'

'I flooded the Metasphere with angry Uploaded,' said Jonah. '*Hungry* Uploaded.' *Don't think about that,* he told himself. *You came to Hong Kong to rescue your dad, and that's what you did. If you hadn't…*

If he hadn't come here, Jonah realised with a chill, then his dad would have been dead by now.

Dead again.

He held onto that thought. He had told Jason to message him when he was safe. Perhaps that message had arrived already, he thought. He plugged a datapad into the plane's computer terminal, let it scan his thumbprint.

An urgent red message window popped up on his pad. I AM REBORN, it said. RESURRECTED ON THE OTHER END OF THE NYLON THREAD. TELL AK. MEET ME @ THE SHOP.

The message wasn't signed, but it didn't have to be. Jonah knew whom it had come from. He read the words through three times more, and each time they made him feel a little colder. He showed the message to Sam.

'Does that mean what I think it means?' she asked.

Jonah was at once excited and afraid, but the two sensations cancelled each other out until only a dull numbness remained. 'It means trouble,' he said.

21

Jonah's humatar flew low over Venus Park.

He hadn't been to this part of the Metasphere in what felt like an age. He was surprised at how little had changed. Couples still strolled together in the shade of the cherry blossom trees. They still threw coins in the Japanese fountains.

Don't they know about the Uploaded? thought Jonah. *Don't they know they're in danger?*

Then Jonah's thoughts returned to his father's message. *Reborn.* Had his father really given into the hunger and usurped another's avatar? Did he log off and awake in someone else's body? Jonah shuddered at the idea. He was excited that his dad might actually be back in the real world but terrified that he had given in to the hunger and become one of the monsters he was trying to fight.

Jonah looked down at the empty lot where his family's gift shop had once stood. His heart felt heavy as he set down in front of it. An interactive signpost promised a new development on this site soon and – because the Guardians controlled this area now – asked passers-by to vote on what it should be.

'You should have told me.' Jason's great red dragon

descended, folded in his wings, and looked sadly at the vacant space. 'You should have told me it was gone,' he said.

'I didn't want to upset you,' said Jonah.

'That shop was meant to be your inheritance.'

'I don't need it, Dad. I have you back.'

'What happened?' asked Jason.

Jonah didn't feel like relating the whole story right now. He boiled it down to one word. A name: 'Granger.'

Jason clenched his front claws in anger. 'I'm sorry,' he said.

'What for?'

'That man has done nothing but harm to our family – to you – and it's all my fault. I should have thought more about my responsibilities when the Guardians asked me to join them. I should have let someone else try to save the world.'

'You did what you thought was right,' said Jonah. 'It took me a while to understand that, Dad, but I do now.'

Jason nodded, smiling proudly. 'Yes, son. I know you do. And…what about the message I sent you? Did you understand that?'

'I think so,' said Jonah.

'You passed the message on to Axel?'

'I haven't seen him yet. Sam and I are flying a plane, in the real world.'

'You're flying?'

'With *your* memories, Dad.'

'That's amazing, Jonah,' said Jason. 'You're a pilot now! Say, let's call in at the Icarus? You remember, the old pilots' bar? God, I've missed that place!'

Jonah shook his head. 'The Icarus has gone too, Dad.'

Jason didn't speak again for long seconds. Then, he sighed and said, 'I guess a lot of things have changed while I was away.'

'Let's take a walk,' said Jonah. 'Let's... Let's talk about your message and what it means, and... And about what we do next.'

One of the joys of the Metasphere was its unlimited variety. You could walk to the end of a crowded city block and come to a beach or a jungle or an alien planet.

In Jonah and Jason's case, their wanderings took them from Venus Park to an Old Western ghost town called Progress.

They strolled past clapboard houses, swing-doored saloon bars and a blacksmith's shop. In the dusty main street, a crowd had gathered to watch a gunfight. Two cowboys drew their pistols and fired at each other. One was shot in the stomach and went reeling into a horse trough. The audience applauded happily.

The fallen cowboy picked himself up, unharmed, and demanded, 'Best out of three!'

'He feels right at home here,' said Jason.

'Who?'

'Luke,' said Jason. 'I'm reborn in his body, in the real

186

world. But it's funny, I can somehow sense him inside me.'

He spoke in a casual, matter-of-fact way, but his words were like a punch to Jonah's gut. So, it *was* true, after all. Everything that Jonah had feared, and hoped for.

They heard a scream. A delicate pink rose was cowering in fear, shouting, 'Uploaded! He's Uploaded!'

But she wasn't pointing at Jason. The terrified rose pointed a trembling leaf at a pig standing on its hind legs, which itself looked afraid as it was surrounded by angry avatars.

'She's got it wrong,' the pig squealed. 'I'm not Uploaded, I'm alive, I swear it!'

'He was telling me about himself,' the rose insisted, 'but he started to forget things. Just like the Uploaded do!'

The mob was turning ugly, closing in around the pig. Jonah thought they might rip him apart. Then, with a flap of his dragon's wings, Jason hopped over their heads to land beside their would-be victim.

'Leave him alone!' he commanded. 'This man has done nothing wrong!'

'How do you know that?' a member of the mob challenged him.

'Yeah,' another agreed. 'The little rose could be right, for all you know. The pig could be Uploaded. There's no way to tell the difference.'

'You're right,' agreed Jason. 'There's no way to tell. The pig could be Uploaded. So could you. For that matter, so could I.'

Jonah winced. He felt his dad was sailing too close to the truth there.

'The point is,' said Jason, 'there are probably fewer Uploaded around than we think – and if we let our fears rule us, if we turn on each other, then we're lost.'

No one could argue with that. The angry avatars dispersed, with only a few disgruntled murmurs. The pig, relieved, thanked Jason and scurried away.

'That was brilliant, Dad,' said Jonah. He remembered his own failed attempt to reason with a mob, in the Chang Stadium. He wished he had his father's way with words – not to mention the sheer presence of his avatar.

'I just told them the truth,' said Jason.

'Can you still sense…? I mean, is that how you knew…?'

Jason knew what his son was asking. 'No, Jonah,' he said. 'I meant what I said. I don't know if the pig was Uploaded or not. I can no longer sense life, because I'm no longer hungry for it. I'm no longer Uploaded.'

'You've been…' Jonah couldn't say the word. The word his father had used in his message. Every time he thought about it, it made his stomach sick with horror.

'Reborn,' said Jason. 'Yes, I have.'

'In Luke Wexler's body.'

'Yes,' said Jason. 'In Luke's body.'

Jonah stared at his father, not knowing how to react.

'Jonah, I walked outside today,' Jason continued, filling the silence between them. 'I walked outside, with real legs in the real world. I breathed real air. I smelled real flowers. I even felt real rain on my cheeks.'

'You can feel all those things online,' Jonah suggested.

'It's not the same. Once you've lost the real world, the virtual world just isn't enough.'

'You stole his body,' muttered Jonah. 'You took over his mind! And you know that's not right, Dad.'

An especially noisy pop-up advert exploded between them. Annoyed, they brushed its debris aside in unison.

'Listen to me, Jonah,' said Jason. 'Everything that has happened – it could be a blessing in disguise. I'm... You know where I am, don't you?'

'*The other end of the NYLON thread,*' said Jonah. 'Your old route, New York–London. I always wanted to go with you.'

'Now you can. Don't you see? That's why I had to do it. So I could get inside Manhattan. Do you know what that means?'

'Yeah,' said Jonah. 'It means we can go for the Western Corner.'

'Exactly!' said Jason. 'You can bring the Guardians here and I can let them in. Working together, the two of us, we can take the Western Corner!'

*

Jonah and his father continued to stroll through the Metasphere and then returned to Venus Park. Jason wanted one last look at the empty lot, once the site of so many happy family memories. But for Jonah, they were now distant memories, painful memories. That was where Sam found them. Her unicorn avatar with its bright red mane came swooping out of the sky.

'The meet-up's arranged,' she said as she landed, carefully keeping Jonah between her and Jason. 'We'd better go.'

'Meet-up?' echoed Jason. His eyes sparked eagerly. 'You mean...?'

'I showed Sam your message,' said Jonah. 'I told her what it meant and she's been assembling the Guardians.'

'Who'd have thought it?' said Jason. 'Axel Kavanaugh's little girl, all grown up and taking charge.' He took a step towards Sam. She flinched away from him. He couldn't have failed to notice.

'We really should be going,' said Jonah, trying to cover the awkward moment.

'You're right,' said Jason. He turned to Sam. 'Are you leading the way?'

'You aren't invited,' said Sam.

She must have realised how blunt that sounded, because she added, 'What I mean is, you haven't been an active Guardian in a long time. Some of the others...'

'It's all right, Samantha,' said Jason quietly. 'I understand.'

Jonah understood too. The Guardians didn't trust Jason. After all he had done for them. After all he was *still doing* for them. It reminded Jonah of the way he had been treated by some of the Guardians lately, and that made him feel angry.

But this time it was different, and he knew it.

'Sam,' said Jonah. 'Can I have a minute with my dad?'

Sam nodded and flew up, beating her wings impatiently.

'I meant what I said,' said Jason. 'It's all right. Really. The Guardians don't trust me. I wouldn't either, in their shoes. The last person to trust me was Lucky Luke, and look what I did to him!'

Jonah swallowed hard. He couldn't speak, because he felt that if he tried he might cry. There was one more thing he had to say, though. One more worry on his mind.

'Anyway, I have work to do in the real world,' said Jason. 'And I'd rather be there – make the most of it while I can.'

'Dad,' said Jonah, 'are you sure about this? About working with the Guardians?'

'Of course I am, son,' said Jason. 'I agreed a long time ago to find the Four Corners for them, and now at last I can—'

'But they killed you, Dad,' Jonah blurted out. 'The airport bombings! I know they were trying to kill

Granger, and anyone else rich enough to be able to fly, but you…'

Jason's eyes narrowed.

'You were Granger's pilot,' said Jonah. 'They must have known you would be with him, but they didn't stop… They killed you, Dad. The Guardians killed you.'

'No, son, someone else murdered me.'

22

Jonah and Sam flew over a labyrinth of narrow streets.

It was always night in this part of the Metasphere, but never dark. Buzzing neon signs touted seedy bars and X-rated experiences. Jonah was distracted by what his father had said. Did Jason really know who killed him?

Sam descended and Jonah followed her into a rain-soaked alleyway, at least Jonah hoped it was rain. Sam knocked three times on a black door with her unicorn's horn. A viewing hatch slid back and a pair of glowing red eyes glared out at them. Sam gave her name and a complicated sequence of letters and numbers. The eyes disappeared, and a moment later the door was opened. Jonah and Sam walked down a short flight of stone steps into a cramped, dingy cellar.

A jazz band was playing on a low stage. The band members were all identical to each other in black suits with black ties. *Probably Artificial Intelligence*, thought Jonah. The room was packed with avatars. They were sitting around tables or hovering at the bar. Jonah recognised many of them. He had seen them below stage at the victory concert.

'Like it?' said Sam, tongue-in-cheek.

'Not really,' said Jonah. 'What is this place?'

'An old-fashioned speakeasy,' said Sam, 'like they had in America in the 1920s.'

A familiar avatar came barging towards them: an eagle-headed gryphon.

'Sam!' cried Axel. 'Thank God you're OK. Never do that again, do you hear me? Sneaking out like that... I was out of my mind with worry!'

'Sorry, Dad,' said Sam. 'It was something I had to do.'

'It was my fault,' said Jonah.

'You bet it is,' snapped Axel. 'I mean, Hong Kong! You could have been killed, the pair of you!'

'But we weren't,' said Sam, 'and Jonah found out something. From his dad.'

Axel glared at Jonah. 'You'd better not be wasting our time again, kid.'

'I'm not,' said Jonah.

'Hey!' The angry shout came from behind Jonah. He turned, and wasn't altogether surprised to find the tattooed humatar, Jez, marching up to him. 'Didn't you get the message last time?' barked Jez, as an animated snake curled around his narrowing eyes. 'No traitors welcome!'

Jonah turned to Sam. 'You didn't tell him?'

She shook her head. 'I didn't think he'd come if I did – and like it or not, Jonah, we need him and his followers.'

Jonah nodded, accepting that. Still, he wasn't about to back down from Jez again. 'When it's your meet-up,

Jez,' he said boldly, 'you can set the guest list.'

Jez reacted as if he had been slapped. He stood blinking for at least ten seconds, during which time a scorpion tattoo climbed his neck to nestle behind his cheekbone.

'I'm outta here!' he snarled, at last. He made for the exit, and at least ten other Guardians got up to follow him.

'That's a shame,' Jonah called after Jez. 'Because I can lead you to the Western Corner. But if you aren't interested…'

He didn't have to raise his voice. The room had gone dead quiet around him.

'Where is it?' asked Axel.

'Manhattan.'

'The Republic of Manhattan?' Jez wheeled back to face Jonah, with a sneer. 'I thought you said you could "lead us" there.'

Jonah stayed calm. 'I can.'

'What, you think they'll just throw open the gates and let us in? You might as well say you can take us to the moon, you've about as much chance of—'

'There is one way in,' said Jonah, 'and that's with a certified invitation from a resident. And I can get us one. Some of you knew…*know* Jason Delacroix, my father.'

A murmur went up around the cellar. He heard the word 'Uploaded' more than once.

Axel laughed. He leaned in closer to Jonah. 'I'm glad you decided to be on our side too, kid. You never did say though – where exactly are these servers?'

'I don't know, exactly,' confessed Jonah.

'I thought he knew where all the Four Corners were!' shouted Axel.

'Dad never saw where Granger went from the airfield,' said Jonah, 'but it's on the island, we know that for certain.'

'You'd better find them, kid,' said Axel, but his beak curled in disappointment.

Jonah was glad to get out of the speakeasy, with Sam.

'You did well in there,' she said as they flew back to Venus Park, to their exit halos.

'You think?'

'You saw Jez's face when you stood up to him,' Sam said. 'Those tattoos of his literally hid behind his ears! If we can pull this off, Jonah, if we can capture the Western Corner, they'll have no choice but to accept you as a true Guardian.'

Jonah wasn't so sure, and he didn't think he cared. He wasn't doing this for the Guardians. He was doing it for only one person: his dad.

Jason was still loyal to his old friends and was convinced that the Guardians hadn't contributed to his death. *Someone else murdered me,* he'd said. Why was he so quick to acquit the Guardians of his death? Jason had no real memories from the moment he copied himself. He had no memory of that terrible day. He wasn't the one who had sat, trembling and tearful, on his bed while his mum had tried for hours to get through to the emergency services, to be told that her worst fears were true.

Matthew Granger had once told Jonah that, when the bombs had gone off at Heathrow, Jason had saved his life. As if he had realised, in that moment, that the Guardians had gone too far and wanted nothing more to do with them. Jonah didn't know if that was true or not, and he knew that Jason would never be able to tell him.

The Guardians would *have bombed the airports,* thought Jonah, *if it helped their cause – and they wouldn't have cared who got hurt in the process. Just like Granger didn't care when he bombed Hong Kong.*

That was the way the world worked, it seemed. The Guardians, the Millennials, even Mr Chang… Everyone was just out for their own agenda. *Maybe I'm no better than any of them*, he wondered. He had blackmailed Delphine to get what he wanted, and he didn't regret it for an instant.

I should have wised up a long time ago, he thought. *All these weeks, I've been trying to work out right from wrong and what side I should be on. Where has it got me? I'm sick of being lied to and betrayed. So starting now, I'll be like everyone else. I'll go after what I want, and I'll use anyone I have to in the process.*

Right now, what Jonah wanted was to get to his dad in New York. He had to sort out this whole mess with the Uploaded and Lucky Luke. *And if that means taking the Guardians to the Western Corner, well, then...* He didn't conclude that thought. Jonah remembered another server farm, another battle. He remembered a girl named Kala, full of life one moment, cut down by a bullet in the next. And he shivered at the thought that, because of him, it was all about to happen again.

23

Granger strode across his operations room and leaned over the shoulder of one of his young programmers.

'Do you have a final tally?'

'Compiling now, sir,' she said, nervously flicking her auburn hair behind her glasses rims. 'It looks like—'

'Don't give me "looks like",' snapped Granger. 'Give me hard data.'

'4.1 million, sir,' said the programmer. 'That's how many avatars entered the Metasphere in the ninety-three minutes that the Changsphere portals were open. Of course, we can't tell how many of them were Uploaded and how many were live. But our best estimates put it at fifty-fifty. We also don't know how many users logged on or off during that time, although—'

'Over two million,' breathed Granger. 'Two million zombies roaming my world.'

'If I may, sir, it appears that many of the Uploaded have settled back on the Island. We could recycle that part of—'

Granger had considered that. 'Too slow,' he said. 'They would see the Recyclers coming and scatter.'

'No,' he said out loud. 'I tried to contain them. Now I will have to eliminate them.' Granger turned, stepped into his private elevator, and by the time he set it in motion he was already formulating a final solution.

The lift silently dropped twenty storeys and opened onto a gleaming medical facility. Granger had had one floor of the Freedom Tower kitted out with the finest equipment available (CAT scanners, laser operating knives and artificial blood supplies), much of it from Manhattan's own private hospitals.

He walked through the decon-arch, which spritzed his entire body with a mint-scented decontamination spray, then joined a dozen doctors and scientists in the centre of the blue-tinted room.

David Foster's body lay on the sliding table, protruding from a tube-shaped CAT scanner. He was strapped to it, in fact, and plugged into a computer terminal. He renewed his struggle with his bonds at the sight of his captor. Granger didn't even glance at him.

'Progress?' he demanded.

He was answered by Erel Dias, a young Brazilian man with a long, mournful face. Dias was a brilliant neuro-cyber surgeon, a one-time child prodigy whom Granger had plucked from the favelas and put into private tutoring, eventually getting him into Princeton at age sixteen. Dias worked for Granger now, in his virtual R&D lab. He was a pioneer in the field of Direct Interface technology, and the patents from his many inventions had more than repaid Granger's small investment in him.

Of course, that wasn't enough for Granger. It would never be enough.

'Our physical scans show no anomalies,' said Dias. 'The patient's brain is within parameters for a man of his age and—'

'What about the brain search?' demanded Granger. 'I want to know what's inside.'

'That's where it gets interesting.'

Dias led Granger to a monitor. Eight wave patterns were bumping and spiking their ways across it. The surgeon thumbed a datapad, and the patterns rearranged themselves into four groups of two, each containing one red pattern and one green.

'At first, as you know,' said Dias, 'the search program would not execute. It returned an error report, which suggested—'

'Yes, yes. The program detected two avatars in David Foster's brain and shut down. But you improvised a patch along the lines I suggested, and…?'

'The green brainwaves belong to our Mr Foster,' said Dias. 'As you can see, there is little activity in the beta frequency, as would be expected from a comatose subject.'

'So, the red brainwaves—'

'—belong to our usurper, Joshua.'

At the sound of his name, the young man on the scanner table snarled and thrashed about. 'I fought for king and country before any of you were born,' he spat. 'You've no right to treat me like this. I only wanted to be alive!'

'Then you've done it,' said Granger. 'You've identified the two distinct brainwave patterns – and that means you can separate them.'

Dias didn't look so sure. 'Identifying the data is one thing,' he cautioned, 'but removing it is another—'

'Is the only thing! Now, extract the foreign data from the host's brain. Delete it if you have to.'

The man in David Foster's body howled in protest.

'It may not be so simple,' insisted Dias. 'I've never used this technology in this way before. It would take weeks, months, of testing before we could be sure—'

'We don't have weeks,' said Granger. 'We may not even have days. I need to reassure the world that the Uploaded are no longer a threat, that the Metasphere is safe again.'

'I understand that, Mr Granger, but I would strongly recommend—'

'You like your life here, don't you, Erel? You're comfortable in your townhouse in the Village? You enjoy Lori Weisberg's endless social functions?'

'Yes I do. But, Mr Granger—'

'How do you think all that is paid for?'

'By you, Mr Granger.'

'Not by me. The Metasphere. The Metasphere funds the lifestyle to which you have become accustomed. And the Metasphere is losing users faster than Greenland is losing glaciers. When I found you in the favelas of Rio, your life expectancy could be measured in months. How long do you think you'd last outside of this emerald city, Dias? How long in the slums of Long Island or the wastelands of New Jersey? How long?'

The surgeon bowed his head. 'I will find a way.'

Jonah sighed as the real world crashed back in around him. He had slept on a virtual beach, basking in the heat of a sun that couldn't burn him. In the real world, he was in the floatplane's passenger compartment. His reclining seat was more comfortable than the ones up front, but still his neck and leg muscles ached.

He stood up, stretched, as sunlight streamed in through the windows. Jonah thought he could hear voices: Sam's and one other, male. He walked through into the cockpit.

Sam, in the pilot's seat, turned to greet him. 'Sleep well?' she asked.

Jonah said that he had. 'I thought we'd be in sight of land by now,' he said. All he could see through the canopy was blue sea and blue sky.

'Don't panic,' said Sam, 'but while you were asleep, I changed course.'

'To where?'

'I couldn't raise any Guardians in the American north-west. I was worried, if we continued to Alaska, we might end up stranded there. Anyway, you said you weren't sure you could land the floatplane there, with all the melting ice.'

'Sam, where are we heading?' asked Jonah.

'California,' said Sam. 'We had a contact from Los Angeles.'

'Do we have enough fuel?'

'I set the autopilot to max our efficiency,' said Sam. 'We've had a good tailwind, so it hasn't affected our flight time much.'

Jonah looked at the fuel gauge. It was showing almost empty.

He sank into the seat beside Sam's. He remembered something about Los Angeles from school. 'Wasn't it abandoned?' he asked. 'Something about lots of troubles, even before the US government went down.'

'This guy who contacted us,' said Sam, 'says he'll sell us all the biofuel we need.'

'A Guardian?' asked Jonah, suspicious of 'this guy'.

'No, just a petrol-hoarder.' Jonah had heard of people like this, hoarding fuel and reselling it at exorbitant prices. They weren't technically illegal, but many were criminals who came by their stash through theft. Jonah let out a frustrated sigh; more unsavoury people to deal with. 'Don't worry,' added Sam. 'We'll fill up and be gone without ever having to set foot on dry land. It won't come cheap, mind.'

'I've got nothing left,' confessed Jonah.

'I can access an emergency Guardian account,' said Sam.

Jonah saw Sam's datapad lying on a side console. He reached for it. 'What exactly did this message say? Can I read it?'

'It didn't come through the Metasphere,' said Sam.

Jonah frowned. Then he remembered the other voice he had heard. 'Someone called us on *the radio*?'

Erel Dias moved from datapad to datapad, making an adjustment here, a calculation there. The rest of his team watched too, in nervous silence. Never once did Dias ask for help from any of them. This was his burden to shoulder, not theirs.

The only person who spoke, during those tense minutes, was David Foster, or rather the Uploaded presence in his body. His protests took on a desperate, pleading tone. No one could look him in the eye.

Granger leaned over Dias's shoulder and unnerved him as he examined Dias's calculations. 'It seems to me,' Granger said, 'that we are ready to proceed.' Dias's boss had a brilliant mind, but he was more entrepreneur than scientist, and not at all patient with the deliberate method that Dias took comfort in.

'Not yet, Mr Granger, please. I'd like to double-check the—'

'Breakthrough science starts with experimentation,' Granger insisted. 'Execute the extraction!'

Dias glanced at his colleagues, as if hoping for support from them. They gave him none. A couple looked down at their shoes, but they were all too loyal to Granger – or too afraid of him, he didn't much care which – to speak up.

Dias sighed and nodded. He ran his thumb over a datapad, and the screens around the CAT scanner filled up with lines of programming code.

The scanner itself clunked into life and its sliding table retracted. David Foster was carried head-first into the clinical white innards of the machine. 'No,' he yelled, 'please, no. Don't do this to me. Please. You'll kill me. You'll kill me again!'

'That is not my intention,' said Dias. He meant it. 'It is my hope that you – and by "you", I mean Joshua – will be able to live on as before, as a digital—'

'No! Must have…life. I must have…'

David Foster screamed, and his scream echoed out of the CAT scanner and filled the room. It was a scream of incredible pain. The extraction process was ripping his brain in two.

Granger was leaning forward eagerly, scrutinising the nearest screen to him. He was studying the graphic: a circle, with alternating red and green radial stripes.

The machine was making a terrible thumping sound. Dias shouted to its occupant: 'I am transferring your data to a backup drive for now. Once we have cured your "hunger", we will be able to re-Upload you. You can return to the—'

'It's working!' declared Granger. The green stripes in the circle were growing thicker, crowding out the others. Beneath the circle, a progress bar was filling up red as if the red stripes were bleeding into it. Dias hoped he was right.

The patient screamed again, and gave so violent a convulsion that Dias took a step away from him. In his frenzy, David Foster's body broke the strap around his left ankle. Two other doctors rushed up to hold down his flailing leg.

'The patient cannot take much more of this,' protested Dias.

'He should have thought about that before,' said Granger, entirely without sympathy. His gaze was rooted to the screen. The progress bar was half filled with red now.

He may not survive the other half, thought Dias.

24

Jonah took the controls.

He kept a wary eye on the fuel gauge and saw that Sam was doing the same. When the needle pointed to 'empty', Jonah muttered that they were *running on fumes*, a saying that had bubbled up from his dad's memories.

He considered an emergency landing on one of the scattered islands that had begun to appear below them. By now, however, the American west coast loomed large in Jonah's sights, and he began his descent.

The engines sputtered and stalled, but Jonah conjured his father's memories of landing 'dead stick' during RAF training. Jonah glided the plane over Santa Monica Bay and made a perfect splashdown.

They drifted on the waves to the dilapidated pier, and Sam lassoed a post with the mooring rope. A green light flashed on the navigational display. They had reached their destination. Jonah was relieved, but wary.

There was no one waiting for them, no one around at all. 'So much for not setting foot on land,' said Jonah, as he and Sam disembarked from the plane. He was glad, though, of the chance to stretch his legs properly.

They clambered over a low railing, and climbed a short flight of steps. They passed deserted shops and hollowed-out restaurants, their footsteps echoing off wooden planking. 'I don't like this,' said Jonah as they stood at the end of a long boardwalk, facing inland.

'Me neither,' said Sam, 'but there's no going back now. Without fuel, the floatplane's useless to us.'

'So, what do we do? We can't… How far is it to New York from here, anyway? It'd take us weeks to get there over land, even if we could find—'

'We wait a little bit longer, I suppose. In case our contact's been held up.'

'Your contact's here!' The unexpected voice broke the silence like a whip crack. Jonah and Sam whirled around.

They came swarming out of the abandoned buildings: young people, barely older than children, with dirt-caked faces and raggedy clothes, wielding iron bars, chains and knives. Jonah realised that, beneath the grime, they all wore the same colours: purple and gold.

A street gang.

Granger breathed a sigh of relief; the progress bar showed that the parasite in David Foster's body was half extracted.

Then, it all went wrong. Green pixels appeared among the red in the progress bar – more and more of them, beginning to clump together. 'It's destabilising!' moaned Granger.

'This is what I was afraid of,' breathed Dias at his

shoulder. 'The Uploaded and the native data sets are too tightly interwoven. We cannot extract one without the other.'

'Keep trying,' insisted Granger. He had no tolerance for quitting.

'It's too late! The data – both sets of data – are corrupted. We couldn't reverse the process now if—'

'*Mr Dias! Mr Granger!*'

Granger turned at the shout, from one of the other doctors. Even as he did, he smelled burning. A red light was blinking furiously on a server, and Granger heard the whirring of an overtaxed hard drive.

Smoke poured out of the server, out of every seam and socket. An instant later, the whole thing burst into flames. The progress bar on Granger's screen froze, and ugly black shapes invaded the almost-green circle.

David Foster convulsed one final time, then fell still. As one of the doctors grabbed a fire extinguisher, Granger turned to the brainwave monitor. There were only four patterns on it now, all yellow, all flat.

He heard Dias's hollow voice behind him: 'We've lost him. Them. David Foster and Joshua both. I'm pronouncing this body dead at—'

Granger whirled around. Dias had retrieved David Foster's corpse from inside the machine. It lay on the sliding table, its eyes rolled back into their sockets, its chin flecked with foam. 'Find another subject,' snapped Granger.

'But, sir!'

'Breakthrough science, Mr Dias, relies on experimentation. Relentless cycles of experiments to test, learn, tweak, improve and perfect. Find another subject. Tweak the extraction process and try it again. Until you get it right.'

'But how do we know...?' Granger was already striding back towards the elevator. Dias had to shout after him. 'How can we tell who has been usurped?'

Granger stepped into the elevator, stabbed at the controls. 'That's for you to figure out,' he said, as the doors slid shut between them.

'It's an ambush,' Jonah whispered. 'Run!'

But Sam was already running, and Jonah sprinted after her. They didn't get very far. More gang members leapt out of hiding, from down steps and behind a burnt-out burger cart, blocking their way.

Three of them leapt on Jonah. A scrawny, spotty-faced boy raised a monkey wrench to club him. Jonah grabbed his wrist. To his surprise, it was bony, weak, and he was able to twist the weapon right out of his grip. It didn't do him much good.

He was defeated by the weight of numbers, forced onto his knees, his arms pinned behind him. Jonah saw that Sam was faring better. She climbed up onto the boardwalk railing, kicked away two kids who tried to stop her. She was about to jump, Jonah realised, for the shallow water below. Before she could, a gunshot rang out.

The shot had been fired by an older gangster, fourteen or fifteen Jonah guessed, with lank chestnut hair and an angular nose and chin. Jonah wondered if he was the one who had spoken before. He was aiming his gun at Sam from the doorway of the old harbour office.

For a long few seconds, no one moved. Sam was sizing up the gunman, clearly trying to decide if she should jump or not. She chose the latter.

She stepped down from the railing. Immediately, she disappeared beneath a heap of triumphant gangsters. Jonah yelled out her name and tried to break free of his own captors, to get to her, to help her. It was no good. He was held too tight.

Jonah's attackers hauled him to his feet. Two sets of gangsters shoved their captives in front of the gunman, the oldest member of the gang and clearly the alpha. Jonah counted twenty in the gang, but he knew there could be more. They let go of Jonah and Sam, but kept them surrounded. The gunman tucked his pistol into the waistband of his trousers. They were too big for him, secured by a rope belt. He leered at his two prisoners.

'You're wasting your time with us,' said Sam. 'We don't know anyone who can pay you a ransom, so you may as well release us.'

'This ain't Florida,' said the gunman. 'And we ain't pirates.'

Jonah noticed that the gunman's eyes – and those of many of his followers – were sunken, their skin wrinkled.

'Who are you?' asked Jonah.

'We're the Lakers.' The others raised a ragged cheer at the mention of the gang's name. 'I'm Jackson and I'm in charge.'

'Of what?' said Jonah.

'Everything west of the 405. Which now includes you. And you'll be treated just fine, so long as you do exactly as I tell you.' Jackson's manner was blunt, and surprisingly charismatic, but there was no denying the threat that underlay his words.

'If you don't want a ransom,' said Sam, 'what do you want?'

'Same as you,' said Jackson. 'Same as everyone wants: to survive. And to do that, we need your plane.'

Jonah had no choice but to speak up now. 'No,' he protested, 'you can't have it!'

'We need that plane,' said Sam.

'If you only knew…' said Jonah.

'We're on a mission,' said Sam, 'Fighting for the future of the Metasphere, and if we don't make it to—'

'You think I care about your cartoon computerland?' scoffed Jackson. 'We're fighting for our future, for our *real* lives in the *real* world.'

'Maybe they don't know what that's like,' another gang member chimed in. 'They both look pretty hydrated to me.' The others jeered in agreement.

'What's that supposed to mean?' asked Jonah.

'It means,' said Jackson, 'that the two of you are gonna help us. We have a plane; now we need a pilot.'

'No chance!' said Jonah.

'I'm not giving you a choice, kid,' said Jackson. 'Things are tough in these parts these days and we can't afford to carry no slackers. So you're gonna have to prove your worth to us. That means you fly us wherever we want to go, whenever we want to go there – or else you and your foxy redhead will never, ever have another sip of water in what will be a very short, but very painful, life.'

25

Jonah and Sam were marched along the Santa Monica waterfront, past burned-out buildings that looked like they had once been hotels and resorts.

They were taken into the neglected shell of a former boutique hotel and locked in a bare room on the top floor with a single barred window overlooking the ocean. There was a light bulb, but it had blown. The window pane was broken, and the room grew colder as the night drew in.

No one came to see them, although sometimes Jonah heard voices in the corridor. He tried banging on the door, shouting to the people outside. 'Can't you bring us some food?' he cried. 'Or at least a glass of water?'

Muffled voices laughed from the corridor.

That was it, remembered Jonah. His teacher, Mr Ping, had taught a lesson on the decline of the American empire. 'The whole south-west dried up, maybe ten years ago,' he recalled.

'I remember Axel saying something about the entire region being declared uninhabitable,' said Sam.

'Then how come the Lakers are still here?' Jonah wondered aloud.

Sam shrugged. 'Holdouts, I guess. I don't know.'

Jonah paced the small room, frustrated. 'Dad'll be waiting for us in Manhattan. He'll be worried about us. I can't even message him.' He had looked for a Metasphere terminal, but there was none. *No wonder they let me keep my datapad*, he thought. *It's useless to me in here!*

They had taken Sam's rucksack, however, with its arsenal of tools.

The door opened, at last. Jonah looked up hopefully. A girl stood in the doorway. He hadn't seen her before. The girl was younger than Jonah, as grimy as the other Lakers and wearing their colours. Her pointed nose and chin reminded him of someone.

Jackson, he realised. *She looks like Jackson.*

'I'm sorry,' said the girl, 'about my brother. He's only trying to look out for us.'

She dropped an armful of bedding into the room, then ran out. The door was closed and locked again. At least now Jonah and Sam had a pillow each, and a large sheet between them.

Jonah lay on the bare floorboards and closed his eyes.

'How can you sleep?' said Sam. 'We should be figuring out how to get out of here.'

'I'm exhausted,' said Jonah. 'And we need to get the lie of the land before we plot any escape.'

Jonah pretended he was back on the beach. It didn't work. He was shivering. Sam climbed under the sheet but Jonah didn't open his eyes. Without a word being spoken, they huddled closer together beneath the thin sheet.

Jonah was woken once, by a plaintive howl from outside the hotel. He saw that Sam was awake too, her eyes wide open. 'A coyote,' she whispered.

The next thing Jonah knew, it was morning. Heavy footsteps were clumping around the room, and the toecap of a tattered boot nudged his ribs.

'Ahh, look at the little lovebirds,' said an unkind voice, 'all snuggled up nice and cosy together. Sorry to have to pull the two of you apart, but you got work to do.'

Jonah and Sam leapt away from each other. 'We aren't...' said Jonah.

Three Lakers stood over them, mocking them.

'We weren't...' said Sam.

'We were cold, that's all,' said Jonah. 'You only gave us one sheet and—'

'And we're hungry,' said Sam. 'Jackson said we'd be treated well.'

'You want food and water,' said the Laker who had woken them, a tall kid with a shaved head and sunken eyes. 'You earn it like the rest of us. Now, which of you is the pilot?'

Jonah looked at Sam, then nervously raised his hand.

'Jackson's waiting for you at the pier.' Two Lakers closed in around Jonah, prodded him towards the door.

Sam made to follow him, but the first Laker stopped her. 'Not you. You stay here.'

'No,' said Jonah. 'I won't... I can't fly without Sam. She—'

'She stays,' growled the Laker. 'Your girlfriend is our insurance policy. So long as we can off her whenever we feel like it, we know you won't try anything stupid.'

Jonah hardly recognised the floatplane when he saw it again.

The Lakers had pulled it up onto the beach. They had grafted a big tank to its belly, between its pontoons, and several smaller tanks to its wings. At first, Jonah thought it was a fuel tank, but he didn't see an intake hose to the engine.

The gang swarmed over the plane with spanners and welding torches, making final adjustments. Jackson was supervising, leaning against a pier strut, chewing on a matchstick. He straightened up as Jonah was brought towards him.

'What took you so long, Kobe?' asked Jackson.

'The lovebirds were sleeping in,' laughed the tall kid with the shaved head.

Jonah decided not to bother explaining that he and Sam were just friends, he was too worried about the modifications to the floatplane. 'I don't think it'll fly like that,' he said.

'You're the pilot. It's your job to see to it that it does.'

'Even if it does,' said Jonah, tapping into his dad's memories, 'you know you've increased the load, especially if you're planning to fill up those tanks. Fuel efficiency will be shot; you won't get nearly so far on—'

'Fuel is one thing we ain't short of,' said Jackson. 'But you can't drink fuel.'

Jonah could smell petrol fumes. There were fresh tyre tracks in the sand, which he guessed must have come from a fuel tanker.

'Anyway,' said Jackson, 'we ain't going too far.'

'Where *are* we going?'

'The course is programmed in. You just follow it, keep your mouth shut, and fly.' Jackson pushed past Jonah, shouted to the other Lakers, 'All right, move it, you guys. The sooner we get this bird into the sky, the sooner we can all drink.'

His words enthused his followers, galvanised them into action. Within a minute, most of them had packed up and leapt off the floatplane's hull. 'Magic, Kobe,' barked Jackson, 'you're riding in the back. You two as well.' He pointed to two pairs of Lakers, who snapped to attention and climbed aboard the plane.

Jonah looked around. No one was watching him. This was his last chance to make a break for it. If he weaved between the pier struts, he could make himself an almost impossible target. But what if Kobe carried out his threat?

What if the Lakers did something to Sam, before Jonah could get back to her?

It was too late. Jackson ushered Jonah into the floatplane's cockpit, took the co-pilot's seat for himself. He leaned out, shouted back to the Lakers still on the beach. At Jackson's instructions, they lined up, put their shoulders to the wings of the plane and pushed it back out to sea.

Jonah thought they would sink at first, with the weight of the new tanks. The floatplane's pontoons scraped the seabed, threw up silt to cloud the water. Then it was picked up by a gentle wave and carried out of the cheering Lakers' hands.

'Well, what are you waiting for?' asked Jackson. 'An engraved invitation? Let's get those engines fired up!'

Sam heard footsteps on the stairs. She waited beside the bedroom door. She had decided to go for it, rush that door when it was opened.

The hotel had been quiet all morning. Most of the Lakers, Sam guessed, were at the pier or off who-knew-where in the floatplane. If she could overpower her visitor, she could be downstairs and out of the door before anyone else knew about it.

She had considered the risk to Jonah. She was confident, however, that Jackson wouldn't hurt him. He needed him. It would be better for Jonah, anyway, if Sam was free. Then the Lakers would have nothing to hold over him.

The door was unlocked from the outside. The knob turned. Sam tensed.

The door opened. Sam was about to spring when she recognised the young girl from last night, Jackson's sister. She had come alone. She was carrying a yellow Pro-Meal pouch and a glass of brownish liquid. She froze, afraid, as she saw Sam looming over her. Sam stepped back, raised her hands, smiled to show that she meant no harm.

You idiot, she thought. *That was your chance. You should have gone for it!* She knew she couldn't have hurt the girl, though.

She accepted the food and drink and sat on the floor. The water was murky, brown, but Sam needed it too much to be fussy. 'Thank you,' she said.

The girl didn't speak, but nor did she leave. She watched as Sam took a slurp of banana-flavoured protein.

'Do you want some?' asked Sam.

The girl shook her head.

'I'm Sam. What's your name?'

The girl stared at the floor for a long time, and finally raised her sunken eyes to meet Sam's.

'Kit. My name's Kit.'

'I guess your brother really fooled me, huh?'

Sam felt like an idiot for being for being lured into

Jackson's trap. When his voice came over the radio, she had been tired, exhausted and not thinking straight. She and Jonah had refuelled in Guam, thanks to a Guardian outpost, but once over the vast Pacific, with Jonah plugged in, she didn't want to become another Amelia Earhart. The siren song of fuel came through the radio and she jumped at it. And now, here she was, locked up in a part of the world long since dubbed uninhabitable.

'Don't feel bad,' said Kit. 'Jackson's really smart.'

'Maybe I should recruit him into the Guardians,' joked Sam.

'I don't know what that is,' said Kit, embarrassed about not knowing.

'What?' said Sam. 'You don't know what a Guardian is? We're... I'm a Guardian, Kit. We're freedom fighters. Against the Millennials. You must have heard of...?'

'Like a gang?'

Sam thought about it. Kit was right; the Guardians would never call themselves a gang, but from Kit's point of view, that's what they were.

'Maybe, but more like a network of people all around the world fighting for the same ideal. Our turf is the Metasphere.'

Sam noticed Kit's blank stare. 'Have you ever been online, Kit?'

'Jackson says it's too dangerous. He says the onliners dreamed themselves to death. What... What's it like in there, Sam?'

'The Metasphere?'

'Anywhere. Anywhere but here.'

'I don't understand,' said Jonah. 'Where *are* we going?'

'All you have to do is—'

'—follow the programmed route,' said Jonah in a monotone voice, 'shut up, and fly.' Jonah guided the plane higher into the sky, fighting the drag caused by the modifications. 'You do know we've just come around in a big semi-circle? We're...' Jonah broke off the sentence. The floatplane had hit turbulence, and he had to fight the control stick to keep it level.

The tanks were creating a constant drag and Jonah hoped Jackson was right about having no shortage of fuel.

'We took a detour out to sea,' said Jackson, 'so the inland gangs can't track us. Man, if the Clippers or the Raiders knew we had wings...'

Jonah understood.

They were headed a fairly steady north now. The abandoned urban sprawl of LA lay beneath them; different from any city Jonah had seen before. It was empty like Hong Kong, but sprawling and seemingly endless like London. There was no haze of pollution in its air, no lights on any of its buildings. The freeways were clear of bicycles and rickshaws and were mostly grown over, as if the earth itself had sent up tendrils to strangle the last remnants of civilisation.

Jonah saw the odd shadow flitting across the ground. It was hard to tell from up here, but he didn't think some of them were human. He remembered the coyote he had heard last night, and he shivered.

'Why are you still here?' he asked. 'I mean, there was an evacuation, right? Why didn't you leave?'

'You think it was that easy?' sneered Jackson.

'I don't know,' said Jonah, wishing he had paid more attention to real-world affairs. 'But…but surely, by now, you could have found a way to—'

Jackson scowled. 'If you know what's good for you, kid, you'll—'

'—shut up and keep flying, right?' sighed Jonah.

A minute passed in silence. Then, quietly, Jackson said, 'The gang looked after me when I needed it. It's my turn – my duty – to look after them now.'

'By finding water for them?'

Jackson looked at Jonah sharply.

'You let it slip before, on the beach. Something about getting the floatplane in the air so we could all drink. I've been looking at the map. There's a huge freshwater lake to the north of here – Lake Tahoe – and we're headed straight for it.'

'Well, ain't you the little boy genius!' Jackson muttered.

Jonah looked at his captor, really looked at him for the first time. He knew now why Jackson and the rest of the Lakers were so scrawny and wrinkled. They were malnourished, sure, but it was more than that. They were chronically dehydrated.

When asked what they wanted, Jackson had said, *Same as you. Same as everyone wants: to survive.*

He had meant it too. The problem was, for all its bolted-on tanks, the floatplane could only carry...what? Enough water to quench the Lakers' thirst for a few days? A week? There would be more trips north after this one. Many more.

The Lakers needed the floatplane. They needed it for keeps. That was why they had lured Jonah and Sam to the Los Angeles desert with the promise of fuel. And now that they had a plane, a way to fetch fresh water, they wouldn't ever let them go.

Jonah thought about Jackson's words: *to survive*. If Jonah were to survive, he and Sam would have to escape. Or they'd die trying.

26

Jonah brought the floatplane to set down on the south end of Lake Tahoe. As its pontoons were just about to touch the water, Jackson placed his hand over Jonah's own, pulled back on the control stick, eased them back into the air. 'A little further in,' he said.

Jonah did as he was told. The lake was kilometres long, and its crystal-clear water sparkled in the sunset. Jonah hadn't realised how dry his throat was until now. Of course, he hadn't had anything to drink all day.

'Now?' he asked. Jackson nodded, and Jonah lowered the plane until he was floating in the freshwater.

He heard delighted whoops from the passenger compartment. Jackson undid his seatbelt, pushed himself to his feet. Jonah prepared to cut the engines, but Jackson shook his head. 'Best we keep moving, kid,' he said.

'Why?' asked Jonah. Jackson didn't answer him.

The other four Lakers crowded into the cockpit, asking if it was time. When Jackson gave them the word, they pushed open the doors and climbed out onto the pontoons. They primed the pumping mechanisms and filled the plane's new tanks with as much fresh water as they could hold.

'Not too much,' Jonah called back over his shoulder. 'I don't know how much more weight we can...' No one was listening to him. Anyway, he had just noticed something else. A more immediate problem. 'Jackson...'

They weren't alone.

A gunboat was steaming across the lake to meet them. It looked like a smaller version of the Millennial warship Jonah had seen in Hong Kong – and, just as with the warships, he could tell that it meant trouble.

'Time to earn your purples, kid,' said Jackson, leaning over Jonah's shoulder. 'Those patrol boats—'

'You mean there's more than one?'

'Tahoe treats water theft as a capital crime,' said Jackson. 'But don't worry, they won't sink us if they can help it.'

'This just keeps getting better,' said Jonah.

'They don't want to risk contaminating the lake with biofuel and airplane parts. Nah, they'll try to corner us, and then kill us later. So long as you keep us moving—'

The patrol boat was moving to cut them off. Jonah heard an angry voice, amplified through a loudhailer, demanding that he prepare to be boarded.

Jonah stamped hard on the right rudder pedal, brought the floatplane around in a wide U shape, and drenched the oncoming boat in its spray.

For an instant, plane and boat were almost hull to hull. Then the plane was speeding southwards, back the way it had come. 'That's the way, kid,' whooped Jackson.

'We're not out of trouble yet,' said Jonah. 'And it's not "kid", it's Jonah. Jonah Delacroix.'

He could see more patrol boats setting off from the shore. 'I think you'd better call the others back inside,' he said. 'I'm taking off.'

'Not yet.'

'This plane is not built for manoeuvrability on the water,' said Jonah. 'And those boats are working together, herding us to the edge of the lake.'

'I'm not leaving,' said Jackson, 'until those tanks are full.'

'We might not have a choice.'

'We need this water! My people—'

'Will get nothing,' snapped Jonah, 'if we're captured and killed.'

Four patrol boats were forming a circle around the floatplane. In a few more seconds, they would have it completely penned in. Jonah turned the plane back to the north, gunned the throttle and made for the biggest gap he could see – but that gap was closing fast.

'Hold on!' he yelled as he yanked the control stick back hard. Jonah could hear cries from the Lakers outside the plane, as they found themselves airborne. He couldn't think about them now, they'd just have to hold on. Jonah had to get them all out of the range of the gunboats or they'd all be dead.

The pontoons left the water as the plane rose up.

The engines screamed with exertion, Jonah feared

they might stall, and still… Still, the plane was too low. He could see the terrified crew of the converging boats ahead of him, see them in close-up detail. They were scattering from the decks, leaping in vain for cover. He saw two men jump overboard.

Jackson howled with laughter and shouted, 'Suckas!'

The stick was juddering in Jonah's palm. It almost flew out of his grip. He pulled back on it even further, held his breath. He felt the floatplane's port pontoon scraping against something – a tall mast? Then, the plane rose into the sky, breaking through the cordon, leaving the patrol boats behind and below them.

Jonah eased the pressure on the stick, and let the floatplane level out. He was sweating and shaking. He didn't quite know how he had survived the last few seconds. His instincts had taken over. *No*, he reminded himself, *not* my *instincts. Thank you, Dad!*

'Now,' said Jackson, 'let's get down there again and—'

'No!' said Jonah. 'It's too risky. I won't do it!'

'You don't give the orders here, kid.'

'We're carrying as much water as we can lift. You'll have to make do with that.'

'I wasn't thinking about the water,' said Jackson. 'My boys are barely hanging on out there. We gotta set down somewhere, so's they can—'

He was interrupted by a series of dull crumps, like fireworks going off. Jonah didn't have to look back to know that the patrol boats were firing on them, after all.

'Somewhere,' he said, 'not here. They'll just have to hold on a little bit longer.'

A shell whistled past them as he spoke, convincing Jackson to argue no further. Jonah was still fighting that port-wing drag, worse than ever now with the water tanks half full. They had made it to the south end of the lake, though.

Jonah pointed the floatplane at the purple-grey Sierra Nevada mountains, and soon they were weaving their way between them, and out of firing range.

They returned to Santa Monica to a hero's welcome – at least, Jackson did. The Lakers mostly ignored Jonah. He and Sam were given an upgrade to a better hotel room, however, so it wasn't all bad.

They each had a bed of their own now, which would spare them any further embarrassment. *Do we really look like we could be a couple?* Jonah asked himself, eyeing Sam across the room.

And, of course, there was plenty of water. The Lakers brought it from the floatplane at the pier, by the bottle and the jug and the panful.

'Drink as much as you like,' said Jackson expansively as he brought a jug into Jonah and Sam's room. 'There's more where that came from, right, kid?' He looked at Jonah with his lopsided grin. 'We go back tomorrow,' he said. 'Tomorrow and the day after that, and every day.'

Jackson left and locked the door behind him.

Sam listened at it, to check if there was anyone outside. She couldn't hear anyone, but kept her voice to a whisper anyway as she told Jonah about Kit. 'We had a long chat today,' she said. 'It sounds like she's being kept here against her will too.'

'She told you that?'

'Not exactly. Her brother's all she has, and Kit's devoted to him. All the same...'

'If she wants out of LA, maybe others want out too?'

'Exactly,' said Sam, 'but Jackson won't let them go. He tells them that things are just as bad everywhere. At least here they rule the streets. Outside of LA, they're nobody.'

'So, how does that help us?'

'We have a plane, Jonah.'

'No, Sam. We *had* a plane. Jackson has it now.'

'But with Kit's help – and a few other Lakers who want out – maybe we could take it back. I think they'll help us, Jonah. I really think they might. I told Kit about some of the places we've seen, better places than this, and—'

Jonah shook his head. 'No, Sam. She's just a kid! And she's Jackson's sister. We can't trust her!'

'She's our best chance to escape!'

'And in return for her help, what? We take her with us? And to where? We can't bring Kit and a bunch of gangsters to Manhattan. And Jackson's right, they're nobody outside of LA. They probably wouldn't even survive—'

233

'That's their choice,' said Sam. 'Kit wants to be free, deep down, and isn't that what the Guardians are all about – fighting for people to be free?'

Jonah wanted to protest: *I'm not a Guardian!* Instead, he said, 'We bide our time, wait for the right chance to sneak out of here, steal the plane and get to Manhattan, ourselves.'

'There may not be any more time,' said Sam, hesitantly.

'What do you mean?'

'Something Kit said. She didn't mean to let it slip, but...'

'What is it?'

'Jackson plans to kill us. As soon as he doesn't need us any more.'

'But he *does* need us,' argued Jonah. 'Who else is going to fly the plane for him?'

'I'm just repeating what Kit said. We aren't Lakers, Jonah. As far as Jackson is concerned, we're just two more mouths to water.'

Jonah lay back on his bed, sighed. 'You'd better talk to Kit, then.'

'Tomorrow,' said Sam. 'She said she'd come back tomorrow. It'll probably be when you and Jackson are out in the plane again.'

'We need answers from her,' said Jonah, 'like how many other Lakers we're talking about here and when they might be ready to act. No more hints and maybes.

Kit needs to be sure of what she wants. If we're going to do this—'

'Yeah, I know,' said Sam. 'We need to do it soon.'

No one came to fetch Jonah the next morning. No one came to the bedroom door at all. 'Jackson must have changed his plans,' said Sam. 'I wonder why?'

'He said there were other gangs in LA,' said Jonah. 'He said he didn't want them knowing about the plane. Maybe... I don't know, maybe there's been some trouble.'

That could be exactly what we need, he thought. *A distraction.*

'I just hope...' said Sam. She didn't finish the sentence, but Jonah knew what she was thinking. *What if Jackson has found another pilot somehow?*

But Jonah's fears were allayed – and his hopes dashed – after sunset, when Jackson appeared at last, along with several other Lakers as usual.

He tossed Jonah and Sam a pink Pro-Meal each, but gave them no water. He must have thought they had had their fill. 'Thought we'd make the water run a bit later today,' he explained. 'Should keep the lake patrols on their toes. And anyway, it'll be harder for them to get a lock on us in the dark – right, kid?'

'Yeah, right,' sighed Jonah, slurping his strawberry-flavoured protein.

He hauled himself to his feet and followed Jackson out of the room.

27

Jonah sat beside Jackson once again, in the floatplane cockpit. He followed the same course as before, flying out to sea and then circling back over the arid land north of Los Angeles.

Every time Jackson looked in his direction, he felt nervous. *Is that why he keeps sitting up here with me?* Jonah wondered. *He's watching what I do, so he can learn to fly the floatplane himself and replace me.*

Jonah fiddled with the instruments, making unnecessary changes. He muttered pilot's jargon from his dad's memories to confuse his observer. It appeared to work and eventually Jackson leaned back in his seat and closed his eyes.

They came upon Lake Tahoe at last, glittering black in the moonlight. Jonah killed the floatplane's lights as they came in to land. If it weren't for the moonlight reflected on the water's ripples, Jonah could have ploughed the plane straight into the water.

At least Jackson had been right; the patrol boats couldn't find them in the darkness. Jonah kept the plane puttering about the lake, avoiding their questing searchlights. The other Lakers worked efficiently too, and the thirsty water tanks were soon filled. They were gone before the boats could narrow down their location. A single gunshot rang out as the floatplane took off, but it was hopelessly off-target.

Jackson didn't say a word, but when Jonah glanced at him he was deep in thought.

They were halfway back to Santa Monica when the Lakers' leader broke his silence. 'We tried to leave,' he said quietly.

Jonah looked at him, surprised, not sure what he was talking about.

'You asked me yesterday,' said Jackson, 'why we didn't leave LA ten years ago. We tried. My parents tried.'

'What happened?'

'There weren't enough places for everyone. The government said there would be, but there weren't. We were scheduled on one of the last airlifts to Canada. I was six, Kit was still a baby. When we came to board the plane...' His voice tailed off. Jonah didn't say anything. He waited for Jackson to compose himself and continue.

'Another family took our seats. Bought our seats. Stole our seats. A family with more money and more influence.'

Jonah sensed the familiar anger of injustice in Jackson's voice.

'What did you do?'

'What could we do?' said Jackson. 'We went home, that's what we did. Mom and Dad kept us holed up in our trailer while they went out scavenging for what little there was out there. One day… One day, they didn't come back.'

'I'm really sorry,' said Jonah, sympathetically.

'The Lakers caught me,' said Jackson, 'tryin' to steal a bucket of rainwater from them. They could have offed me there and then, but they took me in instead. Let me work as a runner for them, and I worked my way up to the top. Now that I'm the leader, I'm the Jackson.'

'That isn't your real name?'

'It's my name now. It's tradition for the leader to be named after one of their first leaders, a famous overlord from the olden days in LA.'

'Must be a lot of responsibility,' said Jonah.

'The Lakers are my family now. They took good care of Kit and me when we had nothin'. It's my turn to look after them.'

Jonah thought he understood. In some ways, Jackson's story was similar to his own. He too had been orphaned by an unfair world. He too had found himself taken in by a gang – the Guardians in his case – to whom he now felt a huge debt. Jonah too was just trying to do what he thought was right.

The one big difference between them was that Jonah didn't think he could kill another person, and certainly not in cold blood. *Maybe Jackson won't do it either*, he thought. *Maybe Kit was wrong about him. I mean, why would he have opened up to me like that if he still planned to…?*

Jonah didn't want to go there. Jackson had fallen silent again. He was staring out through the cockpit canopy at the night sky, pensively. Jonah couldn't guess what he must be thinking, feeling. He had never thought himself especially blessed, growing up in a cramped London flat – and later, after his dad's death, on the top deck of a dilapidated bus. He had always had the three essentials of life: food, water and Metasphere access. He didn't like to imagine what his life would have been like without those things.

Jonah didn't like to think about what he might have done – what Jackson might have had to do – to survive in a place like Los Angeles.

There were more water runs on each of the next two days, as Jackson had said there would be. They took place at different times of the evening and night, in order to keep the Tahoe patrols off-guard.

Jackson didn't go along on either run, sending other Lakers in his stead. Jonah was relieved, hoping that Jackson was no longer interested in learning how to fly the plane, until Sam mentioned that perhaps Jackson was simply distancing himself from Jonah to make killing him easier.

The second night brought an especially close call with the lake patrols. Landing back in Santa Monica Bay, Jonah saw that one of the water tanks had been blown clean off the floatplane's starboard wing. He felt that his luck couldn't hold out much longer, and he told Jackson as much when he saw him on the pier.

'We got lucky tonight,' Jonah said to Jackson, who was waiting for them on the pier. 'Those patrol boats were ready for us. I think we should postpone the next run for a few days.'

'Not a chance, kid!' said Jackson. 'We're on a roll and our tanks need filling.' Already, the Lakers were starting to look healthier – and, through Kit, Sam had learned that they were talking about trading water with the inland gangs for food and medicine.

Sam claimed she'd been making progress with Kit – although, to Jonah, it felt unbearably slow and unreliable. It was one thing to talk about escape, apparently, another for Kit to commit herself to leaving her brother, and the only life she had ever known, behind.

The next afternoon, however, Kit paid an unscheduled visit to the captives. Jonah could tell right away that something was wrong, but it took Sam a few minutes to find out what it was. Kit was nervous of Jonah, who was still a stranger to her, and Sam had to coax her into confiding in front of him.

'You remember how you told me,' said Kit, 'about your Metal world.'

'The Metasphere,' said Sam. 'But it isn't just our world, Kit. The Metasphere belongs to everyone – at least, it should.'

'I think… I think Jackson's been going there. He's been "going online". A lot.'

Jonah's ears pricked up. 'How?' he asked. If there was Metasphere access in this wasteland, Jonah wanted on. He was panicked about how long they'd been off-line for, five days now, and worried about his father. Jason had seemed so eager to prove himself to the Guardians, Jonah dreaded that he might do something rash that would get him killed again.

'He doesn't want anyone else to know,' whispered Kit. 'But Jackson's been trading water with the Clippers.'

'And they have Metasphere access?' asked Jonah. Kit nodded.

'What's he up to?' asked Sam.

'He won't tell me,' said Kit. 'He thinks I'm still a little kid.'

'But you're not, are you?' Jonah prompted.

Kit looked at him, hesitated for a moment. 'Some of the others…' she said. 'I overheard them talking and they said… I don't know if this is right, but they said Jackson's been…learning to fly. Can you do that in the Metal Sphere?'

Jonah groaned, put his head in his hands, his hopes dashed. 'Flight simulators,' he said. 'Plenty of them in the Metasphere.'

'And they said,' continued Kit, 'he's been getting good at it. Magic said, tomorrow night, he's going to fly the real plane instead of you.'

'Which means,' Jonah filled in the gaps, 'that tonight's run is my last.'

'You know what that means, don't you, Kit?' said Sam, urgently.

Kit nodded. 'I do. It means I have to leave my brother.'

'You have to tell the other Lakers,' said Sam, 'the ones who want to leave. Tell them we're out of time. We have to make our move tonight.'

'Otherwise said Jonah, 'they won't have a willing pilot any more. Once Jackson is sure he can fly that plane without us, I'll be dead.'

Sam looked at Kit and held her hand. 'We'll both be dead.'

Jonah was taken to the pier as usual that night. He swallowed dryly at the sight of Jackson waiting for him in the moonlight.

'Thought I'd fly with you tonight,' said the Lakers' leader as they tramped down the beach together. 'I've missed your sparkling conversation.' His tone was light enough, but his smile didn't reach his hard eyes.

There was no doubt about it now, not in Jonah's mind. Apart from Jackson's presence, everything seemed perfectly normal. The same as it had been last night, and the night before. Four Lakers – Jonah only recognised one of them, the one with the shaved head whom they called Kobe – climbed into the back of the floatplane. Jackson got into the cockpit with Jonah, watching him with keen eyes.

What if Kit's had second thoughts? he asked himself. *What if she's decided she can't go through with the plan? What do we do then?*

Sam heard footsteps on the landing.

She leapt up off her bed. *Kit?* she thought. *Or someone sent by Jackson?* Now that Jonah had left the hotel – for the last time, most likely – the Lakers didn't need her.

She wouldn't go down without a fight.

She didn't recognise the two Lakers who unlocked and opened the door. They weren't carrying weapons, though, as Sam had expected they would. Perhaps they hoped to surprise her. She tensed, waiting for them to make their move.

'We're with Kit,' one of the Lakers whispered.

'Where is she?' asked Sam. She wasn't sure if she trusted this.

'Ssh! It's time to go.'

They crept out of the room and down the stairs. Sam could hear raised voices and laughter from what must have been the old hotel bar. She held back while the Lakers went ahead to check that the way was clear for her. It was.

They hurried outside and along the waterfront. After days cooped up inside, Sam was grateful to be breathing the cool, fresh sea air. Shadows shifted in the corners of her eyes, and she tensed, expecting an ambush – but the shadows were of more allies, who streamed out of the buildings to join them.

By the time they reached the pier, they were ten-strong – with two more shadows waiting on the beach for them. Neither of them was Kit.

These final two Lakers had acquired four inflatable dinghies, blown them up and laid them out on the sand, each with a single oar. In four groups of two and three, the Lakers and Sam took to the tiny boats and paddled silently out to sea.

Sam scanned the night sky for any sign of the floatplane's lights, listened for any sound of its engines. She felt helpless, bobbing in the ocean, surrounded by strangers who were counting on her to lead them to a better life. But right now, there was nothing more she could do, only wait. The rest was up to the Lakers aboard the floatplane.

Up to them, and to Jonah.

28

Jonah tensed as two Lakers, Kareem and Shaq, came into the floatplane cockpit.

This is it! he thought. *Either they're here to kill me or...*

'What do you two want?' asked Jackson.

The Lakers exchanged a glance, long enough for their leader to know something was very wrong. He punched his seatbelt release button, jumped to his feet, went for his gun. The Lakers were on him before he could draw it, but the back of Jackson's seat was in their way and they couldn't hold onto him.

Jackson tore himself free of the Lakers' grip, held his pistol on them, swore at them. 'Don't fire in here,' cried Jonah. 'You might hit something.' *Someone*, he meant. He wished there was more he could do. But the plane wasn't stable enough for him to let go of the control stick, even for a few seconds.

'We don't want no trouble,' said one of the Lakers.

'You got a funny way of showing it,' sneered Jackson. 'Do you wanna be the Jackson, is that it, Shaq? Do you think you got what it takes to lead?'

The other Laker spoke up: 'It ain't like that, Jackson. We just want the plane.'

Jackson snorted. 'You "just" want...? I never trusted

you, Kareem. I never trusted either of you. Who'd you sell us out to? The Clippers? The Dodgers?'

'No one. We ain't sold out to no one,' said Shaq.

'We just want out, Jackson,' said Kareem. 'Out of the gang. Out of LA. And we ain't the only ones.'

'And where you gonna go, huh? Who'll look after you if I—?'

'Up north,' said Shaq. 'The kid said he could fly us to—'

'Oh, did he now?' snarled Jackson.

And now he turned his gun on Jonah.

'And how's the kid gonna fly you anywhere with a bullet hole in his head?'

Jonah did the only thing he could think to do. He slammed the control stick hard left, throwing the plane into a steep bank. Jackson was caught off guard, as were the other two Lakers. All three of them stumbled, and Jackson's pistol discharged into the roof.

Shaq and Kareem seized their second chance. They overpowered Jackson quickly, snatching the weapon from his hand.

Jonah brought the floatplane level again. His hands were shaking. *Did Jackson really try to kill me?* he wondered. *Or did he pull the trigger by accident as he fell?*

Jackson was still struggling, although he was pinned down on the floor. 'I say we shoot him now,' said Shaq.

'I say we open the door and throw him out of the plane,' said Kareem.

'And I say we don't,' said Jonah. He was concentrating on his flying, but he could feel the Lakers' stares burning into the back of his head. 'No one dies on my plane,' he said, 'or I won't take you anywhere.'

'He planned to kill you, you know,' grumbled one of the Lakers.

'I know,' said Jonah quietly. He brought the plane around, headed back the way they had come. To Santa Monica Bay. If all had gone to Kit's plan, then that was where Sam would be waiting for him. *If all has gone well...*

'Who's behind this?' spat Jackson from the floor. 'I know it ain't either of you two, you ain't got one brain between you. Whose idea was it to—?'

'It was mine.' The voice was Kit's, and it silenced her brother in mid-word.

She must have snuck aboard the plane before me or Jackson boarded, thought Jonah. She stepped into the cockpit.

'It was my idea,' said Kit.

Jackson was struggling again. 'No, I don't... I won't believe you!'

'I had to, Jackson. I'm sorry.'

'You wouldn't turn against me. Not unless... Tell me, sis. Tell me who it is that's making you do this, and I'll—'

'It's *you*!' Kit cried. 'You made me do this...*Tony*! You did!'

'I never made you do a thing. I've looked after you all your life.'

'But you never listened to me, Tony. You never…' Kit choked on her words. At last, she turned and hurried out towards the passenger compartment, with a tearful parting shot: 'You never listened to any of us!'

And, for the next few minutes, the only sound to be heard was the droning of the floatplane's engines. The Lakers – Jackson especially – had nothing more to say.

As Jonah circled the bay, he spotted four rubber boats and scanned for Sam. He saw her waving and he let out a sigh of relief. Sam was right where she was supposed to be: drifting out on the bay with the rest of the defecting Lakers. Jonah put the floatplane down alongside them, and they paddled their dinghies up to it and climbed aboard.

Sam joined Jonah in the cockpit. To his surprise, she threw her arms around him and hugged him tightly.

'Smoochy-smoochy,' laughed Kareem.

Jonah broke away from her, embarrassed, then wished he hadn't. 'I'm glad you're OK,' he said.

'I'm glad you're OK,' Sam said.

Soon, everyone had boarded, leaving four empty dinghies drifting on the sea.

'Just one more thing to take care of,' muttered Shaq, and he and Kareem picked up Jackson from the cockpit floor and dragged him to the open hatch.

'No, wait,' said Jackson. 'Where's Kit? I need to talk to my sister.'

'She's in the back,' growled Shaq, 'and she don't wanna see you. None of us wanna see your ugly face again. Now, jump!'

'Take me with you,' said Jackson. Everyone stared at him for a moment.

Then Shaq pushed Jackson out of the plane.

He landed sprawled across a dinghy with his legs in the water. He scrambled up onto the rubber raft, almost capsizing it. 'Please,' he pleaded, 'for the Lakers! I know… I know you don't like me a whole lot right now, but you've gotta believe that everything I did, it was for us. *To survive!* Maybe I went too far, but you know what'll happen if you leave me here.'

'What will happen?' asked Jonah.

'As soon as the Clippers find out Jackson's lost his gang—' said Kareem.

He didn't need to finish the thought. Everyone knew.

'Could it be any worse?' asked Sam. 'Any worse than what Jackson had planned to do to Jonah and me?!'

And I can't just leave him to die, Jonah thought, *no matter what he might have done.*

'I think we should let him come,' he said. 'But that's up to Kit.'

He waited for the expected protests to die down and Kit joined him in the cockpit. Then, quietly but firmly, Jonah said, 'I've never had a brother, or a sister, and I know you're more than angry at him right now, and you have every right to be, but I honestly think that everything he did was to protect you, and to make sure you two survived down there. But now you have a chance to start again.'

Kit turned to the open hatch and motioned to Shaq and Magic to haul Jackson inside the plane. Jackson hugged his sister, and looking back with a glance, Jonah spotted him crying. When Jonah's eyes met Jackson's, the deposed gang leader gave Jonah a subtle nod of acknowledgement and thanks.

'Shaq, Kareem,' called Jonah. 'Get those tanks off the plane before we take off!' Jonah turned to Sam. 'We'll need to conserve fuel for our journey.'

'Where do you want to take them?' Sam asked.

Jonah had the image in his mind's eye, pulled from his father's memories, of a sparkling lake surrounded by steep, snow-capped mountains. 'There's a commune, in Canada, and someone my dad knows lives there. It's a start.'

'And it's better than here,' said Sam.

'I'll need to get online once we're airborne. Can you handle the plane while I go in?'

'Of course,' said Sam. 'But what if Jackson tries something?'

'He won't,' said Jonah.

*

Once the tanks were shed, Jonah took off again and stayed overland as he headed directly north. When they reached their cruising altitude, Jonah put the plane on autopilot, handed control over to Sam, and locked the cockpit door from the inside. He tapped out a message for his father: BEEN DELAYED. NOW BACK EN ROUTE. MEET ME AT THE SHOP.

Jonah waited nervously for the ping-ping of the reply: GOING IN NOW.

'I'm going in,' he said, as unwrapped a new adaptor and plugged the cold piece of plastic into his spine. He tapped in the eight-digit coordinates for the gift shop and fell out of the real world with a blur.

Jonah materialised on the edge of Venus Park and was instantly enveloped by two massive red wings.

'I've been so worried, son,' Jason said.

'We're OK,' Jonah said, happy to be in his father's reassuring embrace. 'We just had an unexpected... detour.'

Jason retracted his wings and Jonah felt something was wrong. At first, it was the sound, or the lack of any sound. Then, Jonah looked around and saw...nobody. Venus Park was completely deserted.

'Where is everyone?' he asked.

'Scared. Terrified,' said Jason. 'Too frightened to go online.'

'Because of...'

'Yes, Jonah. Because of me, and those like me.'

The emptiness of the Metasphere sent a shiver down Jonah's spine. It was one thing to witness the Changsphere emptied out, but here, in the Metasphere, which had always been so full of life, Jonah shuddered at the thought of a world where people were too afraid to go online. It was the opposite of what had happened with real-world flying. People became too afraid to fly after the airport bombings, and so they flocked to the Metasphere. If fear drove them off-line again, there'd be nothing left of the virtual world. It preyed on Jonah's heart, and he knew that he'd have to stop the Uploaded from hunting the living. But right now, he needed his father.

'Dad, do you remember you told me about that man who helped you copy yourself?'

'Yes, it's one of the last things I do remember before the big blank.'

'He's in Canada, in the mountains, right? I need to find him.'

'Jonah, he may not want to be found,' warned Jason. 'What's this all about?'

'I need to make one more, um, detour, before we reach Manhattan. I need to make good on a promise.'

'His name is Sal Vator,' explained Jason. 'He is part of a commune of farmers. They're good people, former coders and programmers who gave up on technology, left the virtual world behind to live off the land.' Jonah was relieved that this man wasn't a Millennial contact from his dad's tenure as a double agent. 'I'll send you an encrypted message with his RWL, if that's what you really want.'

'It's what I need, Dad.'

'And when will I see you in the RW?'

'I'll message you when we're close, but we should make it by tomorrow morning.'

'Fly safe, son.'

'I will,' promised Jonah. 'Thanks to your memories.'

With that, Jason extended his great wings, flew up in the sky and dived through his exit halo. Of course, Jonah remembered, it wasn't his exit halo at all.

Matthew Granger sat across from the old woman and tried his best to be patient and understanding.

'Why don't you begin by telling me what you told Octavio, here?' he said gently, signalling to the Millennial agent standing by the door of Granger's new wood-panelled study.

'Is like I said,' she began. 'When *señor* woke up from his computer sleep, he was not the same man.'

'How do you know, Luisa, is it?'

'I know, I just know,' she said. 'I've cleaned his house for twenty years, since before the rebellion. And I know when he's been possessed by the devil.'

More and more reports of usurping were coming in. To some people, the metaphobes who didn't go online, these were viewed as possessions. But to Granger, he knew that the Uploaded were getting loose in the real world. And this house-cleaner was reporting the third case of usurping in Manhattan this week, and he wanted to hear the details for himself.

'There are others,' Luisa continued. 'All of us cleaners and maids, we know what's going on. The devil is among us. And the young man there says you can help us.'

'Yes, Luisa, I believe I can.'

'*Madre!*'

'Tell me one thing. Is your master planning to attend the gala launch of the Luke Wexler game this week?'

'*Si, señor.*'

'Then that is when we will exorcise his demon.'

'*Gracias, señor.*'

'No, Luisa. Thank you.'

'Do we have a destination?' asked Sam.

Jonah readjusted his eyes back to the real world, and looked out the cockpit window to see the parched land below. He looked at his datapad, decrypted the message from his father, and punched the coordinates into the autopilot.

'We do now,' said Jonah. 'Let's hope it's the right one.'

A knock on the cockpit door interrupted Jonah's train of thought. Jonah looked through the security viewfinder to see Jackson and Kit. Sam shot Jonah a look as he opened the door.

'Can I talk to you?' Jackson asked.

Jonah was about to invite him into the cockpit when Sam stated, 'From right there.'

Jackson didn't take one step further and said, 'I just wanted to thank you. For sticking up for me back there. You didn't have to do that.'

'No,' agreed Jonah. 'I didn't. What will you do? Will you stay with the other Lakers?'

'I dunno. If they want me to, maybe. But they've made it clear they don't need me any more. And that's fine with me.' Jackson sounded bitter. However, when Jonah next glanced at him, he was smiling to himself. 'You know, it really *is* fine,' he said. 'I feel like... Like a weight's been lifted from my shoulders.'

'Yeah,' said Jonah, 'I can imagine.' And he wondered, *Could Jackson be a different person – a better person – away from LA and the gangs? Away from the weight of other people's expectations?*

'They don't need me any more,' said Jackson. 'No one needs me. For the first time in a long, long time, I feel... free.'

Jonah almost envied him.

Jonah crested a ridge of British Colombia's Rocky Mountains and spotted the Y-shaped Quesnel Lake below. He circled the plane above the lake and brought them down gently in the stem of the Y.

It wasn't long, of course, before the gunboats found

and surrounded them. The locals were as wise to water theft as were the owners of Lake Tahoe.

The three boats herded Jonah's plane to a small pier, where armed men and women, dressed in long, brown robes were waiting. They signalled to Jonah to come out of the plane.

'Stay inside,' pleaded Sam, gripping Jonah's arm.

'It'll be OK,' said Jonah, as he stepped out of the cockpit, through the hatch and onto the bobbing pier. 'My name is Jonah Delacroix, and I'm looking for Sal Vator.'

One of the women laughed. 'Aren't we all!'

The others joined in her laughter and Jonah forced a grin.

'We disturb no one up here,' said a man with long, braided hair. 'Why do you disturb us?'

'He helped my father once, and now I need his help. We're carrying, um, water refugees, children mostly, from—'

'And are you not a child?' asked the man.

'I'm just trying to help,' said Jonah. 'And I'm hoping you will too.'

'I am not the *salvator*,' said the man. 'I am merely a servant. But we know the name Delacroix here. He is a friend to our community, and helped us when we needed it. You can tell him that we will honour our friendship by helping out his child.'

'Thank you,' said Jonah. 'But I'm not a child, really, I'm...'

'We are all tomorrow's children,' said the woman, pointing to the pier. 'And if your charges will work the land to earn their keep, live at one with the land, then we will welcome them here.' She looked past Jonah to the plane and asked, 'Will you join us?'

Jonah turned to see Kit standing at the hatch. She jumped onto the pier and stood bravely beside Jonah.

'We've come from Los Angeles,' she began. 'And Jonah has helped us escape. We just want to survive.'

The man with the braided hair knelt down to look Kit in the eyes. 'You have a brave spirit, my child,' he said softly.

He rose to address the other robed men and women. 'We will welcome these newcomers. These children will take lessons alongside our children. They will farm and nurture the land alongside our children. And they will be one with our way of life. So it is said.'

The others bowed their heads, and repeated his words. 'So it is said.'

'Thank you,' said Jonah.

'You are a Delacroix,' said the man. 'And you are their saviour. And we will honour that.'

'Thank you,' said Jonah. 'My father was right about you and your people.'

'I would ask you to stay with us as well,' said the man. 'But I know you are still walking your path.'

'Tell me about it,' said Jonah with a sigh, thinking to all that awaited him in Manhattan.

'Perhaps you'll return here to the mountains to complete it?'

Jonah didn't know what to say. He knew he had to get to Manhattan quickly, and that a war was waiting for him. But as he watched the Lakers deplane and marvel at the great mountains and immense lake of fresh water, he wished, for just a moment, that he could shirk his responsibilities and remain in this hidden Eden.

Kit gave Jonah a hug and the Lakers slapped his hands with heartfelt high-fives.

'Thanks, kid,' said Jackson. 'We'll be OK here. You and your girlfriend get goin'...'

'She's not my...' Jonah started, and then simply shook his head and muttered, 'and it's not *kid*.'

'It never was,' said Jackson, slapping Jonah on the back and joining his sister and the others as they walked up the slope of the mountain.

'You were right, Sam,' Jonah said as he took his place in the cockpit beside her. 'About Kit. I'm glad we helped her and the others.'

'You too,' said Sam. 'You were right about Jackson, about not letting them kill him. And...and, Jonah... Maybe you were right about the other thing as well. About Granger. Maybe you were right to spare his life.'

Jonah thought about what it meant for Sam to say that, to admit that not killing her sworn enemy was all right by her.

'That... That means a lot,' said Jonah. 'More than you know.'

They didn't discuss it further, but Jonah felt that something had changed between him and Sam during their captivity. He felt they understood each other better now, that their bond had become stronger and deeper.

They took off eastbound along the long stretch of Quesnel Lake and set their heading for Manhattan Island, three thousand miles away.

Jonah was glad to have his friend at his side.

29

For Axel Kavanaugh, it had been a long week.

He'd hitched a lift with a dozen Guardians on a Chinese Food Aid plane to northern Florida. From there, they'd travelled in convoy up the lawless American continent by road, and he'd worried that he would never reach Manhattan in time. They were heavily armed, and more than once had to defend themselves against bandits on the crumbling interstate motorway. But nothing was going to stop Axel from reaching the Western Corner, and seeing his daughter again.

By the time he'd reached New York, he'd located Jez at a makeshift Guardian outpost in Queens, across the East River from Manhattan. It had been over two months since the American government fell, and gunfire and explosions still filled the night air.

Jez had taken over an abandoned garage, and had assembled almost 150 Guardians, but he was growing impatient with Sam and Jonah.

'For all we know,' he had said, 'your kid and her traitor friend have sold out to the Millennials. There could be an army of them on their way here right now to—'

Axel had grabbed Jez by his gnarly dreadlocks, and

dragged him up to the edge of a foul-smelling grease pit. 'You don't ever – *ever* – talk about my daughter like that!'

Jez had torn himself free, glowering at Axel. He seemed to know he had overstepped the mark, though, and didn't make an issue of it.

'Just a few more days,' Axel had said, addressing all the assembled Guardians. 'Let's give Sam and Jonah a couple more days. I think we owe them that much, at least, after what they did – what they both did – at Uluru.'

The reminder of that previous victory had raised morale a little. The Guardians, even Jez, had agreed to wait – and that night, Axel had been messaged by Sam. She and Jonah had been held up in LA, she had said, but they were back on course now and would reach Manhattan by the next morning.

Jonah grinned at the sight of the shimmering island ahead of him.

'I've always wanted to come here,' he said, guiding the floatplane towards it.

'What, to Manhattan? Really?' said Sam. 'To a real-world city?'

'I know. Not like me at all, huh? But Dad used to talk about this place all the time, about this city that reached to the sky, and then I saw it in his memories.'

'Yeah, my dad used to love flying here too.'

'He used to say it was better than anywhere in the Metasphere,' said Jonah. 'I never actually believed him, didn't think that was possible, but still...'

They descended towards the New York harbour area, at the island's southern tip. Sam sighed as they swooped by the headless remains of the Statue of Liberty, toppled years ago by anti-immigration activists.

'We might find a few things have changed,' she said, 'since Jason and Axel flew this route.'

They followed instructions from an air traffic controller to dock at the Battery Park Ferry Terminal, where they were met by a swarm of armed men in dark blue uniforms. Manhattan's private police force.

Jonah and Sam were separated, scanned for explosives and frisked for concealed weapons. They were taken, one at a time, into an antiseptic-smelling room for a thorough health screening, and fingerprints and DNA swabs were taken from them.

Jonah tried not to look too worried. As far as the Manhattan authorities were concerned, he and Sam were 'Jonah and Samantha Wexler' and they had a certified invitation from a resident. It would mean big trouble, both for them and for Jason, if the truth was discovered.

At last, the sergeant in charge – a heavyset, moustached man who until now had done nothing but glower at them – marched up to them both. Unexpectedly, he beamed through his bushy moustache, and said in a cheerful voice, 'Welcome to the Republic of Manhattan!'

Jonah and Sam exchanged grins of relief. They had passed their tests.

They stepped out onto the pavement, to be greeted by a man they had never met before, but whom Jonah instantly recognised. He was tall and handsome, dressed all in black, wearing a trademark black cowboy hat.

'Jonah! Samantha! Mighty good to see you two again. My, haven't you both grown!' The cowboy opened his arms and enveloped both of them in a bear hug.

'*Dad?*' whispered Jonah.

He knew he should have been prepared for this, prepared to see Jason Delacroix in Lucky Luke Wexler's body. But deep down, Jonah had hoped that somehow he might see his father in his own real-world body once again, even if he knew that was impossible.

'Hush up,' Jason whispered. He indicated the watching cops. 'In front of those guys, I'm your uncle and you're brother and sister. Now, let's vamoose outta here before they wise up.' He didn't even talk like Jason!

A yellow auto-cab stood waiting for them. They climbed into the back, and Jason tapped in a destination into the onboard datapad. The cab door slid shut, and the vehicle eased out into the roadway.

They headed north, through the bustling financial district. They glided through the shadow of the famous Freedom Tower, and Jonah craned his neck out of the window to see to the top of its spire. A large airship, bigger than the one that first took Jonah away from England, was docked at the pinnacle of the building.

Once they were alone in the cab, Jason hugged Jonah tightly. 'You kids had me worried sick,' said Jason, in Luke's Texas accent.

'I'm sorry, Dad.'

'It's all right now,' said Jason. 'I just can't believe I'm seeing you, son, with my own eyes!' Jonah wanted to correct him, but closed his eyes and pretended that Luke's arms were his father's arms and for a moment, he was transported to a time, three years ago, when his dad would return home from a long flight, pick him up, and squeeze him in a hug until he pleaded with his dad to stop. Now he wished he'd never asked him to stop.

Finally, Jason let go as the cab weaved north though the city.

'You were right, Dad,' Jonah enthused. 'Everything you ever said about this place. It's clean and not too crowded, and… Look at all the shops and the parks, with real trees and bushes and… It's like… It's like a virtual city, but it's in the real world!'

'Yeah,' agreed Sam. 'Pity you have to be a billionaire to enjoy it!'

They motored past the Art Deco façade of the Empire State Building, and then drove up 7th Avenue, through Times Square, where hundreds of animated billboards dazzled the senses. Finally, they turned onto

West 59th Street, and pulled up to the kerb across from Central Park. Jason winked at Jonah. 'Wait till you see my flat,' he said.

'It's incredible!' gasped Jonah.

Luke's loft apartment filled three floors, overlooking the park. It was open-plan, with walls that could be slid across to create smaller rooms. There was a hot tub set into a raised platform, plasma screens everywhere and four giant leather off-line gaming chairs.

'It's like…it's like the ultimate—' said Jonah.

'—gamer-geek-chic—' Sam put in.

'—And this is where—?' started Jonah, thinking about exactly how his father gained this amazing apartment; by usurping Luke.

'This is where I woke up,' confirmed Jason, 'after I… when I used Lucky Luke's exit halo. It gave my nurse quite a fright, I can tell you.'

'Your nurse?'

'Luke's nurse. He came in when I…when *Luke* was trapped in the Changsphere, to keep his real-world body fed and cleaned and free from bedsores.'

'And he didn't suspect,' asked Sam, 'that you weren't…?'

'That I'm not Lucky Luke?' Jason shook his head. 'I told him the truth, at least an edited version of it: how one of the Uploaded protected me from the others until we found a way out. He had no reason to disbelieve me.'

'What about the rest of Wexler's staff?' asked Sam. 'What about his friends? He must have friends in Manhattan.'

'Now, don't you be fretting yourself none, little missy.' Jason spoke in the same exaggerated Texan accent he had put on at the ferry terminal. 'I've been playing my part in public. Got pretty good at it, as it goes. 'Course, I have lots of Lucky Luke's memories rattling about in this new head of mine.'

Jonah had found a shelf full of gaming industry awards. He picked up one, and accidentally activated a tiny hologram of a brain-sucking zombie. He almost dropped the award in surprise as the monster roared and clawed at his throat.

'Oh yeah,' said Jason, 'that reminds me. We've a shindig to attend tomorrow night. The launch of my new game.'

'That's tomorrow?' Jonah whirled around to face his dad. 'But we can't... I mean, you can't go, Dad. You can't play Lucky Luke online. Your avatar—'

'Who said anything about online?' Jason smiled. 'Online is off-limits right now: all those hunger-crazed Uploaded, terrorising living users.'

'Then where—?'

'My gala premiere tomorrow night,' said Jason, 'will be held in the real world. Right here in Manhattan. And we'll all be going, the three of us, because this is the chance we've been waiting for, maybe the best chance

266

we'll ever get.'

'To do what?' asked Sam.

'To find the Western Corner, of course.'

Sam was dismayed. 'You don't know where it is yet? But you told Jonah you could find it. You said—'

'I know what I said, Samantha. I've been doing my best. I've been asking around when I can. I know that the server farm is somewhere in this city.'

'A lot of good that does us,' snorted Sam. 'There are thousands of buildings here. It could take us months to search them all, and the Guardians—'

'We're already running late, Dad,' said Jonah, 'and the Guardians won't wait too long. They're worried this might be a trap.'

'I've been doing all I can,' said Jason. 'I just need a little—'

'Someone must know something,' said Sam. 'Someone must have seen something. This is hardly the Australian desert. How do you hide a huge server farm here?'

'If you'll let me finish,' said Jason, 'I've been thinking about that. And I think we should follow the power.'

'The power?' echoed Jonah.

'The Western Corner runs one-quarter of the Metasphere. It must soak up power like a sponge, and that demand must show up on a report or a readout somewhere.'

'OK,' said Sam. 'Now we're getting somewhere. So,

who would see those reports? Who controls the power grid?'

'It's all run through the co-op,' said Jason.

'The what?'

'The co-operative board that governs Manhattan. Fourteen men and women. All of whom will be—'

'—at the launch tomorrow night,' Jonah realised.

Jason tipped his black Stetson hat in his direction. 'Now you're getting it, son. I can't question all those fine folk myself. Lucky Luke has lived here almost two years; it'd be odd if he got curious now. But two inquisitive newcomers...'

Jonah looked at Jason. He looked at Sam. He looked down at himself, at his jeans and the rumpled old hoodie top he had been wearing since Sydney.

He looked at Sam's black overalls, with their frayed sleeves and ripped pockets. 'We're going to need some new clothes,' he said.

After Jonah enjoyed a hot shower – his first in what felt like forever – and Sam relaxed in a herbal bath in another of Luke's four bathrooms – Jason took Jonah and Sam shopping on 5th Avenue.

Jonah couldn't believe how opulent the shops were.

'You could fit four bus-flats in here,' he said. He tried on, and Jason purchased, with Luke's thumbprint, a set of new jeans and shirts, and was measured for his very first dinner jacket. Sam tried on a series of dresses, somehow not happy with any of them until Jason finally urged her to make a choice.

'Let's see?' teased Jonah.

'I look stupid,' called Sam from the changing room. 'I'm only doing this for the mission.' But she refused to show Jonah and Jason the dress.

Later, they dined at a posh uptown restaurant, again courtesy of Luke Wexler's thumbprint. They had a booth to themselves, and Jonah marvelled at the taste of his first real beef burger. He would have enjoyed it more had the waiting staff not been quite so attentive. He feared that his dad would slip up and give himself away.

Jason's performance, however, was impeccable. He got Luke's booming voice and outsized personality to a T. He even knew everybody's name.

'I got a message from Jez,' said Jonah, once they were alone at last. He showed the message to the others on his datapad. It said, ASSEMBLED AND WAITING.

'You should message him back,' said Jason. 'Tell him we're a go for tomorrow night, details to follow.'

'Are you sure? But what about—?'

'We'll find it,' said Jason. 'We'll find the Western Corner at the game launch. Failure isn't an option, son. If we don't do this now, we'll never get a better chance. We'd be leaving a quarter of the Metasphere under Granger's control, and I know that's the last thing either of you wants.'

Back at the apartment, Jonah and Sam plugged into a closed-system version of *Brain-Sucking Zombies 2* with sharper and smoother graphics than either had seen before. Then they dived into Lucky Luke's collection of fully immersive movies and ate too much popcorn. Jonah wished he could live like this forever, not just for a day.

That night, he slept on a racing car-shaped waterbed beneath a holographic vista of a clear night sky. In the morning, a cook arrived to prepare pancakes and real bacon for 'Luke' and his guests, and Jonah lay in bed and enjoyed the delicious smells wafting from the kitchen. A perfect moment of calm. Before the storm.

His dad had sounded so sure of himself last night – so sure that they were doing the right thing, choosing the right side – and his enthusiasm had been infectious.

Jonah *wanted* to do this. He wanted to help the Guardians – because if his dad supported them, then he should too, right? All the same, he felt a familiar queasiness in his stomach at the thought of what that meant.

Everyone was counting on Jonah. Again.

30

Jonah had never worn a dinner jacket before.

It felt tight around his shoulders, loose around his wrists. He couldn't help feeling that his own body was to blame for being not quite the right shape.

His bow tie was choking him. Jason had had to tie it for him, after Jonah had tried for almost twenty minutes.

Jason's own tux, on the other hand, fitted perfectly – as if he had been born to wear it. *As if* Luke *was born to wear it*, Jonah corrected his own thoughts. *It's Luke's jacket, not Dad's. Luke's body, not Dad's!* How easy it had become to forget...

He looked down at his father's polished black shoes. 'Oh, Dad,' groaned Jonah, 'don't you know anything?' He marched into a walk-in closet, which was bigger than any room he had ever lived in, and found a row of cowboy boots. Jonah picked the least scuffed-looking pair and took them to his dad. 'Lucky Luke only ever wears cowboy boots. You'd be found out for sure if you turned up at his launch in dress shoes.'

As Jason pulled on the boots, Jonah found Luke's trademark black Stetson hat balanced on the back of a chair. He placed it onto his father's borrowed head. 'There,' said Jonah. 'Much better.'

271

He heard a small sound behind him: a polite clearing of the throat. He turned, and his jaw dropped open.

Sam stood at the foot of a narrow spiral staircase. She was wearing a formal, single-shoulder dress, dark blue, and carrying a matching handbag. The long dress followed every curve of her body, in a way that her own clothes never had – and she had combed her red hair in a new way too, parting it and adding a butterfly-shaped clip.

If Jonah had passed her in the street, he might not have recognised her.

'Do I look as stupid as I feel in this?' she asked.

'You look, um…' said Jonah. *Amazing*, he thought. 'Different,' he said.

'I knew it,' said Sam. She crossed the room with a less-than-elegant gait. 'How anyone can walk in high heels like this, I will never, ever know.'

'You look a billion meta-dollars,' said Jason. 'You both do.'

'I just hope nothing goes wrong tonight,' said Sam, 'because if I have to run I will probably break my ankles and tear this straitjacket right up the back.'

'Nothing will go wrong,' said Jonah. 'We all know our parts.'

The datapad at Luke's door chimed and Jonah looked over to see the icon of a black limousine flashing.

'I think our ride's here,' said Jason. 'Shall we go?'

As Jonah followed Jason and Sam through the door,

he took one last look around Lucky Luke's flat. If all went well tonight, he knew he would never come back here, probably never set foot in a place like this again.

Jonah tried not to gasp when he saw the sleek, black auto-limo. Someone might have been watching, so he had to play his part. He was a member of a wealthy family, after all. He was a Wexler.

Once he was inside the vehicle, however, behind its tinted windows, he relaxed into the soft leather upholstery and put his feet up. Despite the jacket and bow tie, he didn't think he had ever been so comfortable in his life.

Sam, in contrast, had never looked so awkward. She fidgeted on the leather and complained that the dress was too tight.

They cruised down Fifth Avenue, past department stores and jewellers, fashion houses and some of the world's few remaining art galleries. Their limo took up more than half the road, but no one got in their way. The smart grid system saw to that.

A screen in front of Jonah featured the famous video blogger Bryony, who was broadcasting from outside the *Brain-Sucking Zombies 4* gala:

'...most exclusive event yet of the year, now set in the real world, here in the playground of the rich and famous, Manhattan. And I'll bring you, my dear followers, the juiciest gossip and the hottest celebrities. Trust me, I'm

Bryony. Oh, and here comes the man of the hour now…'

They pulled up outside a magnificent building, all arches and columns and statues of mythical heroes. 'Grand Central,' said Jason. 'The greatest entertainment venue in the world. Of course, you two are too young to remember when it was a railway terminal.'

A skinny man in a grey and red uniform scuttled forward. He opened the limo door, and bade 'Mr Wexler' and his associates a good evening. Jason stepped out of the car first, onto a red carpet. Sam stopped Jonah from following, whipping out a comb and trying to flatten his stubborn tuft of hair. She couldn't, of course.

They followed Jason along the carpet. On one side, the paparazzi and vloggers clamoured to get a look at Jason. Jonah spotted Bryony waving. On the other side, the fans cheered, many of whom were the cooks, cleaners and shopkeepers of Manhattan, who weren't welcome inside the venue. Jonah felt like he had in the Changsphere, like a celebrity. He had to remind himself that the cheers weren't for him. They were for his dad.

No, they aren't, he reminded himself. *They're for someone else altogether!*

The station's main concourse was a cavernous space, with passages branching away from it. It teemed with men and women in formal dress, many of whom broke off their conversations to applaud the arrival of the star of the show, Lucky Luke.

People swarmed Jason, congratulating him and asking when he was going to make his big speech.

'There ain't gonna be no speeches,' said Jason. 'Y'all know why we're here. Let's get this wagon on the road!'

The guests applauded that sentiment with even more gusto.

An orchestra started playing on a balcony at one end of the concourse. Waiters dressed as zombies weaved their way through the crowd with blood-red drinks on trays. Ticket booths had been put into service as cloakrooms. Hanging from the ceiling was a giant tricolour flag, blue, white and orange. Jonah's eyes, however, were drawn to the off-line gaming chairs that had been set up everywhere.

Lucky Luke's new game, he thought. *I could be one of the first people in the world to play it.* He sighed to himself. He had work to do.

A young woman approached them. At first, Jonah thought she was much older, with her long black hair pinned up in a formal, almost fierce way, but as she got closer, flanked by two massive bodyguards, he guessed that she was actually only a year or two older than he was.

'Now, here's someone you'll want to meet,' Jason muttered.

He stepped forward with a broad smile, and kissed the young woman's hand. 'President Lori Weisberg,' he said, 'may I introduce my niece and nephew from

London, Samantha and Jonah Wexler.'

President? thought Jonah.

'Absolutely delighted,' said Lori Weisberg. She shook Sam and Jonah's hands in turn. 'I hear you're following in your uncle's footsteps,' said Lori. 'Another superstar in the making.'

It took Jonah a moment to realise she was talking to him. 'Um?' he said.

'That's sure as shooting, ma'am,' said Jason, 'Jonah here is on the bleeding edge of next-generation programming. He'll make me obsolete before I'm thirty-five, my oath he will. You tell the lady, kid.'

'I...um, yeah,' said Jonah. 'I've been working for... my uncle here for a while, but...' He glanced up at his dad to check he was saying the right thing.

'But now he's fixing to set up on his own,' said Jason, 'maybe right here in Manhattan if you'll have him.'

'I'm sure there'd be no objections from the board,' said Lori. 'I would be happy to make a personal recommendation.'

'Uh, right,' said Jonah. 'Thing is, the games I create, they need a lot of processing power to run them. I mean, an awful lot. That's why—'

'That's why you must build your games lab here,' said Lori. 'I hear the national grid in England has become as erratic and unreliable as most countries' are these days.'

'But Manhattan is different?' asked Sam, eagerly.

'Can you supply the power Jonah needs?'

Lori grinned. 'This is a party, not a sales pitch. But I'll make you a deal.' She was looking at Jonah. 'Let's move this discussion to the dance floor, and I'll tell you a little secret about power.'

Jonah wasn't too sure about being alone with Lori. What if she asked him a question he couldn't answer? But he glanced at his dad, and was reassured by his little nod. He let Lori take his hand and lead him along the concourse.

'I'm not much of a dancer,' mumbled Jonah.

'Don't worry about that,' said Lori. 'I'll lead. But I'll make it look like you are.'

As Jonah glanced back over his shoulder, he noticed Sam rolling her eyes.

Sam watched as the glamorous president led Jonah through the crowd.

'I wouldn't worry too much about Lori,' said Jason.

'I'm not worried,' said Sam, too quickly.

Jason grinned. 'She probably just smells money. Her father was one of America's leading financiers, you know. She learned at an early age how to get ahead and stay there. Well, look where she is now: President of the Republic!'

'I'm not worried,' Sam repeated. 'I just hope... I hope Jonah can get something out of her, that's all. Is something wrong? You seem a bit...'

Jason was craning his neck, scanning the crowd around him.

'Are you looking for someone?' asked Sam.

'Someone I don't want to see,' said Jason. 'It's OK, I don't think he's here. I never really expected him to show.'

'Who? Who are you talking about?'

'Granger.'

'Matthew Granger?' hissed Sam. 'Here? In New York?'

'It's OK, really,' said Jason.

'How can it be OK? Granger's here? And you never thought to mention this?'

'I didn't know myself until a few days ago. I haven't even seen him. Apparently he's been spending his time shut away in the Freedom Tower downtown. This doesn't have to be a problem, Sam. Sure, Granger's met Luke before but the way Lori tells it, he can't stand him so I reckon he'll give me a wide berth.'

'But Jonah,' said Sam. 'He knows Jonah.'

Jason frowned. 'What do you mean?'

'They met in the real world,' said Sam. 'Granger knows what Jonah looks like, and that he's with us. With the Guardians.'

Jason turned pale.

'We have to get him out of here,' said Sam. She stood in her high heels, trying to spot where Jonah and Lori had gone.

'Without drawing any attention to him,' said Jason.

'It might be too late.' Sam was already pushing her way along the crowded concourse.

She called back over her shoulder, 'He's dancing with the president.'

31

A dance floor had been set up at one end of the concourse, in front of the orchestra. No one else was using it. Lori whisked Jonah out onto the floor, took his hands in hers. She held her body close to his and guided him through the steps of a slow waltz.

Jonah had to keep apologising for his two left feet. 'I, um, spend more time programming than dancing,' he mumbled as he trod on Lori's toes for the third time.

'Try to relax,' she advised. 'Move your body with the music.'

That was easier said than done. Jonah was nervous, not just because he was trying to play his part, but because he was the centre of attention. All eyes were on the beautiful president, and him, as he awkwardly tried to keep up.

Jonah could almost hear the crowd thinking, *Who's that gawky-looking kid dancing with the president?* They were even being taped by the function's official cameramen. *This is probably going to end up on all the vlogs!*

The waltz ended, and the crowd applauded Jonah and Lori politely. The band struck up a more upbeat number, and to Jonah's relief more couples joined them on the floor, taking the spotlight off him.

Lori had been right. Now that Jonah relaxed a little, he was far more graceful. The best thing, he thought, was not to think about his feet at all, just let them do their thing. He might not win any prizes for style, but at least he wouldn't bruise his partner any more than he already had.

Sam had the dance floor in her sights. She saw Jonah and Lori between the other whirling couples. The president's hands were all over Jonah's body!

Jason hadn't followed her. He must have been intercepted by another party-goer keen to talk to the man of the moment. Sam was on her own.

She started towards Jonah, but suddenly there were two men in her path. They were dressed in dinner jackets, and so had been invisible among the crowd until they had made their move. They glowered down at Sam, their arms folded.

Bodyguards! she groaned inwardly. *Of course, the president has bodyguards – Secret Service.*

'I was just…' she said. 'I need a quick word with my brother. He…' She gestured toward Jonah. The two men were unmoved. Sam sighed. She turned and walked away, and the guards melted back into the crowd.

She had to get past them. The guards were almost certainly part of a larger team. Now that Sam really looked, she could pick out a few more of them. She could see it in their eyes, always alert, scanning their surroundings. The dance floor was hardly off-limits, though. Sam had just approached it wrongly, in a suspicious-looking way.

She scanned the crowd and found a group of young men, apparently unattached. They were talking about stock options and laughing raucously. Sam tapped the nearest of them on the shoulder, and put on her sweetest smile. 'Would you care to dance?' she asked.

'It's a brilliant place you have here,' said Jonah.

'Why, thank you, Jonah,' said Lori.

'The whole island,' said Jonah. 'I mean it. If the rest of the world was run like this...and you're the president! The President of Manhattan, and you're so...'

Lori grinned. 'Young?' she asked. 'It's a young person's world, Jonah. You of all people know that. The future belongs to people like us.'

'I guess so.'

'You don't sound so sure. It must be the same in your line of work?'

'I guess... I never thought about the future all that much. I never knew what I wanted to be. I always thought there'd be more time to decide, but now...'

'Let me guess,' said Lori. 'You got pushed into the family business, and you're not so sure it's what you really want.'

Truer than you know, thought Jonah.

'I know how you feel,' said Lori. 'My mom did this job before me. Well, sort of. She was the Mayor of New York City, you know…of the old New York.'

'She was?'

'You never heard of her? Terri Weisberg? She helped draw up the plan for Manhattan to secede from the Union. She was one of the "Founding Mothers" of the new Republic. If it weren't for Mom…'

Jonah was only half listening. He had just spotted Sam. She was dancing with a tall, straw-haired guy with a jutting chin. *What's she doing up here?* he wondered. He didn't think she was the dancing type. Then again, neither was he.

Sam was mouthing something at him, but Jonah couldn't make it out.

Lori had stopped talking. Quickly, Jonah scanned his memory for the last thing she had said to him. 'Where is she now, your mother?' he asked.

'Dead,' said Lori. Jonah froze. It was not the answer he was expecting. Lori nudged his arms, motioning him to keep dancing. 'Assassinated.'

'Oh. I'm sorry.'

'Ten years ago, and I still miss her every day.'

'Me too. My mum was murdered too.'

'That's what made my mind up in the end,' said Lori. 'That's why I ran for president. Mom was killed by the United States government, trying to cling onto their power here. I can't prove it, but I know it. I figure I owe it to her memory to keep her dream alive, or else she died for nothing.'

'I know how you feel,' said Jonah. This time Lori stopped dancing. She looked at him suspiciously.

Suddenly, Sam slid in between Jonah and his now stationary dance partner.

'Do you mind if I cut in?' she said and, before Lori could object, Sam took hold of Jonah's arms and dragged him away.

'What are you doing?' whispered Jonah. 'I was just—'

'Ssh,' said Sam. 'Keep dancing. Granger's here. *Ow!*'

'What?'

'No, don't look around.' Sam was leading, guiding Jonah to the edge of the dance floor. A clutch of Secret Service men were watching her, suspiciously. They had started forward when Sam had approached the president, but they backed off now.

'Where is he?' asked Jonah.

'I don't— *Ow!* You kicked my ankle again!'

'Sorry. I'm not used to...'

'You were dancing well enough with her,' said Sam.

'She was leading,' Jonah shot back. 'And she's good at it.'

'Granger's here, in Manhattan,' Sam said. 'And he's on the guest list.'

'Oh no,' Jonah said. 'Have you seen him?'

'Not yet. We have to get you out of sight in case he turns up.'

'But I...' Jonah looked across at Lori. Sam followed his gaze.

The president was dancing with Sam's former partner, the big-chinned guy who looked like he'd just won the meta-lottery. Lori shot Jonah a frown as if to ask him what was going on. He shrugged helplessly and mouthed: *sisters*.

Sam spun Jonah around so that he had his back to Lori.

'I was starting to get somewhere with her,' he said.

'I bet you were,' coughed Sam.

'No, I mean...' Jonah decided to start again. What was Sam so mad about? 'She was opening up to me.'

'Don't you understand, Jonah? Granger's here! If he sees you—'

'I know. I know. But if I can get the information we need, we can both get out of here.'

'It's too big a risk,' said Sam. 'If he sees you—'

'You and Dad can keep a lookout. If Granger walks in here, Dad can stall him, distract him, as Luke, while you signal me and—'

'There are too many entrances,' said Sam. 'We can't cover them all.'

'A couple more minutes, Sam, that's all.'

They exchanged partners again. The big-chinned man

looked resentful at being torn away from the president. Sam danced with him for another ten seconds or so before she excused herself and left him standing.

'What was all that about?' asked Lori. 'What did your sister want?'

Jonah made up something about a problem in London, which he had had to deal with. 'Which, um, reminds me...'

Lori smiled with mock chagrin. 'You want to talk business. Everyone always does.'

'If that's OK,' said Jonah. 'I'm curious about your "little secret".'

'Oh, that.' The president winked at Jonah. 'Wave power.'

'Wave power?'

'We're on an island, Jonah. We're surrounded by waves. Our scientists finally figured out how to harness them into reliable electricity.'

'Wow,' said Jonah.

'We capture wave energy off the coast, transform it into electricity out on Long Island and then pipe it into the city through the old subway tunnels.'

'Isn't that... Isn't wave energy unpredictable?'

'We store up enough power in the high tides to see us through the low. In the early days of the revolution, Washington cut our power and we had to become self-sufficient in energy and—'

'Subway tunnels,' said Jonah. The orchestra had

finished another number, and were taking a break. Jonah and Lori joined the other dancing couples in applauding the musicians.

'Train tunnels, you mean,' said Jonah. 'Like the old Underground in London?'

'Well, of course the trains don't run any longer,' said Lori. 'Our residents don't care much for *public* transport. We have the smart grid and auto-cabs now.'

Jonah's brain was working furiously.

'Should we hit the buffet table?' asked Lori. 'I'm starving.'

'I… Not right now. Thanks. I… Thank you for the dance, Lori, but I'd best be getting back to Uncle Luke and Sam.'

'OK. Well…'

Was it Jonah's imagination, or did Lori seem disappointed?

'Your uncle has my contact details, if you have any more questions about our set-up here, or if you just want to talk. I mean it, Jonah. I'd love to see you make a move to Manhattan.'

'You know,' Jonah said with an awkward smile. 'I'd love that too.'

Sam was waiting for Jonah by an old information kiosk. It was topped by an ornate clock with four faces, looking out each way across the station concourse.

Sam made Jonah face the kiosk, so his back was to

the crowd. Jason joined them shortly, and Jonah repeated what Lori had told him.

'Maybe I'm being dense,' said Jason, 'but I don't see how this helps us.'

'The Western Corner,' said Jonah. 'It's underground. It has to be. It's in the old subway system.'

'There would be plenty of room down there,' conceded Sam.

'And it'd explain how Granger kept it hidden all this time. Not only that, he'd be able to siphon off the incoming electricity—'

'—before it reached the city grid,' Sam realised.

'There'd be no record of the drain,' said Jonah. 'So no one in Manhattan – not the president, not the board – would know about it. It all fits!'

Jason mulled that over, then nodded. 'OK. We need to check this out pronto. I can't leave my own party, so you two will have to—'

'We'll do the recce,' said Sam. 'You said this place was once a rail terminal?'

'Nice thinking, Sam,' said Jason. 'Yeah, there should be a way down into the subway tunnels from in here. Just remember, if the Western Corner *is* down there—'

'It won't exactly be unguarded.'

'Don't worry, Dad,' said Jonah. 'We'll just get close enough to be sure, then...'

'Then we'll signal the rest of the Guardians,' said Sam, 'and bring them in.'

They hurried across the concourse, eager to prove their theory. Sam was better at wending her way through the crowd of partiers, and she quickly outpaced Jonah.

He lost her for a moment. He looked around in confusion, and stumbled into another guest. The man was holding a glass of champagne, which he spilled down the front of his dress shirt. 'I'm sorry,' Jonah mumbled. 'I didn't mean to…'

He caught sight of Sam again, and hurried after her. He didn't look at the man he had collided with, never did see his face. But the man had seen him.

Granger furrowed his brow and narrowed his eyes as he glared after the departing Jonah.

Jonah Delacroix…

Originally, he hadn't planned to attend this party. He loathed Lucky Luke, and had endured enough of Lori Weisberg's social niceties in his short stay on Manhattan Island. But once his agents discovered that several of Manhattan's best and brightest had been usurped, it was the most public forum to unveil his Uploaded detector and prove to the world that he was in control. And the best part was that that gossipmonger Bryony would vlogcast the entire unmasking to her mindless followers.

But as an awkward teenager scurried past him, causing him to knock half of his champagne down his front, he saw the last person he expected to see at this event.

Jonah Delacroix.

He reached for his datapad and tapped in a message to the night watch of the Western Corner, his secret server farm beneath the Manhattan streets.

Go to full alert status. Attack may be imminent.

Then he turned to Erel Dias.

'It's time to scan this crowd.'

32

Jonah and Sam clambered over a disused ticket barrier, and tiptoed down a motionless escalator. They could still faintly hear the music from the party above them, but this part of the old Grand Central Terminal was deserted. Fading signs pointed to the old subway platforms. Jonah and Sam descended the stairs, two at a time, only to be blocked by a newer-looking brick wall across the bottom of the steps.

Jonah ran his hands along it. 'There must be a way through,' he reasoned.

'If the Western Corner *is* somewhere down here,' said Sam. 'It must be in the subway tunnels, else why would anyone have built this wall at all?'

'To hide it,' guessed Jonah.

'That doesn't mean the entrance is here in Grand Central,' said Sam. 'It could be in any one of hundreds of subway stations across New York.'

'Or there could be many entrances,' said Jonah, 'so the Millennials can come and go as they please without being seen.'

Sam stood back, inspecting the obstacle in their path. 'If only I still had my rucksack,' she complained, 'with my tools and explosives.'

Jonah's questing hands had found something. At least, he thought they had. 'I think it's a seam,' he speculated.

If he hadn't been looking for something exactly like this, they would never have noticed it. Jonah and Sam looked at each other, then scrabbled at the seam with their fingertips.

Jonah's heart soared when he managed to pry three bricks from the wall. One by one, he and Sam pulled all the bricks down, covering them both in red-brick dust.

'So much for our new outfits,' said Jonah, wiping the dust from his face. His heart sank again when he saw what was behind the wall: a sturdy-looking metal door with a combination lock.

Sam was already searching her blue handbag. She pulled out a device that looked like a metal spider with a keypad on its back. Jonah looked at it, amazed, and Sam grinned. 'You didn't think I came completely unprepared, did you? I had a few things left in my overall pockets.'

She touched the metal spider to the door lock and it stuck. Jonah realised it must be magnetic. Sam tapped a few keys, then stepped back.

'It's an automated safecracker,' she said. 'Dad picked it up in Zurich this one time. It runs through about two hundred combinations per second, until it finds—'

The metal spider beeped twice and then Jonah heard

the heavy clunk of the door lock disengaging. Sam retrieved her safecracker, returned it to her bag, and pulled out a small but powerful torch. She pushed at the door and opened it to reveal only darkness beyond. She switched on the torch and looked back over her shoulder at Jonah.

'Are you ready?' she asked.

Granger looked at Dias and repeated, 'It's time to scan the crowd.'

'Mr Granger, this device has not been properly tested yet.' Erel Dias cradled the square contraction like a baby. Trailing from it by a black umbilical cord was a small, green torch-like device. Granger snatched this from Dias and inspected it. It looked simple enough to use: a 'scan' button and a readout screen.

'But it works?' Granger asked.

'There's no reason why it shouldn't,' said Dias. 'I cannibalised the back-up CAT scanner like you said. Of course, this handheld version is far less functional than the full-size machine, but it should serve your purpose.'

Granger pointed the device at Dias. He pressed the button. Nothing happened.

'It only has a short range,' said Dias, 'but I'm working on—'

Granger held up the device to the neuro-cyber-surgeon's temple. He pressed the button again, and this time the screen lit up with a single green brainwave pattern.

'If the screen shows *two* brainwave patterns,' began Dias, 'that would mean—'

'Yes, thank you, Erel. I had managed to work that out for myself.'

Eight of Granger's Millennials, clad in combat fatigues, moved into the room and took their positions around Granger and Dias. Granger held up the scanner to each of them in turn and pronounced them all clear.

Then he moved to the centre of the great room, yanking on the scanner's cord so that Dias had no choice but to scuttle awkwardly after him.

'It's time,' declared Granger, 'to show the world that Matthew Granger is going to be their saviour.'

After nearly an hour in the abandoned train tunnels below Grand Central, Jonah and Sam stopped to investigate another platform between two underground train lines. As Sam turned, the light of her torch played across dusty, once-white wall tiles. Other than that light, it was pitch-black down here. The dust was making Jonah's nose itch and he tried to contain a sneeze.

'Do you hear that?' whispered Sam.

'What?' asked Jonah.

'A sort of humming sound,' said Sam.

'Like computer equipment?' asked Jonah, hopefully.

'Maybe. I don't know. You don't hear it?'

Jonah stood still, listened. He thought there might have been a humming, but he couldn't be entirely sure. It might have been his imagination. He couldn't tell, in any case, which way it might have been coming from. Sam stepped up to the platform's edge, shone her torch along the left-hand line.

'I can't see anything,' she whispered. Nor could Jonah. Sam's torchlight was swallowed by the subway tunnel in each direction.

There were so many tunnels down here, it seemed. Jonah had begun to despair of ever finding the right one.

He stifled a sneeze and suddenly thought of something. 'Wait,' he said. 'No, Sam, stand still. Shine your torch on the floor down here. That's right.'

'What are you——?'

'You see that dust?'

'Yeah,' said Sam, 'I do. It's everywhere. But what...? Oh, I see.'

They had left footprints along the left-hand edge of the platform. There were no more ahead of them, though. The dust lay undisturbed there. They crossed the platform quickly and Sam shone the torch in front of them. Jonah grinned.

There were footprints in the dust on this side too – but Jonah and Sam hadn't stepped there. 'Someone's been this way,' announced Jonah, 'and recently too.'

Sam stood still and listened for a moment. Then she picked a direction and strode along the track purposefully. Jonah had no choice but to hurry after her or be left alone, lost in the dark.

The brick tunnel walls closed in around them as they passed the platform's end. It was freezing cold down here, and Jonah felt claustrophobic.

There was something ahead of them. A glint of light. Sam snapped off the torch and they stood in the absolute blackness, trying not to breathe too hard.

For a minute, nothing stirred. Sam took hold of Jonah's hand and they crept forward. Jonah's eyes had begun to adjust, just a little, and he could make out a monstrous shape almost filling the tunnel. He squeezed Sam's hand hard, bringing her to a halt. He pointed, although he wasn't sure if she could see him.

Another silent minute passed.

Not silent, Jonah realised. He *could* hear that humming sound, low but persistent. It seemed to fill the air around him, to come from everywhere and nowhere.

Sam turned on the torch again, making Jonah jump. She shone it at the looming shape and Jonah almost laughed with relief.

A train! It was an old subway train, plastered with graffiti, abandoned on the track. Sam's torchlight must have glinted off its window.

They squeezed past the train and reached a point where the tunnel split in two. Jonah stopped and listened closely. He pointed to the left-hand fork. They had only travelled a few metres along it when Sam's torch beam found a row of computer servers.

They stretched as far as Sam's light could reach, on a long, low wooden platform that had been constructed over the tracks. The servers stood with their backs to the left-hand tunnel wall, almost scraping its roof.

Jonah and Sam ran their hands over the cold metal surfaces as if to reassure themselves that the servers were real. Jonah looked at Sam and her eyes shone with excitement.

'We've found it,' she whispered.

The Western Corner!

'How far do you think these things go?' asked Jonah.

Sam shrugged. 'Remember how many floors there were inside the Southern Corner, in Uluru? Thousands of servers. I wouldn't be surprised if there's a whole network of tunnels filled with them here, right under the streets of Manhattan.'

'Right under their noses,' said Jonah. 'I wonder what Lori would say if she knew about—'

'Not her again,' scoffed Sam.

'Are you *jealous* of her, or—'

Sam clamped her hand around Jonah's mouth. 'Shut up and get down,' she whispered.

She flicked off her torch, but Jonah could still see light: a glaring white light, streaming out of the tunnel wall, growing bigger and brighter by the second. And he could hear footsteps and low voices.

Jonah grabbed Sam's arm, pulled her back along the

tracks. They paused at the tunnel fork and Jonah looked again. Two men stepped out of a gap in the tunnel wall, the mouth of a narrower service tunnel. Two men with guns.

One was holding up a halogen lamp, far more powerful than Sam's feeble solar-powered torch. It bathed the two men in a harsh spotlight and bleached the shadows around them, almost reaching to Jonah's feet.

Jonah held Sam's hand, and with the other he felt for the split in the tunnel, guided them around the corner and into the tunnel of the right-hand fork.

'—toldja it was only a drill,' one of the men was saying. 'The big Gee wants to keep us on our toes, especially after what happened down under.'

'I hope you're right,' said the other. 'But let's check down the line anyway.'

Jonah and Sam watched the two men from the darkness as they peered into the abandoned train and continued down the line.

'I think we've seen as much as we need to see,' she said.

Jonah nodded his agreement.

'Time to call the cavalry,' said Sam.

33

Jason thought it was odd that the orchestra stopped playing in mid-number. One by one, the party-goers in the Grand Central concourse fell silent and turned to see what had happened.

Jason had been cornered by a woman called Bryony – whom he recognised from the limo screen on the ride over. He was glad of the interruption to her prying questions about Luke Wexler's private life. Until he saw who was standing at the microphone.

'Madam President,' said Matthew Granger, 'fellow esteemed residents of Manhattan.'

Keep calm, Jason told himself. *Keep playing your part. As long as you can do that...*

'I apologise for this interruption to your celebrations,' said Granger. 'I assure you, I will only take a few minutes of your time.'

Jason slipped away from Bryony while her back was turned, heading for the nearest exit. *Time for this cowboy to hang up his spurs!* He stopped himself when he saw that the door was guarded by a man in black combat fatigues, holding a semi-automatic weapon. The man's left arm boasted a single-letter logo with an ever-watchful eye in the loop of the *M*. A Millennial.

'What is the meaning of this, Mr Granger?' A score of Secret Service men had moved to surround Lori Weisberg, but she pushed her way out from between them.

'Again, Madam President, I apologise,' said Granger. 'However, I have good reason to believe that one of your residents has been usurped by an Uploaded.'

That caused a stir. Now, everyone was looking at the person next to them.

'That's a serious accusation,' said Lori. 'Can you prove it?'

'I can do better than that, Madam President.' Granger smiled. He held up a green, torch-like device. It was tethered to a box-like contraption held by a man in a lab coat. The man had a long, mournful face. He held the box to his chest and looked nervous. Jason had seen this look a thousand times before among Granger's Millennials.

'With this device, I can scan each person here and find the dead in our midst.'

The crowd didn't know what to make of that. There were some protests about invasion of privacy, shouted down by others asking, 'What have you got to hide?' A few people looked to Jason for guidance – this was Lucky Luke's party, after all – but he didn't speak up for fear of drawing suspicion upon himself.

He was just glad that Jonah and Sam had got out when they had. But if Granger's device could do what he claimed...

Lori marched up to Granger, bodyguards in tow, and she waved them away as she squared up to Granger. 'Then you can start with me,' she announced.

'As you wish.' Granger smiled. He held his scanning device to Lori's temple, checked the screen and declared, 'You are who you appear to be.'

Lori nodded, took the microphone from Granger, addressed the crowd.

'My fellow residents,' she began. 'I know this is an intrusion to our celebrations, but my first duty as your president is to protect the residents of Manhattan...and your property value. Please remain calm and let Mr Granger scan everyone in the building.'

This caused a few disgruntled murmurs – but, now that Lori had shown a lead, most people were content to follow.

Granger moved into the crowd with Dias trailing along behind him. He held his scanner up to each party-goer in turn. Jason's eyes darted to the door again, but he knew he had missed his chance to make a break for it. If he tried now, he had no doubt that a hundred people would bring him down before he could take two steps.

A cold dread crept over him. Granger was coming closer, ever closer – and Jason could see no way of avoiding him. As soon as Granger scanned 'Luke Wexler's' brain patterns, he would know the truth. Jason would be exposed.

Jonah crouched near the top of the defunct escalator and called up to Sam, 'What's happening?'

When they emerged from the tunnels below, Sam had said she thought it was too quiet. She had crept ahead to the main concourse to take a look. She hurried back to Jonah now, looking worried.

She didn't speak until she had reached him. Then she whispered one word – a name – and Jonah's stomach sank. 'Granger!'

'He's in there now? What's he doing?'

'He's with the president,' whispered Sam. 'He had some kind of a machine. I couldn't see what it was. There were guards everywhere. I didn't dare get any closer.'

'What about my dad? Did you see my dad?'

Sam shook her head. 'Maybe he got out before—'

'He's in trouble,' said Jonah.

He started towards the concourse, but Sam dragged him back. 'You might be right,' she said, 'but we can't help him if he is. We can't let Granger see you, remember? If he does, and if someone connects us with Lucky Luke—'

'Yeah, OK,' said Jonah, frustrated but knowing that Sam was right.

'Jason can look after himself,' she said. 'We still have a job to do.'

There was a row of antiquated payphones by the

wall. Of course, if that was all they had been, they would have outlived their purpose years ago. The phones were actually public datapads, providing a rudimentary, non-Direct-Interface connection to the Metasphere.

Sam went up to the nearest of them and tapped in a string of numbers, followed by her message. The message she left was for Jez, with a copy going to Axel. It was succinct but complete, detailing everything that she and Jonah had found in the subway tunnels.

'Now come on,' said Sam. 'It's time we got out of here.'

'But—'

'For your dad's sake, Jonah. If he has been found out, it won't be long before they look for us too. We need to lie low until we can figure out what's happening. We can't help Jason if we're locked up in a jail cell with him.'

She was right, again.

They found a door that led from the station directly out onto the street. It was chained from this side, and padlocked. Of course, Sam had a bolt cutter in her handbag.

Jason's eyes widened as Granger's scanner let out an alarm ping.

Granger withdrew the scanner from the man's forehead and Jason stole a look at the terrified man, who was in thick, black glasses, heavyset and sweating. The Secret Service men drew their guns, marched forward.

They surrounded the man, whose three chins shook as he trembled, and seized him by the arms.

'There must be something wrong with your machine,' the man pleaded.

One of the Secret Service men pressed the man's thumb to the scanner and announced, 'Borzecki, Allan. Upper East Side. Resident for seven years, three months and twenty-two days.'

'I'm flesh and blood,' Borzecki continued to argue. 'I'm as alive as any of you!'

'Now, Mr Borzecki – or whoever you are in there – that's not exactly true, is it?' Granger smiled his predator's smile – and, just a couple of metres away from him, Jason shivered. He hadn't seen that smile in years.

'So…so what if I *am* Uploaded? I've done nothing wrong. I just want to live.'

Jason realised he had met this 'Mr Borzecki' only a few days ago at a dinner, and had no idea he was actually an Uploaded like him. Jason hoped his own disguise was as robust, but feared the inevitable moment when Granger placed that scanner to his head. He had to get out of here. Fortunately, Mr Borzecki's protests provided a useful distraction.

People were starting to move again, either backing away from the usurper in horror or craning closer for a better look at him. It meant that Jason was free to move too.

He moved to the door, his hand to his head, feigning

a headache. As expected, an armed Millennial stepped into his way.

'Look, pardner,' he said, 'you know me. Everyone in this room knows me. I'm Lucky Luke and this here's *my* shindig.' He touched the brim of his cowboy hat, shone Luke Wexler's dazzling grin upon the guard. He knew it wasn't going to work. He had only one hope. If he could take the guard by surprise, hit him hard enough to stagger him, be through that door before anyone else could react...

'Going somewhere, Lucky?'

Jason stifled a groan, unclenched his readied fist, and turned to find Granger behind him, scanner in hand. The entire concourse fell silent.

'Heyyyy,' said Jason, elongating the word to give him time to think, to access Lucky Luke's memories, '*Matty*. Have a word with your gorilla here, won't you? You've found your infiltrator now, so why keep the rest of us corralled like cattle? I can't speak for the rest of these fine folk, but it's been a long night and I'm ready to hit the trail.'

'I understand, Luke,' said Granger. 'And, of course, you may leave.'

Jason couldn't believe his luck. He tried not to show how surprised and relieved he was. 'Then I'll be moseying—'

'As soon as you have been scanned,' said Granger.

Jason opened his mouth, but there was nothing

more he could say. He looked guilty enough already, and Millennials and Secret Service men were closing in around him.

He sighed, held up his hands, let Granger approach him and hold the scanner to his temple. For a second, Jason harboured the hope that the device might not work, might not be completely reliable.

Then, the scanner pinged urgently, and a gasp went up from the onlookers. The game was up.

Jason met Granger's gaze defiantly: it was all he could do. Granger turned the scanner around, showed Jason the readout screen on its back with its two brainwave patterns, one red, one green. He smiled his predator's smile, leaned in closer to Jason and whispered in his ear, *'Gotcha!'*

34

If there was one thing Axel hated, it was waiting around.

He paced the garage forecourt, just to exercise his muscles and burn off some nervous energy. Sam had been in touch earlier in the morning, to say that everything was going well and that the Guardians should be ready to move tonight.

Her message, Jez had noted sourly, had been suspiciously short on detail.

Still, the Guardians had greeted the news with a refreshed sense of optimism and a flurry of preparation. Both had worn off as the minutes ticked by like hours.

Jez was leaning against the side of the car wash, smoking.

Axel leaned against the wall beside him. 'For what it's worth,' he said, 'I think you're doing a good job with them.' Jez shot him a suspicious look.

'I mean it,' said Axel. 'You got a hundred and fifty people here, for a start. They took the Southern Corner with less than half that number.' He had wanted to say we, instead of they. Axel felt like he'd let everyone down back then by his sudden disconnection from the Metasphere, which had put him into a comatose state and caused him to miss the fight.

'Maybe,' said Jez, gruffly, 'but that was two months ago. The Millennials have had time to bring in reinforcements of their own.'

Axel sighed. 'I know that, Jez.'

'Don't kid yourself, Kavanaugh. This will be no easy victory.'

'But we *can* win, Jez. We did it once before. What's wrong with you? I thought you wanted this fight. I thought you were the great Millennial-hunter!'

Jez flicked away his cigarette butt and squared up to Axel, angrily. 'You just watch me, Kavanaugh. You just point me towards those sons of slugs and see what I do. We might capture the Western Corner tonight, we might not – but either way, Granger and all his little suck-ups are gonna know I was here!'

Axel grinned and nodded approvingly. He had taken an instant dislike to Jez, but over the past few days, he'd come to admire his dedication and focus, even if it did come with an unhelpful dose of surliness and pessimism. Axel had heard that the Guardians' struggle was personal for Jez, as it was for a lot of the Guardians. Jez blamed the Millennials for the death of someone very dear to him.

A cheer went up from inside the garage.

'Kavanaugh,' called a female voice from inside. 'Your little girl's on the datapad!'

Axel and Jez looked at each other, then turned as one and ran for the doors. They were met halfway by Jez's girlfriend Liv, a pixie-thin woman covered in tattoos. She was holding up Axel's datapad with an encrypted message from Sam blinking on the screen.

Axel grabbed it and pressed his thumb to the smart-glass screen, and the pop-up message appeared:

W CORNER IN SUBWAY TUNNELS UNDERNEATH CITY. FOUND SERVERS BETWEEN 42ND STREET AND 39TH. MILLENNIALS ARMED & ON GUARD. B CAREFUL.

'Listen up, people,' he called. 'The location of the Western Corner – it isn't in Manhattan, after all.'

The group let out a collective, incredulous groan. Jez stared at Axel with an incredulous look, his eyes hardening with disappointment and betrayal.

Axel smiled and boomed, 'It's *underneath* it!'

Breaking into the nearest train station was no problem.

A tiny amount of plastique blew the gate right off its hinges. Nor did the bang bring anyone running. *Why would it?* thought Axel. *The night was filled with gunfire and booms.*

The Guardians followed Jez along the train tracks. This far out of the old New York City centre, they ran above ground, alongside the roads, and Axel fretted about being seen by the dangerous Queens nightlife.

He was relieved when the subway system began to live up to its name, at last.

The tracks of the disused number-seven subway plunged into a long, dark tunnel, and the Guardians got out their torches. Axel drew his pistol, alert for any sign that they weren't alone down here. Several times, he heard a scuffle or a squeak and found himself taking aim at a rat or a cockroach or a bat. The vermin had become used to having these tunnels to themselves, and they didn't seem at all pleased at this invasion of their territory.

Jez had downloaded an old subway plan to his datapad, and he negotiated his way around the system confidently, leading the Guardians in the dark, through the tunnels under the East River. In a couple of minutes more, they would be underneath Manhattan Island.

Once they'd reached the underbelly of the city, they were as cautious and as quiet as they could be. They turned off all but three torches, and fanned out as widely as they could in their cramped confines. They snuck along the train tunnels six abreast, and Jez sent scouts along the narrower maintenance tunnels than ran between them.

They came to a tall barricade of wood and barbed wire, and Axel crept ahead of the others to check that it wasn't manned.

It wasn't, so Jez detailed six Guardians to take the barrier apart. They began to do so slowly, carefully, mindful that any noise would carry a long way down here. Fidgety with impatience, Axel checked his pistol for the seventh time and let his eyes rove up and down the tunnel.

Something caught his eye, and made him catch his breath. He grabbed the arm of one of the torchbearers, directed his beam upwards. Axel cursed.

'They're watching us,' he said.

The camera was small, peeking out from behind a busted signal light. Axel had only noticed it because a torch beam had glanced off its lens.

It was probably infrared.

Axel caught Jez's eye and signalled to him, clasping his hands together and then fanning them apart. Jez nodded and pulled the Guardians away from the barrier while Axel called up a young woman named Janz, whom he knew was carrying explosives.

There was no point in sneaking any more.

Jonah was cold, tired and cramped.

He was crouching, with Sam, behind a bush just inside Central Park. They had been here for hours, watching Lucky Luke's apartment building. To begin with, they had hoped Jason would come back here. But there had been no sign of him at the entrance doors, and Luke's windows had been dark all night. Jonah didn't know what they were still waiting for.

But now, as a pre-dawn glow lit the sky to the east, he got his answer.

Four white vehicles sped up to the apartment building

from different directions. They had blue stripes down their sides, flashing lights on their roofs.

The vehicles braked and their doors flew open. Four blue-uniformed cops leapt out of each of them. They drew their guns, and one of them swiped a plastic card through the building's security keypad.

'That settles it,' said Sam, as the cops poured into the apartment building. 'They know.'

'They're looking for Dad,' said Jonah.

'Maybe,' said Sam, 'but I doubt it. I think it's more likely they have Jason already – and now they're looking for us!'

'What do you think they'll do with him?'

'If we're lucky,' said Sam, 'they'll lock him up for the rest of his life.'

'And if we aren't?'

'Luke pays a lot of money in co-op fees here,' said Sam. 'They're going to want him back. That means… Somehow, that means they have to expel the Uploaded presence from his brain. Jason's presence. And the only person who might know how to do that is—'

'Granger,' said Jonah, feeling sick. 'They'll give him to Granger!'

'Downtown,' said Sam. 'Your dad said that Granger's base of operations is in the Freedom Tower. That's where he'll be.'

'Then that's where we're going,' said Jonah.

*

312

The explosion made Axel wince.

He had stood well back and plugged his ears, but the noise echoed off the tunnel walls and almost deafened him. He was blinded too, by a thick cloud of smoke. He heard the other Guardians spluttering behind him.

Axel raced forward, anyway. He knew that every second counted. With his long legs, he even outpaced the eager Jez. He vaulted the smouldering remains of the Millennials' barricade. Their explosives expert had done her job well, using just enough to clear the obstacle from their path without bringing down the roof.

Jez had found his voice and was bellowing out orders: 'Come on, forward! No loitering back there. We've lost the element of surprise, so our best tactic is to hit this place hard and hit it fast. I want us spread out across these tunnels. You see anyone you don't know, you shoot first and don't bother with questions. And remember, we're looking for the control centre, that's the prize here. Move it! Remember why we all volunteered to do this. For the Guardians! For freedom!'

Axel's vision had begun to clear. He found a maintenance tunnel and hurried along it, six or seven other Guardians following close behind him.

They emerged onto another set of tracks. In the light of torch beams from behind him, Axel saw computer servers. Elated, he raced for them, and almost into a barrage of gunfire from somewhere ahead of him.

Bullets pinged off the server casings, striking bright sparks off them in the darkness.

The Guardians ducked, scattered, pressed themselves against the tunnel walls. Axel squeezed his wiry body into the recess of a blocked doorway. He found his enemies by their muzzle flashes; they were crouching among the servers.

He poked his pistol around the edge of the doorway and loosed off six shots. 'Cover me,' he whispered to the Guardian opposite him, and then he quickly looked around the edge, noting that he'd downed two Millennials, but three others stood with guns ready. He fired three precision shots and felled the three remaining Millennials.

He wasn't about to shy away from this fight.

35

Jason sat on the floor of a tiny cleaner's cupboard, handcuffed to a shelving rack.

He had been left here for hours, in the dark. His left wrist was raw from his attempts to work it free. He knew he was in the famous Freedom Tower. He had been brought here by three Millennials in a yellow auto-cab.

The president had wanted Jason in police custody, but Granger insisted otherwise. Only he had the equipment and the expertise, he had claimed, to deal with the Uploaded interloper inhabiting Luke Wexler's brain.

As the Millennials cuffed him, President Weisberg marched up to Jason and looked into Luke's eyes.

'I don't know who you are in there,' she'd said, 'but you're squatting in the body of a certified Manhattan resident and I'm serving you with an eviction notice.'

Granger had also suggested – within earshot of Jason – that the police find Luke's 'nephew and niece'. He had confirmed from Lori's descriptions of them that they were known terrorists.

Jonah was in trouble, and there was nothing Jason could do to help him.

*

Jonah and Sam ran across a construction site in west mid-town, scrambled over a wall and huddled down behind it. They heard the whine of an electric car passing behind them. Two dogs were barking loudly, not very far away.

'It's no use,' hissed Sam. 'We'll never make it all the way downtown.'

'We have to,' insisted Jonah.

'It's light already,' said Sam. 'There'll be people on the streets soon – other than the police, I mean – and we stand out like a pair of sore thumbs in these stupid clothes.'

'It's not much further now,' said Jonah.

'If we could message Dad and Jez and the other Guardians—'

'We don't have time to wait for them. That's even if they…' Jonah had almost said, *even if they're still alive*. He didn't want to think about what might be happening underground right now.

'What if Granger's found out who Dad is?' he said, scoping his surroundings. 'I mean, who he *really*—'

Sam grabbed him, pulled him back down. They could both hear a new sound: the thrum of rotor blades. They cowered and covered their heads as the shadow of a helicopter flitted over them.

'We must have been seen by someone,' said Sam, 'or caught on a security camera. They know which area of the city to search for us.'

'All the more reason,' said Jonah, 'to keep moving before they can pen us in.'

Sam sighed, but nodded. She took off a shoe and inspected the high heel. Jonah saw that it had broken, probably as she had come over the wall. Sam tore the heel from her other shoe too, to make them even.

'Come on,' called Jonah. He led her through a narrow gap between two buildings and they emerged into a dingy alley and kept running.

Underground, the Guardians were making progress. At least, Axel thought they were. The Millennials might have been expecting an attack, but they appeared to be surprised by its scale, its speed and its sheer ferocity.

Jez led from the front and fought more violently than anyone. Axel caught up with him when a Millennial dropped his gun and raised his hands, but he was too late to stop his assassination. Jez shot the unarmed Millennial in the head and stepped over his slumped body.

'Jez!' Axel shouted. 'We don't slaughter surrendering combatants. We take prisoners.'

'Like they'd show you any mercy,' hissed Jez as he charged forth through the tunnel.

The Guardians pushed forward, splitting their forces at every tunnel fork or junction, and Axel lost track of Jez in the darkness. Axel rounded up a few followers of his own and advanced along a tunnel lit by dull blue lamps – another sign, he hoped, that they were nearing their objective.

A bullet whistled past Axel's ear before he had even heard the gunshot. It struck and killed the Guardian behind him. Axel didn't know which way to jump for cover, so he flattened himself on the train tracks and yelled, 'Get down!'

More bullets zinged over his head, ricocheting off the walls. Axel saw shifting shadows ahead, and realised that the tunnel wall opened out onto a subway platform.

The Millennials had set an ambush, and had the Guardians pinned down.

Jason winced as the bright light from the corridor flooded into the dark cupboard where he was chained up. Two Millennials, silhouetted against the harsh light, stood at the door and uncuffed him. They hauled him outside into the light, where Granger was waiting with two more armed guards.

Jason didn't say anything; he didn't want to give Granger anything he could use.

Granger turned, beckoned to his Millennials to follow him and strode away. The Millennials dragged Jason along in their leader's wake, into a gleaming, antiseptic-smelling room filled with medical equipment and computer servers. In the centre of the room was a large white CAT scanner, with a figure bound to its sliding table.

Jason recognised the portly figure as Mr Borzecki. He was lying on his back, his eyes closed, perfectly still.

While two of the Millennials held Jason, the other two unstrapped Borzecki. They struggled with his heavy body but picked him up and cast him to one side like a sack of rubbish. He was dead.

Jason started struggling, but it was no use. The guards hoisted him onto the CAT-scanner tray and fastened heavy leather straps around his wrists and ankles, cutting into his flesh. Another man in a white lab coat jammed an Ethernet cable into his back and snapped it into place.

'What are you doing?' Jason finally asked.

'The extraction process needs refinement,' Granger said. 'But we are experimenting and learning with each attempt. Who knows, Wexler might live up to his moniker. You might be the *lucky* ones. You might be the first to survive the procedure.'

Jason struggled with all of his strength but it was in vain. The last thing he heard before losing all of his senses was Granger commanding one of his staff to 'execute'.

Jonah led Sam down thirty blocks of Manhattan grid. It was early morning, between night and dawn, and the streets were just starting to wake up. Jonah was tired and filthy, but if Granger had his dad, he wasn't going to give up. They wove their way through SoHo, catching sight of the Freedom Tower. Then they huddled in the last remnants of darkness in St Paul's Churchyard, at the corner of Fulton and Church, just two blocks east of the Freedom Tower.

Jonah heard police sirens and two police vans circled the block. The dragnet was tightening around them. A helicopter buzzed overhead.

'They must've guessed we were coming here,' said Sam. 'They were waiting for us.' Jonah knew she was right. She was always right. He didn't want to accept it, though, because he knew what that would mean.

He hesitated for a moment as Sam set off towards the south, the only way that looked clear. That moment cost them both dearly.

Sam stopped, turned back for Jonah. In the moment that she did, a police patrol with dogs appeared around the corner of Church and Dey, one block south.

'Stop and surrender!' they called.

Jonah almost did. But Sam was already running, so he ran after her instead. The cops didn't shoot as he had feared they would, but they unleashed the dogs. They barked and slavered as they closed on Jonah's heels.

'Split up,' cried Sam. 'Then at least one of us might stand a chance!' It made sense.

As Sam turned north along Church, Jonah jumped back into St Paul's Churchyard, rushed north-east through the park and sprinted across Broadway for the adjacent City Hall Park.

But police dogs came around and cut him off. One of them leapt at him, caught his sleeve between its teeth. Jonah flung it off desperately and doubled back, into the arms of two waiting cops. They wrestled Jonah to the pavement, cuffed his wrists behind his back and held him down until he accepted that there was no point in resisting.

The cops marched Jonah back to Church Street, their dogs snarling at his feet. They met Sam, being hauled along Barclay Street; she was handcuffed too. She looked at Jonah with sorry eyes.

They had come so far, so close, only for it to end like this. They had no hope of saving Jason now. They would be lucky if they could save themselves.

Face down between the train tracks, Axel fumbled in his overalls for the pineapple-shaped grenade. He pulled the pin and lobbed it over his head.

He didn't have the right angle to get the grenade onto the subway platform, but it landed close enough.

The Millennial snipers on the platform leapt for cover as the grenade exploded. Axel scrambled to his feet and led the charge forward through the smoke.

The Millennials regrouped and picked off two more of Axel's Guardians as they climbed up onto the platform. Two of them leapt on Axel. The first took a chokehold on him from behind, while the other snatched the pistol from his hand.

Axel threw himself backwards and crushed the Millennial behind him against the wall. The hold on his throat weakened. A backwards jab from Axel's sharp elbow found soft tissue and finished the job. Axel pushed the limp man at the second Millennial, who was pointing Axel's gun, and grabbed it as the man struggled under the weight of his fallen comrade.

Axel aimed his gun at the second Millennial, a scrawny, middle-aged man with glasses, probably one of the server farm's tech guys rather than a paramilitary, and remembered how Jez had executed the surrendering Millennial in cold blood. Axel grabbed the man's head and slammed it into the tunnel wall, knocking him out. 'I'm doing you a favour,' he said.

The fighting had spread across the platform and Axel looked for a target. He found a trembling, stocky Millennial kid, crouching behind a pillar, facing away from Axel, firing wildly into the melee and not caring who he hit. Axel shot him in the shoulder, neutralising him without killing him.

Out of the corner of his eye, Axel spotted several Millennials panicking and retreating, running back through the tunnels in search of a way out. Axel let them go. His immediate concern was the four armed Millennials who had dropped down onto the tracks.

He called attention to them with a shout, and fired after them. One of the runners fell with a bullet, but the other three escaped into the tunnel, firing over their shoulders.

A single train carriage sat on the track beside a server row, leaving only squeezing space between them. Axel ran up and fired into that space. But it was too late. The Millennials had made it to the back of the carriage, a perfect sniping spot.

He cursed under his breath. From there, they could keep the Guardians at bay for as long as their ammunition held out. Not if Axel could help it!

He stood on the footplate at the front of the carriage, found a handhold, and hauled himself the rest of the way up. There was precious little clearance between carriage and tunnel roof, and he had to lie flat and pull himself along on his elbows and knees. If the Millennials heard him, or guessed what he was doing, if they came up here and saw him, they would have him dead for sure.

But the Guardians and the Millennials were exchanging frantic gunfire around the train carriage's sides.

Axel reached the far end of the carriage roof, peered over its edge. Two Millennials were at one corner of the carriage, one at the other. He tucked his pistol into his waistband, swung himself around and leapt onto the two. His boots struck one of them in the head, the other in the back, sending both of them flying.

He landed between them, flooring one of them completely with a two-fisted punch to his jaw. The second Millennial dropped her gun, and Axel kicked it underneath the train carriage. He wrestled with her: a lithe young woman a head shorter than he was but far stronger than she looked. It was almost all he could do to keep a grip on her, keep the pair of them upright so that the Millennial was between Axel and the still-armed third sniper, a human shield for him.

At last, he managed to slip his foot between hers, to sweep her right leg out from under her. He slammed her head into the back of the train carriage, so hard that the tiny window in its door cracked. With his enemy dazed, Axel got his hands behind her head and pulled her chin down to meet his rising knee. The woman crumpled at his feet, but he knew she had fought well, delaying him for longer than he could afford.

The third Millennial had backed up along the tracks and had Axel in his gun sights. Axel felt for his own pistol, but knew there wasn't time to pull it.

A shot rang out.

The last Millennial stiffened and fell. Axel blinked. He couldn't understand why he wasn't dead.

A man stepped out from behind a server cabinet. He had dark hair and a long, mournful face, and wore a filthy lab coat. He was holding a gun on the fallen Millennial – the dead Millennial – as if afraid he might suddenly rise again. The newcomer's hands were shaking and his forehead was shiny with sweat. He wasn't looking at Axel at all. Axel took the opportunity to ease his own pistol out of his waistband. Just in case.

'Who are you?' he demanded, grabbing the startled man's gun.

The man looked up at him, swallowed. 'M-my name is Doctor Erel Dias,' he stammered.

'You're a Millennial?'

'Not any more,' he said. 'I used to work for Matthew Granger, but I... I've had enough. I just want out. Please let me go.'

Granger dismissed his Millennials from the medical room. With his subject strapped down, he didn't need them any more. The Uploaded in control of Wexler's body was still struggling with his bonds, but Granger ignored him. He wouldn't be struggling for much longer.

Granger yawned as he rewrote line after line of programming code. He had been up all night. He wondered where Erel Dias had got to. He should have been here to relieve him by now. Perhaps it was as well, though. Dias was brilliant in his field, but he lacked Granger's determination, his tenacity. Granger had learned long ago that if he wanted something done right, he needed to do it himself.

He was about to run the extraction program on his former employee when he glanced up at a monitor.

It displayed two distinct avatars, the two that had been identified inside his subject's brain. The first was Lucky Luke's own avatar, the black-clad cowboy. The second...

The second avatar was a red dragon with three horns along the flat of its snout.

His jaw dropped open at the sight of that dragon. He took his finger off the 'execute' key.

He whirled around, stared at the man on the CAT scanner table. The man in Luke Wexler's body. 'You,' he breathed.

He looked at the red dragon on the monitor again. There was no mistake.

'I watched you die.'

36

Axel raised his pistol. He pointed it at the man who had called himself Erel Dias.

'And why should I let you go?' he growled.

Dias looked down at the body of the man he'd just killed and then raised his hands, looking at Axel and trembling. 'I saved your life.'

Another Guardian had appeared around the train carriage, behind Axel. It was Liv. She saw Dias, and raised her gun too. Axel placed his hand on Liv's tattooed arm, pushed it down. 'No,' he said.

'You heard what Jez said, Kavanaugh. Anyone we don't know, we—'

'I'm making an exception here.'

Dias continued to hold both hands in the air.

'What are you doing down here?' Axel asked.

'Trying to escape,' said Dias. 'I invented a machine, and…an extraction process. Mr Granger is using it to murder innocent people.'

'He's a Millennial,' snapped Liv. 'We kill him now.'

'No,' said Axel, and then turned his attention back to Dias. 'What is this *extraction* process?'

'It removes the Uploaded from a host brain.'

'And the machine?'

'It detects the brainwave patterns of the Uploaded. It identifies the parasite.'

Axel didn't like where this was going. 'Have you used it yet?'

'Yes,' admitted Dias. 'That's why I'm leaving. Granger identified two Uploaded at the party—'

'Who?'

'A Mr Borzecki and Mr Wexler.'

'Jason,' whispered Axel.

'Granger is going to extract the Uploaded from them.'

'Who else knows about this?'

'I sent a message to the president. I explained everything. Then I tried to make it out through the tunnels, but you had people everywhere. I couldn't see a way...'

Axel lowered his pistol, extended his hand toward Dias. 'I'll help you. If you help us,' he added.

'How can I...? What...what could you want from me?'

'First, where's the control room? Second, where is Luke Wexler?'

Dias nodded. 'I'll take you to the control room, but as for Mr Wexler, he'll be in my lab, in the Freedom Tower. But I fear—'

'What?'

'He'll already be dead.'

Jonah and Sam were taken to a police car, met by the

same moustached sergeant who had welcomed them to Manhattan only two days ago. He wasn't smiling this time. Sam was pushed down into the car's back seat. Before Jonah could join her there, he heard a voice calling out, 'Wait! Sergeant, wait!'

Lori Weisberg was striding along the pavement, outstripping her black-clad Secret Service escorts.

'Lori,' Jonah greeted her, as the president reached him.

Lori slapped his face, so hard that the cops holding him winced in sympathy.

'I trusted you,' she said, 'and you lied to me. About everything.'

'I… I'm sorry,' mumbled Jonah. 'I…'

'What was the plan, Jonah? Or is that even your name? You try to get close to me, then you kill me like they killed my mom?'

'No! I would never—'

'You deny it, then? You aren't a Guardian spy?'

'No. I mean, yes. Yes, I am a Guardian.' It was the first time Jonah had said it out loud, the first time he had admitted it to himself. 'But, Lori—'

She had turned her back. Jonah strained after her but was held fast. 'Granger has my dad,' he shouted after her. 'Please, Lori. You can do what you like with me, lock me up for the rest of my life, but you know what it's like to lose a parent.'

Lori came to a halt, her shoulders stiff. She wasn't

looking at Jonah, but he could tell she was listening to him.

'I told you about my mum,' he said. 'Well, it was Granger who killed her. He was trying to get to me, but she... Please, Lori. Please don't let him kill my dad too.'

Lori's bodyguards closed in, tried to whisk her away. She brushed them off, turned back to Jonah. 'How can I believe a word you say?' she demanded. 'You're a terrorist!'

'Not a terrorist,' he said. 'I'm a Guardian. They – *we* – only want for people to be free. I thought you'd understand that. It's what your mum died for, isn't it?' Jonah thought, for a second, that Lori might slap him again.

Instead, she said, 'I received a very long and detailed message this morning. From a doctor called Erel Dias. Do you know him?'

Jonah shook his head.

'He works for Granger,' said Lori. 'Worked for him, I should say. Some of the things he told me, I can hardly... A server farm in the subway tunnels?'

'It's there,' said Jonah. 'I've seen it. It's what...' He glanced at Sam, in the back of the police car. She gave him an encouraging nod. 'It's what we came here for, to liberate it from Granger. The Guardians have no quarrel with you or with Manhattan. This was always about that server farm...about the freedom of the Metasphere.'

Lori nodded. 'Your father... He's Uploaded?'

'Yes,' confessed Jonah, 'he usurped Luke's body, but—'

'I think you're right,' said Lori. 'According to Dias's message, Granger will try to extract your father from Luke's brain and—' She stopped herself.

'What?' asked Jonah.

'The process will kill him,' said Lori. 'Again. It'll kill them both.'

'We have to stop Granger,' said Jonah.

'I'm sworn to protect every resident of Manhattan and we've moved on the Freedom Tower—'

'That's why you're here!' exclaimed Sam from the police car. Lori looked at her as if she hadn't noticed her before. Sam struggled out of the car, her wrists still cuffed behind her. Two cops moved to stop her, but Lori waved them away. 'You didn't come to set an ambush for us,' said Sam. 'You came for Granger?'

'To stop him,' said Lori. 'But Granger's militia have taken over the tower. When we tried to enter the building, we...' She paused. 'We lost a lot of good people.' She turned back to Jonah. 'I don't know how convinced I should be by your story, um...'

'Jonah. It's my real name, honestly. Jonah Delacroix.'

'Stopping Granger is the most important thing right now. The question is, how? The Freedom Tower is heavily fortified at ground level. We can't just walk in the front door. We'll be sitting ducks.'

Jonah looked up at the immense glass and steel tower

and remembered the last time he desperately needed to get into a skyscraper.

'We're not going to walk in,' he declared. 'We're going to fly.'

From his prone position, all Jason Delacroix could see was the blue-tinted ceiling of Granger's medical bay. But he could hear his captor tapping away at a datapad and each tap filled him with fear.

'I know I shouldn't be surprised, or disappointed,' said Granger, finally breaking the silence. 'I deduced some time ago that you were a traitor.'

Jason heard the bitterness in his voice. 'To be a traitor implies I was ever loyal.'

'You know, I actually believed we were friends,' lamented Granger. 'The hours we spent on the flight deck, talking about our families and our dreams at thirty-five thousand feet...'

'We were never friends,' said Jason.

'I know that now. You were brainwashed by the Guardians before we ever met.'

'Not brainwashed, enlightened.'

'You enjoyed working for me, though. Don't try to deny it. You were the best pilot I ever had. You saved our skins more than once.'

'I saved my own,' said Jason. 'You just happened to be in the plane.'

'Could you have played your part so perfectly if your

heart wasn't at least partly in it?'

'There may have been a time,' conceded Jason.

'When you had your doubts? When you realised that the Guardians lied about me?'

'No,' said Jason. 'There may have been a time when I thought you could change.'

'You knew me, Jason, like few people have ever known me. You know that I have a vision, a vision for—'

'—a better world,' said Jason, completing Granger's sentence. 'I know your sound bites. And I actually think... I believe you mean them. I believe you set out with the best of intentions, but somewhere along the way something—'

'Nothing has changed,' insisted Granger.

'Everything's changed,' said Jason. 'The power you've amassed has blurred your vision. Your dream of the Metasphere was inspiring. So inspiring that my boy Jonah believed in you. Do you know how hard it was for me to pretend to support his hero, when I saw up close the monster you were becoming?'

'He's a smart kid, that Jonah,' said Granger. 'And he'll join my cause because he's smart.'

'He'll never,' protested Jason.

'It's just a shame you won't be around to see it,' concluded Granger.

Jason thrashed Luke's body and screamed at Granger. But he was screaming into silence.

It was a long time before Granger spoke again, and

when he did his voice was cold. 'I was wrong,' he said. 'You are not Jason Delacroix. He was killed three years ago by a Guardian bomb. You are merely a digital echo of that man, a superfluous data file that should have been recycled long ago.'

Jason heard an ominous clunk behind him: Granger's modified CAT scanner, his brainwave-extraction device. The table on which he lay began to move, juddering as it retracted, sucking Jason into the machine's round, white maw.

Jason was fully inside the white tube now. He remembered back to the Uploading Centre where his took his mother, watched her slide into a similar scanner for her memories to be transferred to the Island of the Uploaded. She died in a tube like this, but her memories lived on.

As Granger started up the machine, and a loud hum pulsed in the tube, Jason realised that he really was going to die here. There would be nothing left of him. No digital memories. Not even his own empty body.

37

Jason awoke in an empty white room.

He was in the form of his avatar, the red dragon. The room was small, and his great wings almost touched the white walls. There were no doors, no windows, and no exit halo.

He didn't know how long he had been here. Great chunks of Jason's memories were drifting away from him. He wasn't sure what he had been thinking about a second ago. He was confused.

How did I get here?

He let out an anguished cry. He thrashed about, tried to break down the confining walls. He concentrated on what he could remember, tried to hold himself together.

It was no use. Jason's mind, his very self, was being ripped apart.

Jonah stood between the struts of a water tower on the rooftop of 140 West Street, facing the vertical façade of the Freedom Tower immediately to the south. Sam was here too, as was Lori, much against the advice of her Secret Service bodyguards. Once the president had decided upon a course of action, she had wasted no time in following it through.

Jonah had explained his plan and the equipment he needed was quick to materialise; the Secret Service men were reduced to fetching and carrying. Two of them lugged a huge drum of steel cable across the roof and set it down beside a pair of canvas bags and a toolbox. Another of them came bearing a harpoon gun.

'Let me see that thing,' said Sam and she inspected the nasty-looking, slender weapon and shook her head. 'Jonah, there's going to be an awful lot of torque on this.' She paid out a little cable from the drum and lashed it to a notched harpoon.

'Then you'd better hold tight,' said Jonah. He stepped to the edge of the roof and sighted across the street.

They were thirty-two storeys up, but still the Freedom Tower dwarfed them, three times that height, its glass cladding dazzling in the morning sunlight. Hoisting the harpoon gun under his arm, Jonah's toe touched the low lip of the roof, the only thing between him and a sheer drop.

'Is he always this brave?' asked Lori.

Jonah tried to stay focused, but heard Sam say, only half jokingly, 'Brave and stupid.'

But just then he felt Sam's arms wrap around his waist, holding him steady.

'And stupid?' Jonah asked.

'Mostly brave,' whispered Sam. She held him tight and Jonah fired the harpoon. He felt the kick of it through his shoulder, but he stood firm, kept his aim steady.

The harpoon streaked towards the tower, unravelling cable in its wake. Its arrowhead smashed through the glass side of the building several storeys down, and snagged on a window ledge the first time. Jonah tugged hard on the cable and Sam double-checked its tautness.

Finally Jonah turned around. Lori nodded her head, impressed. Even the Secret Service men looked impressed. None of them had volunteered to zip-line across. One of them cut the cable, and they helped Sam secure its end to the water tower. Next, Jonah attached a pulley system to the cable, with two dangling rope loops.

'I'll go first,' Sam offered.

'Brave or stupid?' Jonah teased.

'Both,' said Sam.

She pushed her hands through the rope loops, tightened them around her wrists. She stepped up onto the lip of the roof and pushed herself off.

Sam dropped down over the roof's edge, and Jonah's heart skipped. She was at the mercy of gravity now, that cruellest of real-world forces. She was doing it, though, riding their improvised zip-line across the street to the Freedom Tower's broken window. Her momentum ran out a metre short of her destination, and Sam had to haul herself along the cable, stretch for the window ledge, pull herself up over it.

Jonah let out the breath he had been holding as Sam

disappeared into the tower. Two Secret Service men were already tugging on a length of rope, drawing the pulley back along the steel cable towards them.

Lori turned to Jonah. 'I'm putting my trust in you,' she said, 'and God only knows why. Call it instinct if you like. Just don't let me down again.'

'I won't,' he promised. 'Wish me luck.'

Lori pulled Jonah close and kissed him on the lips. Jonah had never been kissed by anyone other than family before, and this was completely different; her lips were soft, and salty, and then gone. She pulled away, resumed her composure of authority and said, 'Luck.' Jonah was shocked. 'Go get him.'

Jonah looked across to the Freedom Tower to check if Sam had seen the kiss. He couldn't tell. *Not that it should matter*, he told himself.

The pulley had returned to this end of the cable, and Jonah fastened the rope loops around his hands. It was his turn to see if he was brave or stupid. Or both.

Deep underground, the battle was almost all over.

Most of the Millennials were unconscious, dead, handcuffed or had fled. They were vastly outnumbered by the Guardians now, and had regrouped to defend a single short stretch of subway tunnel, the one that housed their control centre.

Axel could see it, the silver subway car, covered in graffiti, that housed the controlling computers – the heart of the Western Corner.

Axel was crouched between two server towers, squeezing off the last of his bullets along the train tracks. There were Guardians at the other end of the tunnel too, pinning their enemies down. Axel could smell victory. But it hadn't come without a cost.

As Axel scaled the subway car and surveyed the computers, all intact, a Guardian operative told him that Jez was down and being looked after on a station platform. He didn't know how bad it was, or whether Jez would survive. He hadn't been the only casualty, but was one of the lucky ones to be among the walking wounded.

In Jez's absence, the surviving Guardians appeared to be looking to Axel – the eldest and most outspoken of them – to lead. He felt the burden of it. Leadership was something he never sought, but he wouldn't shy away from his responsibility.

'Secure this tunnel from both sides,' he ordered. 'And get technicians in here pronto. I want full access to this quarter in half an hour. We're halfway to freedom, people!'

The world was about to change forever – tipping the balance of power to the Guardians, and Axel was standing at the precipice. His embattled Guardians hurried around him, clearing any bodies and tending to their own wounds. No one had time to celebrate.

*

Jonah stepped off the rooftop and into thin air.

It wasn't like he had much choice. Apart from anything else, he didn't want to let Sam down. If he was a Guardian now, he should act like one.

He just focused on hanging on.

His progress along the zip-line was slow, jerky. He should have paid more attention to how Sam did it, he thought, pushed himself off harder. For a horrible moment, he envisaged himself stalled halfway across this chasm, stuck in mid-air.

A long, long way below Jonah, the street was clogged with police cars, gathered in front of the Freedom Tower. The cops themselves were tiny blue dots to him, with their faces turned upwards, following his slow progress in awe.

It made Jonah dizzy to look at them, so he focused his eyes ahead, on Sam, waiting for him at the window. He tried to speed his progress towards her, but the swinging of his legs made the zip-line shake.

He juddered to a halt, at last, against the tower's side, an arm's reach below Sam. Now came the most dangerous part.

Jonah had to wrestle his wrist free from a rope loop and hoist himself onto the window ledge. His feet scrabbled against smooth glass, finally giving him an advantage. As he inched higher, Sam reached down and grabbed Jonah under his right arm. He straddled the window ledge, pulled his left arm free of its loop and tumbled gratefully into the building.

'Thanks, Sam,' Jonah said, catching his breath and rising to his feet.

'What?' said Sam. 'No kiss for me?'

Before Jonah could respond, Sam was racing across the office and towards the elevator lobby. He didn't know if she was serious or not.

'This way,' called Sam.

At the lifts, a sign informed them that they were on the thirtieth floor. Lori had revealed that Dias claimed the medical room was on the fortieth floor, so Jonah reached for the lift-call button. Sam stopped him.

'We should take the stairs,' she said. Jonah thought about it and agreed. It would be slower – but, right now, most of Granger's Millennials would be downstairs, holding off the police. A rising lift might alert them to the fact that the building had intruders. Plus, they could easily get trapped inside.

Jonah and Sam took the stairs three at a time. By the time they reached the fortieth floor, Jonah spotted a fire alarm in the stairwell and pulled it. It couldn't hurt, he reasoned, to sow a little confusion.

'Let's split up,' said Jonah. Sam went right, Jonah went left. He threw open each door he came to, finding only a succession of empty offices and store cupboards. With each disappointment, he grew more frantic. It was all he could do to keep himself from screaming out his dad's name.

Jason had been Granger's prisoner for hours. Anything could have happened in that time. Anything could be happening to him now.

Jonah heard voices ahead of him. He pulled up short of the next corner, peered around it. Two people – a young man and an older woman – who looked like medical staff, not combatants, were talking in hushed voices. Jonah listened for any clues:

'—*what if it's a real fire?*'

'*We can't go out there, we'll be arrested by the police, or gunned down by our own—*'

'*We should at least get closer to the ground.*'

At last, they cleared out, ambling towards the stairs, and Jonah resumed his search.

The next door he tried opened into a large, clinical-smelling room with a blue-tinted ceiling and a view of New York Harbour.

It took a moment for Jonah to take in all he was seeing, a moment to realise that there was someone else in the room with him, half hidden behind a row of computer servers on the far side of the room: a man with dirty-blond hair and a cherubic face. A face he recognised but had hoped never to see again.

'Where is he?' shouted Jonah.

'I was wondering when you might show up,' said Granger. 'For a second time, you have sided with the

Guardians against me. I am disappointed, Jonah.'

'What…what did you expect? You kidnapped my dad… You were going to—'

'I am going to save Luke Wexler,' said Granger, 'and all the victims of the Uploaded.'

Jonah heard a violent knocking, even over the fire alarm bell, and traced it to a large, white tube in the centre of the medical room; a pair of cowboy boots stuck out of the tube.

'Dad!' Jonah called, as he ran towards the CAT scanner.

'I wouldn't,' said Granger. He had his finger hovering over a switch on the servers. 'If I pull him out now, he'll certainly die.'

'Isn't that what you want?' asked Jonah.

'Why would you say that?'

'That's what your doctor told the president.'

'Ah,' said Granger. 'So Dias has betrayed me. Well, his process was flawed and I perfected it. The host does not need to die.'

'What about the Uploaded inside?' asked Jonah.

'The process cannot revive one who is already dead,' said Granger.

Something in Jonah snapped.

He was going to kill Matthew Granger.

38

Jonah lowered his head, and charged his enemy like an enraged bull.

Granger ducked behind a row of servers. Jonah circled around to the right, Granger moved the other way, keeping the computers between them.

'You won't solve anything this way,' insisted Granger.

'I'll be rid of you,' spat Jonah.

'You don't mean that, Jonah. You aren't a killer.'

'You don't know me! Stop pretending that you know me!'

Jonah lunged at Granger over a low console, but the Millennial leader's cyber-kinetic legs sprang him out of the way. As Jonah closed in on him again, he saw Granger's eyes darting right, and followed them to the door.

I have been stupid, he realised. *I've let him draw me too far into the room!*

'Oh no you don't,' he said. He ran to block his enemy's path, but was wrong-footed when Granger took off in the opposite direction.

Jonah saw the lift doors, too late.

He doubled back, but knew he couldn't reach Granger in time. Granger slapped his hand against a palm-print scanner on the wall, and the lift doors parted.

'You aren't thinking straight, Jonah,' he sneered. 'Your father is still alive – if you can call what he has "life". He can still inhabit Luke Wexler's body – but not for much longer.'

The fire alarm had fallen silent. The room was filled with the banging of the big, tube-shaped device, the one with Jason trapped inside it.

'The extraction program is running,' said Granger, 'but it can still be reversed. You can save your father, or you can kill me. But you can't do both.'

Jonah glared at his enemy furiously, willing him to be lying. He couldn't bear the smug look in Granger's eyes, longed to wipe the superior smirk off his face. He *had* no choice, though. He knew what he had to do, just as Granger knew it too.

Jonah ran back to the bank of monitors at which Granger had been standing before. He was faced by reams of programming code, indecipherable to him. On one screen, a progress bar was filling up red beneath a red and green circle.

'What…what do I do?' he asked, helplessly.

'That's for you to work out, Jonah,' Granger said, as the lift doors closed in front of him. 'You can't expect me to tell you everything.'

Jonah was still staring helplessly at the monitors when Sam rushed in.

She took in the situation at a glance and hurried to his side. His hand was hovering over the 'escape' icon on a datapad.

'I've pressed it six times,' he said, 'but nothing's happening. I don't know what else to try. I could unplug the pad, or the machine itself, but what if...?'

Sam knew what he was trying to say. She had seen Lucky Luke's cowboy boots, sticking out of the white CAT scanner. *What if terminating the program does permanent brain damage to him? To Jason? To both of them?*

She looked at the most prominent screen, at the graphic of a red and green circle, almost all green now. There wasn't much time left. She seized an idle datapad and pulled it towards her.

'What are you doing?' asked Jonah, as Sam typed furiously.

'I'm messaging Dad. If there's a chance he's online—'

'Axel? What can he do?'

'The Guardians will have people with them,' said Sam, 'computer technicians, experts, to take over at the Western Corner if and when—'

She broke off as a message window popped up on her screen, another right behind it. She quickly scanned the first. 'It's from Axel,' she said. 'It's marked urgent. "Matthew Granger...in Manhattan...Freedom Tower... holding Jason..."'

'Tell us something we don't know!'

'Erel Dias!' exclaimed Sam. 'Dad says he defected to the Guardians. He's with them now.'

'Dias worked with Granger. He knew all about his experiments here. If anyone can—'

'If anyone can tell us how to reverse the extraction process…' said Sam.

She sent the crucial message on its way. Only after she had done so did she think to open the second pop-up on her screen. It was from Axel, too.

PS, it said. WE DID IT, KIDDO. WE WON!!!

The Western Corner belonged to the Guardians. The train tunnels resounded with the noise of their cheers and victory chants.

Axel had joined in the celebrations to begin with, but his thoughts had quickly turned elsewhere. He had pushed his way into the tiny control room and dropped into an operator's chair. He had pulled up a datapad and logged into the Metasphere. He had sent an urgent message to his daughter, and just prayed that she was still around to receive it.

They were piling up bodies in the tunnel outside.

Axel waited for what seemed like forever. Then, a pop-up filled his screen, and he grinned. It was from Sam. He read it quickly and his smile drained away. Axel leapt up, swung his long legs over his chair and pushed his way to the door. 'Dias!' he yelled. 'Dias, where are you? Has anyone seen Erel Dias?'

Axel could see the Brazilian neurosurgeon standing apart from everyone else, at the edge of the tunnel, as if hoping to remain unnoticed. He caught Axel's eye and looked nervous.

Axel grabbed his arm, dragged him into the control room. 'We need you,' he said. 'My friend's life depends on it.'

Axel showed Dias the message from Sam. 'Can you do it?' he asked impatiently. 'Can you save him?'

Dias was already typing on the datapad. 'The extraction procedure can be reversed, yes, for as long as both sets of brainwave data remain intact.'

'How long does that give us?'

'Not long. Not very long at all. I am sending your daughter instructions. She will have to follow them to the letter if—'

'What the hell is that Millennial doing here?'

Axel had only been half aware of a commotion behind him. A newcomer had forced his way into the crowded room, a hateful scowl on his tattooed face.

'It's OK, Jez,' said Axel. 'This is Doctor Erel Dias. He—'

'I know who he is,' snapped Jez. His left shoulder was in an improvised, blood-soaked sling. He was levelling his rifle, one-handed, at Dias.

Axel snatched up his pistol, held it to Jez's head. 'We need him.'

'Are you out of your freaking mind, Kavanaugh?

You can't trust that—'

'Jason's in trouble, Jez, and Doctor Dias is the only one who can help him.'

'Jason who? You don't mean Delacroix? The dead guy?'

'Yeah, that's right,' said Axel. 'The dead guy. The dead guy who just handed us the Guardians' biggest ever victory. My oldest and best friend, the dead guy.'

'And you think this worm can...? Let me tell you about Dias, Kavanaugh. He's one of Granger's biggest toadies, been one all his life.'

'And it's "once a Millennial, always a Millennial" – is that right, Jeremy Aitken?'

'Don't,' pleaded Jez.

'And does that apply to you too? You were once a Millennial.'

The control room fell silent. The other Guardians in there had gone for their weapons too, but they weren't sure where to aim them. For a long, tense moment, Axel and Jez glared knives at each other. Then, at last, Jez lowered his rifle and backed off.

'You're going soft, Kavanaugh,' he grumbled.

'Maybe,' said Axel. 'Maybe you're right, I am. But Erel saved my life today, saved the life of an enemy, and he could save another – and if all he's asking in return is safe passage out of here then I figure that's a price worth paying.'

Dias cleared his throat hesitantly. He had been

sitting, petrified, afraid to speak, but now he had found his voice. 'Actually,' he said, 'I was hoping you might let me stay. With the Guardians, that is. Granger is a monster who must be stopped. I see that now.'

'Do you see a recruiting poster round here, Doctor?' sneered Jez.

'You need me. If I finish the work I started, I can find a solution to the Uploaded problem – a proper, ethical solution.'

Axel realised that now that the Guardians had secured half of the Metasphere, the Uploaded were as much their problem as Granger's.

'We'd be proud to have you,' Axel said, offering his hand.

Erel took Axel's hand, shook it, and said, 'Let's get to work.'

Granger swung himself up the boarding ladder into his airship and shouted to the crew to cast off. He was leaving a lot of loyal followers behind, but he had no choice. Not only the Guardians but President Lori Weisberg and her police force were snapping at his heels, and his own freedom was paramount.

He wouldn't be confined again.

The airship drifted up and away from the roof of One World Trade Center, the so-called Freedom Tower. Granger watched the great glass building falling away beneath him, and he felt an uncharacteristic twinge of regret. Another place to which he could never return.

He heard the pounding of helicopter blades, saw a police chopper banking to follow his flight. He doubted it was armed, and so all it could do was buzz the airship until it had crossed the halfway point of the East River and was out of Manhattan airspace.

The chopper ceased its pursuit, turned back, and Granger sighed and turned and strode into his cabin, where he sat down, alone, and activated his datapad, routing its output to a wall-mounted screen.

The screen filled with waiting reports, both written and verbal, most of them concerning the security of the Western Corner. All of them bad news.

Numbed, unable to process what he was being told, Granger reached for a bottle of vintage spring water from his cooler. He unscrewed its plastic top. Then, in a flash of fiery anger, he hurled the bottle at the wall.

It broke the screen and doused the electrics behind it, triggering an automatic shutdown, leaving Granger in semi-darkness and complete silence.

He wasn't really there, though.

His body may have been in that seat, in that cabin, in that airship, but his mind had fled to a place many miles away from there, and a time long past.

Granger was back in a mangled, burning car in Marin County.

39

Jason noticed a round hole in the white wall. Had it been there all along?

It didn't matter. The hole, he could see now, was an exit halo, but it didn't belong to him. He couldn't use it. He turned his back to it, refusing to let the hole distract him. He had stopped trying to break out of the small, white room. His powerful dragon avatar was no use to him in here. He was squatting on the floor, instead, concentrating on what he could still remember.

My name is Jason Delacroix, he recited to himself again. *I am a pilot and a Guardian and a husband and a son and a...*

He felt a hand on his shoulder, whirled around. There was someone else here, someone in the white room with him. Jason came face to face with a teenage humatar, freckled and skinny with a tuft of dark hair. He felt he was familiar somehow, as if they might have met once a long time ago.

'Dad, it's me,' said the humatar. 'It's Jonah. Your son. I've come to get you out of here. But I need your help, Dad. I need you to work with me, to trust me.'

The look in his father's yellow eyes was torture to Jonah.

He doesn't know me, he thought. *He doesn't know his own son!*

Jonah recgonised that look. His grandmother had had it, sometimes, when Jonah had visited her on the Island of the Uploaded.

'Where am I?' asked Jason. 'What is this place?'

'We're in a closed system, on a server in the Freedom Tower.'

'The Freedom Tower,' murmured Jason. 'In New York? I fly to New York, you know, the NYLON thread.'

'Listen, Dad,' said Jonah. 'They're trying – Granger was trying – to extract your avatar from Luke's brain and Upload it to this room, and according to the man who invented the technology – according to him, it should have worked. But you're fighting it too hard. You don't have to fight it, Dad, not any more. Granger's gone now. You're safe. You can leave Luke's body.'

Jason looked at him, blinked. Jonah couldn't tell how much he understood.

'Let go,' Jonah said. 'And we can transfer you back into the Metasphere, and—'

'No,' moaned Jason. 'I can't... I won't go back there. I'm not ready.'

'It's OK.' Jonah laid his hands on his father's shoulders. 'There's nothing to be afraid of. You've done this before, remember? You copied yourself for me to find. This is really no different. You just have to—'

'Granger sent you here, didn't he?' said Jason.

'What? No, of course he… I'm your son. I love you, Dad, and I'm trying to—'

Jason pulled away from Jonah, raised his claws to his ears, although they wouldn't quite reach. 'You're trying to trick me!'

'I'm telling you the truth. I… Do you remember, Dad, that day we met in the Metasphere and just talked? You said… You had just usurped Lucky Luke, and you said you wished you could bring him back. Well, it's time, Dad. I'm so sorry, but it's time. You have to stop, stop clinging onto someone else's life.'

'I won't,' said Jason, sullenly. 'I won't go back to being that way again, so confused, so lost, just an echo. Please, son. I'm not ready to die again.'

'But you can't…you can't stay in Luke's body. It's not right.'

'I know. I know. I need a little more time; a little more time with you.'

A lump was rising in Jonah's throat. He tried and failed to swallow it back down.

'Please, Jonah,' said Jason. His eyes were perfectly clear again and he was looking at Jonah pleadingly. 'Please, son. Don't make me go!'

It was more than Jonah could bear. He knew it wasn't right for his father to inhabit another person's body, but just as Jason wasn't ready to let go, Jonah wasn't ready to let go of him.

Jonah reached into his inventory space, felt for the new item that he knew would be in there: a large, soft cookie, unevenly baked but brimming with moist chocolate chips.

Jason looked at it, suspiciously. 'What is it?'

'Plan B,' said Jonah. 'Doctor Dias coded it and ported it into my inventory. It will reverse the extraction process.'

'And I can stay in the real world?'

'For now, Dad,' said Jonah. 'A little more time.'

Jason took the cookie in his mouth, tossed his head back and swallowed it whole.

Nothing happened for a moment. Then, a smile spread across the red dragon's face, exposing his sharp teeth. 'I can feel it,' he said. 'I think it's working. The pain… It's not pulling me apart any more. It's letting me go back. *I can go back!*'

Jason's avatar was fading away, leaving only a suggestion of red in the centre of the small white room, and soon not even that. Jonah waited, alone with his thoughts, for a minute or two, weighted down by the now-familiar doubt of a tough choice made.

Then he turned and stepped back through his exit halo.

He resurfaced in Granger's medical room, to the sounds of running footsteps, muffled shouts and banging doors. A woman's face loomed over him, her features blurred. 'Sam?' croaked Jonah.

Not Sam. Her hair was black, not red, and too long. The face was coming into focus now. It was smiling. 'Guess again,' said President Lori Weisberg.

Jonah sat up, unplugged himself. 'Did it work?' he asked. 'Is my dad—?'

'Your sister's checking on him now,' said Lori.

'She's not my sister—' began Jonah.

'Oh,' said Lori. 'I see.'

'No, no, no,' stuttered Jonah. 'See, she's just a friend.' Jonah adjusted his eyes and spotted Sam by the CAT scanner. 'A really good friend.'

He swung himself off the trolley on which he had been lying. The room was filling up with cops, and for a second Jonah feared he was about to be arrested again.

The sergeant in charge marched up to Lori and saluted her smartly. 'This floor is secure, ma'am,' he reported. 'We found another handful of Granger's people, but they surrendered without a fight. We're sweeping the rest of the tower now.'

Jonah slipped past him, to where the tall, handsome figure of Luke Wexler had emerged from the inside of the CAT scanner. He lay on the sliding table, just starting to come round, as the machine fell silent and the lights on its side went out.

Sam was standing over him. 'The readouts look good,' she told Jonah. 'But we won't know for sure until he—'

Jonah was already shaking Jason, tapping his cheeks lightly. 'Come on, Dad,' he urged, 'wake up. You've got to wake up and tell me you're OK.'

'H-hey, keep it down to a dull roar, can't you?' said the figure on the table. 'I feel as if a herd of bison is stampeding through my head.'

'L-Luke?' stammered Jonah.

The figure on the table smiled and reached up to ruffle Jonah's hair. 'Guess again,' he said.

'Dad!'

'I'm still here,' said Jason. 'For a little more time.' He sat up slowly and looked around the medical room, straining to find something or someone. 'Where's that Granger? I figure we both have a score to settle with that—'

'I told you,' said Jonah, 'he's gone. Granger's gone.'

Lori walked over to greet Jason, and explained. 'He escaped in his airship as soon as he knew we were coming.'

'He'll be miles away from here by now,' added Sam.

'He was here,' said Jonah. 'Right here. I could have... I failed again, Sam. I let Granger go because Dad was—'

Sam took Jonah's hand and squeezed it. She smiled at him. She understood.

Lori signalled for two of her officers to approach Jason. 'I'm glad that body is safe and sound, Mr...Delacroix, is it?' she said. 'But your continued occupation of it is a serious crime.'

Lori didn't know that the extraction process was feasible, but Jonah wasn't going to reveal it now.

The Guardians nominated Axel as their spokesperson. That suited him. He would be glad to get above ground again, and especially to see Sam and Jonah after so long.

He had disabled the security door between the subway tunnels and Grand Central. He waited until the prearranged time, then stepped through it.

Axel had three Guardians with him. But the New York cops outnumbered them five to one. They were waiting at the top of the escalators, their guns readied.

A fierce-looking, moustached sergeant addressed the Guardians through a loudhailer. He had them open their shirts to show they had no concealed weapons, and then he gave them permission to approach.

As the Guardians climbed one of the escalators, a matching group – three cops and an elderly member of Manhattan's co-operative board – descended the adjoining one. Erel Dias was waiting to meet them at the bottom. He was taking them on a tour of the secret world beneath their feet.

Jez had protested this arrangement. 'We don't need to kowtow to no bankers and billionaires,' he had argued. 'We took the Western Corner from the Millennials, and we can hold it against all comers.'

'Shut it, Jez,' barked Axel. 'There's been enough bloodshed today.'

Axel trusted Sam and Jonah, and it appeared from their messages that they trusted this Weisberg woman.

He reached the top of the stairs, and held out his hand to the police sergeant, who ran a white, wand-shaped explosives detector over him before he took it.

'Mr Axel Kavanaugh?' said the sergeant. 'The president will see you now.'

Jonah, Sam and Jason were waiting in a vestibule inside City Hall. Sam leapt to her feet as Axel and the other Guardians were brought in to join them. She and her father hugged, then Axel turned to Jonah and shook his hand.

He wasn't looking at Jonah, though. His gaze had alighted upon the tall, handsome man behind him, the man whom Axel must have recognised as Lucky Luke Wexler.

'Is that really…?' he asked hesitantly. 'Jason, is that you?'

Jason was grinning all over his borrowed face. 'It's good to see you, Axel,' he said. 'It's been…well, for me, it's been a lifetime.'

'For me too, mate,' said Axel. 'Me too.' But, as Jason started forward, a wary look appeared in Axel's big eyes, and he flinched away from him.

An awkward, silent standoff followed. Then, Jason threw open his arms and Axel reciprocated. The two friends embraced.

'Thanks for watching out for my boy,' said Jason.

'He's a brave one,' said Axel. 'Like his father.'

They didn't have much time to catch up, however. Two Secret Service agents showed the seven Guardians up the monumental staircase and into the president's office. Lori sat behind an oak desk, as dwarfed by her plush leather chair as she was by the two bodyguards flanking her. The formal surroundings, thought Jonah, didn't suit her at all.

The Guardians sat in a semicircle in front of Lori's desk. Axel did most of the talking. He described to Lori the circumstances that had brought them here.

'Let me be clear about this, Mr Kavanaugh,' said Lori. 'I have no interest in this squabble of yours, between the Guardians and the Millennials.'

'It's more than a squabble.' Sam spoke up. 'We're fighting for—'

'My primary concern,' Lori cut her off, 'is that server farm in my subway tunnels. From what Jonah here has told me, I believe it predates the founding of our republic. It has been down there all this time, leeching off our power, a threat to our security.'

'That's about the size of it, ma'am,' said Axel.

'I want it off my island,' said Lori.

'We're in full agreement there.'

'So, let's get down to brass tacks. There are no outstanding warrants for any of your people here, and fortunately for you we have no extradition treaties with

360

other nations. I am prepared to grant you leave to remain in Manhattan for as long as you need to dismantle the Western Corner – shall we say six weeks?'

'It may take a little longer to—' Axel began.

'Six weeks,' said Lori, firmly. 'After that, you will leave Manhattan and never return.' She glanced at Jonah, with a hint of regret in her eyes. 'All of you.'

Jonah had been wrong before. These surroundings – this seat of power – fitted Lori like a glove. This was where she belonged.

'Which brings us to the next item on the agenda.' Lori turned to fix Jason with a long, cool stare, and he shifted uncomfortably in his seat.

'Mr Delacroix,' said Lori. 'Until you vacate that body, you are under arrest.'

Epilogue

Jonah kicked the football to his dad.

This time, though, it was different. This time, they were playing in the real world, on the sprawling Great Lawn of Manhattan's Central Park. There was no stadium, just a few old towels on the grass to mark the goal lines. No replay windows either – and when the ball was kicked out of bounds, it didn't come back automatically; someone had to go and fetch it.

Jonah's real-world body was less coordinated than his avatar, and less durable. He played too hard to begin with and tired himself out. Then he picked up a grass burn on his knee after a mistimed sliding tackle.

It was a beautiful day, and the afternoon sun reflected off the skyscrapers that overlooked the park.

He was having the time of his life.

They slowed down, kicking the ball gently back and forth between them while they got their breath back.

'Did I tell you,' asked Jason, 'about the time I was shot down over South America by a *GuerreVert* rocket launcher?'

'You know,' said Jonah, 'I don't think you ever did.'

'I had to land with one engine burning in a rainforest

clearing,' recalled Jason. 'I was flying with Granger at the time. He was right there in the cockpit with me.'

'He was?'

'He reminded me of it when he had me prisoner. I saved his life that day. It's funny how things work out sometimes, isn't it?'

'Yeah,' said Jonah. 'It's funny.'

A pair of burly cops were watching them from the edge of the field. They were armed with stun guns. Jason saw Jonah looking at them and shrugged.

'You can't blame them,' he said. 'The last thing President Weisberg can afford is for a dead man to abscond with the body of one of her most valued residents.'

'Are you planning to?' asked Jonah.

Jason trapped the football with his foot and didn't return it. 'Have you checked the news lately?' he said, changing the subject. 'There are more usurping attacks being reported in the Metasphere all the time, and that's only the tip of the iceberg, the incidents we know about.'

'Yeah, I heard.' He hadn't answered Jonah's question.

'Millions of Uploaded have crossed over into the real world by now. In a month's time, who knows? Short of scanning the brainwave patterns of *every* person on this island *every* day, how can Lori ever know who's alive and who is dead?'

'You make it sound like...like nowhere is safe.'

'The world has changed, son. The Uploaded are here

to stay, and that's a fact we'll all just have to get used to.'

Jonah didn't like the way his dad was talking.

He was right, though. Even Lori had had to accept that for now there was nothing she could do to bring back Lucky Luke Wexler. *But what if Lori knew what I know*, he thought, *that the extraction process could have worked...if I had let it?*

'Someone will come up with something, though,' said Jonah. 'Someone like Dias or even Granger. They'll come up with a way to... I don't know, but something.'

'Maybe so,' agreed Jason, and he passed the football back to Jonah.

They took a stroll around the Central Park Lake. The cops followed them at a discreet distance. There were a few boats on the water and a few other walkers, but they tended to steer a wide berth around the two Guardians in their midst.

They talked about all manner of trivial things, and Jonah reminded himself how fortunate he was to have his dad by his side at all.

'You know,' said Jason as if he had been reading his son's mind, 'we *have* been lucky, you and I. Every father wants to build a better future for his kid. I thought I'd missed my chance. I died before I could finish what I'd started.'

'You did plenty,' said Jonah.

'Not enough. But now I've been given a second

chance, and look! Look at what we've achieved already, between us. We're halfway there!'

'Halfway,' said Jonah, with a sick feeling in his stomach. There was still so much bloodshed to come.

'The Guardians have liberated half the Metasphere for its users. We're halfway to getting everything we ever dreamed of.'

'And you want the rest,' said Jonah.

'I know where the final two Corners are,' said Jason. 'And I know you do too.'

'But that could take... I mean, it could be months before—'

'Then we should start making our plans straight away. We've got Granger and the Millennials on the ropes. Let's press that advantage!'

'And...and once we're done,' said Jonah, 'once we've taken the Eastern and the Northern Corners too...will be that enough, Dad? Will that be the end of it?'

'I reckon I can rest easy, then,' said Jason.

'Are you sure?'

'I can return what I borrowed, give this body back to its rightful owner. Just as soon as I know that you're safe, son. Safe and free. Just as soon as I know that the future is in good hands.' He lowered his voice as he spoke, because the cops had increased their pace and caught them up.

'Sorry, kid,' one of them said to Jonah, 'visiting hour's up.'

They took Jason by the arms, pulled his hands behind his back and handcuffed him.

'Do you have to do that?' protested Jonah.

'It's all right, son,' said Jason. 'The next time you talk to Lori, remember to thank her for letting us have this afternoon. And I'll see you again soon, right?'

Jonah watched, his heart heavy, as his dad was taken away from him. And he thought about what Jason had said, about returning Luke's body. One day.

He only wished he could believe him.

Jonah stopped off at an old hostel behind Times Square, in which the Guardians had been billeted. The accommodation was basic – and something of a comedown after Lucky Luke's apartment – but it was convenient and clean.

He grabbed a mango Pro-Meal pouch from the cupboard and joined Sam, who was just leaving.

Jonah ate as they walked along 45th Street. 'I thought you were with your dad today,' said Sam.

'I was,' said Jonah. 'They took him back.'

'Oh. I'm sorry. You know, you could take some time off if you wanted. Even Jez agrees that you've done your share, and we have plenty of people clearing out the subway tunnels. You don't have to—'

Jonah shook his head. 'No. I want to help. The more hands we have, the sooner we can get done here and start planning our next move.'

*

The entrance to Grand Central was guarded, but the cops let Jonah and Sam through. They crossed the main concourse and stepped onto a now-working escalator.

'*Our* next move?' repeated Sam, with a grin and a raised eyebrow.

'Yeah,' said Jonah. 'Us. The Guardians.'

'You're ready to take us to the last two Corners?'

'Yes, we both are. And we have to figure out a way to protect people from the Uploaded, and get my dad out of jail.'

'He doesn't want to give up Luke's body, does he?'

Jonah shook his head.

'That's going to be a problem,' said Sam.

'I know,' said Jonah. 'That's why we're going to have to break him out of here.'

But Jonah knew that would not be enough. He could get his father out of his Manhattan prison, but eventually he would have to coax Jason out of his borrowed body. But life was addictive. None of the Uploaded would give up their host bodies willingly. Jonah realised that the metawar between the Guardians and the Millennials was a fistfight compared to the battle that was brewing, the battle between the living and the dead.

Between father and son.